AMULET BOOKS
NEW YORK

Dr. Critchlore's
School for Minions
Gorilla Tactics

BOOK TWO

SHEILA GRAU

ILLUSTRATED BY
JOE SUTPHIN

Library of Congress Cataloging-in-Publication Data

Grau, Sheila.
Gorilla tactics / by Sheila Grau; illustrated by Joe Sutphin.
pages cm.—(Dr. Critchlore's School for Minions; book 2)
Summary: Cursed to die on his sixteenth birthday, Runt Higgins must find answers at the Great Library, as Dr. Critchlore takes desperate measures to save his monster boarding school from being sold.
ISBN 978-1-4197-1371-2 (hardback)—ISBN 978-1-61312-893-0 (e-book)
[1. Monsters—Fiction. 2. Blessing and cursing—Fiction. 3. Boarding schools—Fiction.
4. Schools—Fiction. 5. Mystery and detective stories.] I. Sutphin, Joe, illustrator. II. Title.
PZ7.1.G73Go 2016
[Fic]—dc23
2015027699

ABRAMS
THE ART OF BOOKS SINCE 1949
115 West 18th Street
New York, NY 10011
www.abramsbooks.com

FOR MY PARENTS, JOAN AND BOB JACK

CHAPTER 1

There can be no dominion without a minion.

—DR. CRITCHLORE, SPEAKING AT

THE EVIL OVERLORDS OF TOMORROW CONFERENCE

Terror arrived that afternoon dressed as a Girl Explorer pulling a wagon filled with cookie boxes. I watched her stride up the long, cypress tree–lined drive as if it were a suburban road and not the grounds of a highly secured minion school. Well, it was supposed to be highly secured. We'd just suffered multiple acts of sabotage and hadn't completely recovered.

She wore a beret over her pigtails, and her vest was covered with colorful badges. When the sunlight snuck through the trees to spotlight her face, I could see the freckles on her nose.

"I hope she has Monster Clump Sugar Bombs," my friend Frankie said. He stood next to me with his creator, Dr. Frankenhammer, and Dr. Frankenhammer's new dragon. They'd been about to take off on a father-son dragon ride, now that Dr. Critchlore's post-assembly reception was winding down.

"That issss no Girl Explorer," Dr. Frankenhammer said, and the look on his face made my heart rate jump to "it's time to flee" speed. Dr. Frankenhammer, with his sunken dark eyes and his wild white hair, was probably the scariest teacher in the school. If a little Girl Explorer made *him* nervous, that meant something was very wrong.

"How do you know?" I asked. What had his highly trained scientific eye noticed?

"Nobody that young could have earned so many badgesss. I was sssixteen before I earned my Excellence in Explosivesss badge."

"You were a Girl Explorer?"

He didn't answer. He stroked his dragon, who had started fidgeting and seemed anxious to get away from the little girl. Frankie reached for his neck and started twisting one of the bolts there, his nervous habit.

As the girl approached, I noticed that the shadow she cast wasn't right. It looked like the shadow of a wolf or some other beast. The cypress trees, normally filled with chirping birds, became eerily quiet as she walked past. I reached for my medallion, resting on the outside of my shirt.

As soon as I touched my necklace, her appearance changed dramatically. The pigtails morphed into horns that curved down around her face. Gray fur covered her body, and her bottom jaw stretched forward, revealing a row of sharp teeth. Claws as big as a velociraptor's scraped the ground at the end of unnaturally long arms. Her hind legs were huge, like a kangaroo's.

"She's a beast," I gasped. "And those aren't cookies." Her wagon was filled with a squirming mass of worms, each the size of a swimming-pool noodle. "They're . . . they're . . . they're spewing!" They coughed up little blobs of phlegm that landed on the ground and smoked.

Dr. Frankenhammer reached into his lab coat and pulled out a pair of glasses with blue lenses. "Those wormsss are the Minion Saboteurs I sent to the Pravusss Academy last week," he said. "Someone hasss put a glamour on them. But how can you see through it?"

"I don't know," I said. "It just happened."

"Dr. Pravus is playing gamesss," Dr. Frankenhammer said. "Returning my failed Minion Saboteurs with one of the Girl Explorers he used to embarrass usss."

"Pravus," I said. Of course this monster was one of Dr. Pravus's minions. He and Miss Merrybench had been behind all the catastrophes that had plagued our school recently. Dr. Frankenhammer had sent the Minion Saboteurs as revenge, but apparently they'd been found out.

"Frankie, I need the MonsssterTrapper," Dr. Frankenhammer said. "Then go alert Dr. Critchlore." Frankie sped off in a blur, ten times faster than a normal human. Dr. Frankenhammer squeezed his dragon's flank, and a ball of fire shot straight at the Girl Explorer. I winced, expecting her to be severely singed, but she opened her mouth and swallowed the fireball.

"Interesssting," Dr. Frankenhammer said. "Higginssss, get everyone to safety."

I would have obeyed immediately, but the monster lunged forward like a missile. I let go of my medallion, and the beast immediately looked like a little girl again. I froze; it was just so bizarre watching a little girl bound forward with leaps that spanned ten meters. Before I could move, she had me pinned to the ground.

Dr. Frankenhammer's dragon took to the sky, nearly ripping off his master's arm in the process. The good doctor looked down at me and then slowly backed away.

I couldn't move. The girl leaned over me, her face inches from my own. Her girl face. I closed my eyes, waiting for the worst while trying not to imagine it. But trying not to imagine the worst just made me imagine it. She was going to eat my face.

"Hey, look! Higgins has a girlfriend." Rufus Spaniel's voice drifted over from the grassy area where everybody was enjoying an outdoor buffet after the assembly. Rufus was the alpha werewolf of my grade, and when he talked, people listened. Or, more accurately, when he taunted, people laughed. The laughter didn't bother me; I was relieved that they'd noticed me.

I could barely breathe. This tiny girl was as heavy as a full-grown troll. Where had Dr. Frankenhammer gone? He was supposed to help me. Wasn't that a Girl Explorer motto? "Never leave a girl behind"?

"C'mon, Higgs," a raspy voice said. Out of the corner of my eye, I could see a pack of imps coming closer, Spanky in front. "Throw her off, ya scrawny wimp."

"Can't. She's too strong."

"She's a child!" Rufus said. "Hey, everybody! Look at Higgins, pinned by a little girl."

Judging by the laughter that filled the air, everyone was watching me now. The girl didn't care. A line of saliva leaked from her mouth and burned my cheek. I twisted my head from side to side, trying to fling it off.

"Help me!" I screamed.

More laughter.

But then the laughter turned to gasps. I opened my eyes and saw the monster, not the girl. She squinted and turned her head to the side, as if someone was shining a bright light in her face. A safe distance behind me, Dr. Frankenhammer held something that looked like a flashlight behind his blue glasses. The beast growled, and I heard the rumble of footsteps as my classmates deserted me.

The monster moved off me and roared at my fleeing classmates, keeping a hand (paw?) on my chest. I tried to push the arm off, but it was like trying to move a tree trunk.

A high-pitched scream tore through the air, much higher than the monster's roar. It was the kind made by girls, or my friend Darthin. A blur of movement swooshed toward my attacker.

Syke!

I'd never seen her look so determined. She crashed into the monster like it was the finals of tackle three-ball and the beast was about to score. But Syke's most powerful tackle didn't budge my attacker. She bounced off the monster, looking dazed.

Claws ripped through my shirt, catching on my medallion. The monster's hand looked so powerful, and those claws could shred my chest with nothing more than a twitch.

"Please," I whispered.

She looked down at me, then back at the wall of my minion friends, now watching from the castle steps. She did a double take back to me, staring at my chest. Her mouth approached my head. I closed my eyes, my heart pounding with panic. She sniffed my hair.

In a flash, she released me.

"You are fameely," she said, her deep voice sounding throaty and hoarse. "Forgeeve me."

I sat up, shaking my head. *Did she just call me family?*

CHAPTER 2

Not everything is as it seems. Like candy-shaped soap.
There's a rude surprise.

—DR. FRANKENHAMMER, EXPLAINING GLAMOURS

W hat . . . who . . . what are you?" I asked the monster, now bowing before me. "Why did you call me family?"

"Waiting for you, young one, to free us from Pravus," she said.

"Me? Why?"

"We are Ohtee," she said. "We were stolen from fameely. Only fameely can free us from Pravus. We want to go home to the broken place."

"You think I'm Ohtee?" I said. "Where is the broken place? What's Ohtee?"

She roared at my classmates, who had stepped closer.

"You're not going to hurt anybody, are you?" I asked.

"No. Orders are to return worms, deleever message to Critchlore. I'm to say, 'Ha ha ha ha ha, you lose.' Make sure it is at least five *ha*s. Then orders say to leave. But you are from the fameely. I take orders from you now."

Huh? I was about to ask another question when a steel trap

snapped shut around her. Dr. Frankenhammer walked toward me holding a Dr. Critchlore's MonsterTrapper™, which had been invented by Dr. Frankenhammer. It was an ingenious device, a bazooka that shot a net of material as strong as steel, but flexible. Once the monster was trapped in the net, the thick steel "strings" expanded until they touched one another, resulting in an inescapable bag.

"Can she breathe?" I asked.

"Does it matter?" Dr. Frankenhammer said. The bag jumped around. "We have to dispose of the beast."

"What? No!"

"Higginsssss, that thing is responsible for the bad press this sssschool has gotten. Remember that embarrassssing video?"

Of course I did. "Epic Minion Fail" showed a troop of Girl Explorers chasing last year's graduates off a cliff. Zombie brains! It made sense now. They might have looked like little girls, but they were really these hideous monsters.

And then I remembered that Miss Merrybench had said that Pravus called the girls land piranhas, and that they could strip an animal to its bones in seconds. I had thought she was crazy (she was), but maybe she knew something.

"She called me family," I said.

"Don't be ridiculousss." Dr. Frankenhammer waved a hand, and four security guards came running. "Dispose of the—"

"Wait! It's true," Syke said. She brushed herself off and stood up next to me. "The monster bowed down to him and called him family."

I looked at her and felt the surprise I should have felt when she'd

9

thrown herself at the monster. Tree nymphs aren't known for their fighting ability, but then Syke was only half tree nymph. I think her other half was Holy Terror from the Skies.

She held a Wind and Fire Wheel, which is a metal ring rimmed with seven curving blades. It looked like a flat silver sun.

Dr. Frankenhammer shook his head, then held out his hand for Syke's weapon, which she wasn't allowed to have because she was Dr. Critchlore's ward, not a minion-in-training. She handed it over with a shrug.

"Take the beast to my lab," he said to the security team. "Keep three guards posted."

The security guards lifted the steel sack, which wasn't moving anymore. I really hoped that thing was okay.

"You two return to the reception," Dr. Frankenhammer said. "Or you can help me round up my wormsss."

We chose the reception. Shocking, I know.

But the party had died down to a handful of ogre-men around a plate of maggoty cheese dip (ogres like it maggoty). That was fine with me because I wasn't in a party mood. I needed to figure out how I could talk to that monster again.

I knew I should thank Syke for trying to save me, but I was still mad at her and didn't want her to think this fixed everything. She was going back into the Runt Higgins Shun Box. I stopped at the grassy ledge next to the castle wall and sat down, turning my back to her. I pulled a piece of paper out of my pocket and wrote on the bottom.

"What's that?" Syke asked, nudging my back. I felt her chin on my shoulder as she peeked over. "A to-do list?"

I turned farther away. She was right; it was a to-do list. My foster mother, Cook, told me that if I wrote things down, it would help keep me focused.

"I have one too," Syke said to my cold shoulder. "It only has one thing on it, though. 'Get Runt to forgive me for not telling him he's not a werewolf.'"

Well, that's not going to happen.

"Actually, there's another thing on it. 'Tell Runt I'd never do anything to hurt him, and I'm going to spend every free moment helping him find his family, whether he talks to me again or not.'"

She hopped off the ledge, leaving.

"Wait," I said.

I know, I know. My Shun Box is useless. It never stays closed.

Syke turned around, smiling, and pointed to my list. "What's on yours?"

"'Number one, find out where I'm from,'" I read. "'Number two, find out who cursed me. Number three, ask him-slash-her to remove the curse.'"

When I'd arrived at the school eight years ago, Mistress Moira could tell that I was cursed to die on my sixteenth birthday. I'd only just found this out. It sounds terrifying, but I had Dr. Critchlore's staff working to find answers. In other words, the best and the brightest were on the job, so I wasn't too worried.

"And now number four," I said. "'Find out why that monster called me family.'"

I looked down at my medallion, wondering if I'd missed something in the thousands of times I'd examined it. This little metal disk with a wolf's head in the middle and the funny writing around the edge was the only clue I had to where I came from. What had the beast seen in it? Why could I see through her glamour when I touched it?

"So weird," Syke said. "I mean, clearly you're not related."

"But what if we are?"

"Don't be an idiot, Higgins." Syke called me an idiot all the time, but I didn't care, because she was like a sister to me. "Don't start imagining you're something you're not again."

I think she regretted saying that the moment the words left her mouth. Yes, I had been an idiot, thinking I was a werewolf. A tremendously huge idiot.

"I mean . . . ," she chattered on, but I wasn't listening. All I could hear was my anger and humiliation boomeranging back at me, just after I'd let it go. Finally, I interrupted her.

"Why didn't you tell me, Syke? You of all people?" We'd grown up at the school together. I knew everything about her: that she hated the dungeon because it smelled of "root rot"; that her favorite color was green—pine-needle green, not moss green; that she had a crush on Frankie; and that she had stolen Professor Portry's keys so she could sneak into his Battlefield Implements classroom and "borrow" his—er—implements.

And she knew me better than I knew myself. Obviously, because I had thought I was a werewolf and she had known the truth.

"Runt," she said, "I'm sorry. I couldn't tell you the truth. It . . . being a werewolf . . . it was everything to you. I didn't want to hurt you."

"Don't you think it's worse finding out you're the laughingstock of the whole school?"

I stuffed my to-do list in my pocket and walked off, not waiting for an answer.

CHAPTER 3

If two roads diverge in a wood, one of them is probably a trap.
—ADVICE FROM DR. CRITCHLORE

I went straight to Dr. Critchlore's office. He was the only one who could persuade Dr. Frankenhammer to let me talk to the monster.

I was surprised to see Professor Vodum behind the secretary's desk. Professor Vodum had recently been in the necromancy department, but it'd lost its raw materials (dead bodies) in a cemetery explosion. Prior to being in necromancy, Vodum had bounced around many positions, doing a horrible job at each of them. He was married to Dr. Critchlore's cousin, so Dr. Critchlore had to find a job for him somewhere.

Vodum's attention was focused on a pad of paper. I stood in front of the desk, waiting for him to notice me, but he didn't. I glanced at the paper and read:

Positions I am best suited for:
1. Assistant headmaster
2. Professor of advanced topics in strategy
3. Director of business development for Critchlore-trademarked products

He looked up as he thought of a fourth position, and we made eye contact. He quickly looked down to ignore me again.

"Excuse me, Professor Vodum?" I said. "Are you Dr. Critchlore's secretary now?"

"Temporarily," he said. Then he leaned toward me. "Runt, did you know that my wife and Dr. Critchlore are cousins?"

"Yes."

"First cousins," he said. "They are both grandchildren of Nicholas Critchlore. Dr. Critchlore doesn't own this school—it's a family business. But he's appointed himself headmaster, while my wife has no say over operations at all. It's outrageous."

Nobody knew the school's history as well as I did. "It was Dr. Critchlore's idea to open the school," I said, wanting to defend him.

"I should have known you'd take his side," Vodum said. "You're such a suck-up."

"I need to see Dr. Critchlore, if that's okay?"

"Fine with me." He returned his attention to his list.

Dr. Critchlore's expansive office/library/study was dim, his shades drawn. He liked to work surrounded by darkness, saying it increased his focus. A desk lamp provided the only light in the room, shining on a large poster board he was studying. I approached, edging around Pizza (his chocolate Labrador retriever puppy), who was sleeping on the rug in front of his desk. The rug hid a trapdoor, so I was happy to stand to one side.

I looked at the poster, a blown-up picture of the front gate, but with something added beneath the school's name as it arched over the entrance gate. Now the sign read: "Dr. Critchlore's School for Minions and Models."

"Are you changing the school sign?" I asked.

He glanced at me. "VODUM!" he yelled. "You useless pile of dragon droppings. I said NO INTERRUPTIONS!"

"My bad!" Vodum yelled back. "Perhaps I'd be better at another position!"

"Should I leave?" I asked.

"Hmm? Hand me that gold pen," he said, pointing to the edge of his desk.

When I did, he added some fancy edging to the letters.

"'And models'?" I asked.

"A temporary adjustment. We have visitors coming to see their children. It's such a bother, first the hamadryads checking on Syke, and now this."

"Who?"

"The Siren Syndicate." He shivered.

"But why change the sign?"

"When I recruited the sirens, I might have given their parents the impression that I ran a modeling school." Dr. Critchlore shrugged, like he'd made a tiny mistake and not outright lied. "It was the only way I could lure them away from that hoity-toity finishing school they usually attend."

"That's crazy," I said. "You're famous for running a minion school. How could they not know?"

"Well, businesses are always branching out. And surprisingly, some parents will believe anything if you tell them you'll make their children famous."

"But they must have talked with the girls in the two years they've been here." Most of the sirens were third-year students, like me.

"Sirens aren't really the nurturing type," he said. "Which is one of the reasons why I selected their girls. I could have gone with elves; they are just as pretty, though not as good at singing. I need good singers. Evil Overlords love a pretty girl who can sing. Wingut Thrasher once paid a famous singer her weight in gold to perform at his birthday gala. And I didn't lie; they will be famous when they sing at the Evil Overlord Council in the spring, right before I petition for a license to sell my line of Critchlore Minion Apparel and Weaponry products. Imagine the press I'll—er—they'll get. It'll be fantastic."

I had no doubt.

"But first we must prepare for the visitors," he continued, placing his own to-do list on top of the poster. "They're expecting a fashion show. I need to check on Mistress Moira. She's making dresses for the girls to model."

"All the girls? That's a lot of dresses."

"No, just the sirens, maybe a few other third-years. Whoever's interested. Syke will be in the show. She's my ward; it's only proper."

Syke wasn't going to like that. I don't think she'd ever worn a dress.

As shocking as this development was, I needed to focus on why I'd come.

"Dr. Critchlore—" I said.

"Shh," he said, holding up a hand as he added more things to his list, softly mumbling as he did. "Reception for the sirens, school tour, security . . ."

I had to see the monster, and quick. Standing there quietly was torture, like when you know the answer in class, but the teacher won't call on you anymore because, in her words, "your enthusiasm borders on annoying."

At last he looked up at me.

"You know that minion Dr. Frankenhammer caught?" The words raced out of my mouth like bats leaving the dungeon at sunset.

"Yes, of course," he said. "Dr. Frankenhammer has the beast in his lab. I told him to dissect it before Pravus comes to reclaim it."

"What? No! You can't." I put my hand on his paper so he wouldn't ignore me again. "She knows where I'm from. And she won't hurt anyone—I promise."

"I'm sorry, Hilton," he said, removing my hand, "but I trust Dr. Frankenhammer's opinion. If he says she's dangerous, then she's dangerous. Now, please, I have a lot of work to do."

I was about to remind him that I'd saved his life and his castle, and he owed me a favor, but Mrs. Gomes, the school's head of security, hustled into the office. She'd been frazzled by all the sabotage in the past weeks, but she seemed to be back to her normal take-charge self. Her hair was once again a perfectly styled helmet of poufiness.

"Before you say anything," she said, "I assure you, gate security is now reinforced."

Dr. Critchlore raised an eyebrow at her.

"Yes, it was a lapse," she said. "But I have girls of my own, and I like to support these types of fund-raising activities."

"But she wasn't a Girl Explorer selling cookies," Dr. Critchlore said. "She was an enemy agent. This was a dangerous mistake on your part."

"I agree," Mrs. Gomes said. "Which brings us to our arriving

18

guests. Measures must be taken to protect the school from the sirens. I have some ideas." She looked at me in a way that said this was none of my business, so I left.

Frustrated, I stopped in the anteroom, wondering how I was going to talk to that monster.

Mrs. Gomes's voice drifted out of the office: ". . . added patrols for the perimeter; aerial surveillance, probably using dragons, preferably Puddles or Tinkles, not Plopper. The safety stations should be equipped with earplugs, in case the sirens start singing."

"Professor Vodum?" I said. When he looked up, I asked, "Why are they so worried about the siren mothers visiting?"

"Really, you don't know?" He shook his head. "Other than the EOs, the members of the Siren Syndicate are *the* most powerful people on the Porvian Continent. Over the centuries, the sirens have taken their ability to make ships crash on rocks and turned it into a complete monopoly on ocean and river trade. They control who gets what and when. The Grand Sirenness herself is on many EO Council Committees and regularly hobnobs with the big EOs."

"Why would Dr. Critchlore lie to them about this school?"

"I asked him the same thing. His answer: 'Without great risk there is no great reward.'" Vodum shook his head. "I think he may have *seriously* miscalculated here. The Critchlore family is very concerned." He leaned closer to me. "If a majority of family members decide they have no confidence in Dr. Critchlore, they can get someone new to take over."

He smiled, and then added a fourth position to his list: "Headmaster."

CHAPTER 4

Farmers in Torvay report that attacks on their livestock, in which the animals were stripped to their bones, have ended. The culprits, nicknamed land piranhas, were never found. Some believe that a minion school was illegally training the beasts outside of Stull.
—ARTICLE IN *MINIONS TODAY*

I headed down the stairs to the castle foyer, intending to continue down to the dungeon so I could beg Dr. Frankenhammer to let me talk to the monster. Once I hit the steps, I saw Syke running my way.

"Runt," she said, breathing hard. "I was just in Dr. Frankenhammer's lab—"

"But you hate the dungeon," I said.

She waved a hand. "Doesn't matter. I wanted him to let you talk to the monster, but she went berserk. The lab is a mess. He sent her to the holding cells."

"The holding cells. Rats."

Seriously, there were tons of rats on the lower level. It was way creepy.

I pointed to her hand. "What's in the can?"

She held it up so I could read the black label: "Dr. Critchlore's Tornado in a Can™."

"I found it on the floor and decided to pick it up for him," she said.

"And steal it?"

"I thought it had been opened and that's why the lab was such a mess. I only just realized it's a live one."

"Really," I said, not believing a word of it.

She stashed the can in her backpack. "Hey, I was trying to help you."

"I know. Thanks."

"And, Runt? Dr. Frankenhammer is furious. He said . . ." She looked away, unable to finish.

"What?"

"He said he's going to dissect her as soon as he cleans his lab."

Oh no. I whipped out my to-do list, moving "Save the Monster" to the number one spot. I underlined it twice and put some stars and exclamation points around it.

"I'm going to the holding cells," I said.

"I'm coming with you."

"You don't have to," I said.

"I do. Runt, I meant it when I said I'd do anything to help you find out where you're from. So let's go."

The lower levels were as dungeony as the dungeon got: rocky walls, spiderwebs, the hallways heavy with darkness, and the dank, musty smell of centuries-old skeletons.

"Hey, Gilbert," I said to the skeleton carrying a bucket of fish to the grotto.

He lifted a bony hand to wave at us, and then continued on his way.

We headed for the holding area, a long hallway lined with small cells. The holding cells weren't used anymore, ever since we got a visit from the People for the Ethical Treatment of Minions (PET-M, pronounced "Pet 'em"). They'd inspected the castle and called it inhumane to punish minions by locking them up. Now punished minions got detention. Don't get me started on which is worse: detention or dungeon imprisonment. If I had a choice, I'd pick the dungeon over spending the afternoon with Professor Vodum.

Three ogre-men guards sat on stools in front of the holding-area entrance. Two were playing cards, while the third read a book.

"Hi," I said.

"Scram, kids," one of the card-playing guards said.

"I just want to see the prisoner. She knows who I am," I said. "She won't hurt me."

They laughed. "Only person getting in is Dr. Frankenhammer. Critchlore's orders. Run along."

He stood up, filling the hallway. Syke and I took a step back. She nodded to her backpack and whispered, "It could get windy down here. Just say the word."

I shook my head and pulled her out of there.

At dinner, Frankie, Darthin, and I sat with Eloni Tatupu, who was as huge as an ogre-man but 100 percent human, and Boris Tumble-wrecker, who had the brain of an ogre, but was puny, like me.

I couldn't eat. I was so nervous about what was going to happen to the monster.

"Higgins, she's dangerous," Darthin said. "Dr. Frankenhammer knows what he's doing. We need to know more about her in case Dr. Pravus uses one on us again. As far as we know, he has a team of them. Do you know what that means?"

"The Pravus Academy is going to crush our Mixed Monster Arts team," Frankie said. The Pravus Academy had crushed us in just about every interschool athletic competition lately: MMA, tackle three-ball, stealthball. Even the Dead Games, which were played by zombies, mummies, skeletons, and ghosts (Pravus had excellent ghosts). Waterdragon polo, combat archery, and chess too.

"No, Frankie," Darthin said. "Worse than that. Dr. Pravus is going to run us out of business."

"But the monster has answers I need," I said. "I have to talk to her, but she's in a guarded cell."

"Then break her out," Eloni said.

I gulped. "I can't . . . can I?" Breaking her out would be an Act of Disobedience. Minions do *not* disobey. It gave me the shakes just thinking about it.

"'Course you can. Pravus, Critchlore—they break rules all the time," Eloni went on. "Look at the mess we're in right now. Do you think it's because Pravus follows the rules? As we say on the island—if you've got a problem, it's up to you to resolve it. Nobody's gonna help you but you."

"I've got to break her out," I said, trying on the words to see if they fit. They didn't. I needed more convincing. And then I repeated something Dr. Critchlore had said. "'Without risk, there is no reward.' And I can't just let her die."

Boris kept munching on his food. "Boris thinks you should do it," he said.

I smiled at him, but inside I cringed. Boris was kind of an idiot. His agreeing with me didn't really seal my case.

"It's an Act of Disobedience, Runt," Frankie said, twisting his bolt. "If you got expelled, where would you go? You don't have another home. Don't do it." I felt bad for stressing him out, but despite his thin frame, Frankie was stronger than ten men, and faster than a cheetah. If I was going to break the monster out, I would need his help.

"I'm not saying I'm going to, but if I was"—I turned to all the guys—"how would I get by the guards?"

"Hypothetically?" Darthin asked.

"Sure."

"Well, Critchlore knows you've been asking to free the monster. If she escapes, you're going to be the prime suspect. So first off, you need an alibi. It's movie night. You should go to the movie with Syke, as usual. Make sure everyone sees you. When the lights go down, get Boris to take your spot."

"Syke won't like that," I said. Boris looked so much like me it was eerie, but he was an ogre-man, and had the manners to prove it. Syke would do it, though. She owed me. She owed me big for not telling me I wasn't a werewolf.

Darthin continued to explain a very elaborate plan, one that I probably should have paid attention to. Unfortunately, I saw Dr.

Frankenhammer leave the teachers' dining room with a wicked smile on his face and his trusty scalpel in hand.

"Gotta go," I said.

I caught up with Dr. Frankenhammer in the castle foyer. I thought he'd be heading for the dungeon, but he walked straight for one of the two curving staircases that led upstairs.

"Dr. Frankenhammer?" I called.

He turned, one hand on the railing. "Yes, Higginsss?"

"I was wondering—um . . ." I stopped. He looked at me with raised eyebrows. "Are you going to dissect the monster now?"

Dr. Frankenhammer smiled. "You want to watch? Earn yourself a little extra credit?"

Ew, no. Even the thought of watching that made me dizzy, but he took my silence as a yes.

"You'll have to wait. I'm exhausted after all that cleaning. I was just going to my quartersss to read before bed. I like to do my dissectionsss when I'm fresh."

I tried to mask my relief as disappointment. "Okay."

"Good night, Mr. Higginsss," he said, and continued up the stairs.

CHAPTER 5

We dream of a world where everyone is treated equally.
—PET-M MISSION STATEMENT

See? They're a dangerous bunch of nut jobs out to ruin the world.
—THEIR DETRACTORS

Movie night was held in the ballroom for the regular-sized minions, while the minions of impressive size watched outside on the giant screen by the boulderball field. That night's movie was a classic horror tale called *Beauty and the Beast*. It's the story of an awesomely cruel and angry monster who takes a pretty girl prisoner, but she ends up turning him into a human through singing and romance. It is *so* tragic. I've seen monsters leave the theater shaking in fear after watching it.

I met Syke in the foyer. "Are you sure you want to do this?" she asked. "Runt, you've never broken a rule in your life, and you don't do anything without asking an adult if it's okay. I've heard you ask permission to turn your homework in early."

"She called me family, Syke," I said. "She knows where I'm from. I will die unless I find out who I am, and who cursed me."

"I know," she said. "I just wish there was something more I could do."

"You *do* know I'm going to sneak out and you'll have to watch the movie with Boris, right?"

"Yeah," she said. "I meant to say, I wish there was something different I could do."

We laughed, but really, we were both nervous. I took my seat, saying hi to as many classmates as I could, so they'd remember I was there. I wore my black cargo pants, boots, black T-shirt, and dark gray Critchlore tackle three-ball sweatshirt. I put on a beanie that Cook had knitted for me last winter. It had the logo of my favorite tackle three-ball team, and earflaps with dangling strings.

The lights went down.

"Gotta pee," I said loudly. I edged my way out of the row, ran down the aisle, and found Boris waiting near the foyer, wearing the exact outfit as mine. I thrust the beanie on his head. "Remember, be nice to Syke," I told him.

"Syke," he said. "I like Syke."

Yikes.

Rufus Spaniel walked up to us. Even though we were both third-years, he was twice my size. I got nervous whenever he was in the same room as me, much less talking to me.

"What are you twinsies up to?" he asked.

"Movie night," Boris said. "We watch a movie on movie night." Boris wasn't trying to be sarcastic, but Rufus thought he was and growled at him.

"Where's Janet?" I asked, trying to change the subject.

"Why do you care?" Rufus said, angry now.

"Just wondering," I said. "You two usually watch movies together."

"She's saving my spot," he said. He sneered at me one more time, then put an arm around each of us to lead us back inside. "The movie's starting, boys."

I ducked under his arm. "Gotta pee," I said. I darted into the bathroom, hoping he wouldn't follow. I waited a few minutes before peeking out, but I didn't see Rufus anywhere.

I ran to the boathouse by the lake to meet Frankie, Eloni, and Darthin. Not many people know about the secret entrance to the dungeon in the boathouse, under a box labeled "Engine parts." When I got there, only Frankie was waiting inside.

"Darthin said he had an emergency study session or something," Frankie said.

"He chickened out?" I said.

"Pretty much."

"I don't blame him," I said. "If he got kicked out, his whole family would be put in jail."

"I'm so glad I'm not from Upper Worb," Frankie said. "Or some other place where the EOs keep your family hostage to make sure you come back."

"What about Eloni?" I asked.

"He told me he had a movie-night date with Elise. Then he said 'Elise!' again so I would understand it was a big deal."

"She's really nice," I said. Everybody liked Elise.

I was disappointed, but I couldn't blame him either. "Listen, Frankie, you don't have to do this. This school's your only home too."

"So if we both get kicked out, at least we'll have each other," he said. "Let's go."

Frankie was the best. I pushed aside the box, and we climbed down a shaft that had a ladder built into the side. The reverberating clang of our footsteps echoed in the space, making it sound like someone was following us.

We reached the floor. "This way," I said, pointing. I didn't have my Dungeon Positioning System (DPS), because I'd given it to Boris. If anyone looked for me, they would see that I was at the movie. Fortunately, I knew my way around the dungeon. We had to go past the underground grotto, past Dr. Critchlore's steel-plated safety bunker, and then down another flight of stairs to the lower level and the holding cells.

The crunch of our footsteps seemed amplified in the quiet, and the darkness was so thick it smothered the feeble light of my flashlight. My whole body felt prickly with fear as we passed dark crevices in the rough walls, hiding who knew what kind of creatures.

I was so grateful that Frankie followed me. There's nothing like having a superstrong minion watching your back in times of danger.

We continued on, faster now. I just wanted this to be done. When I reached an intersection, I turned to say something to Frankie, but, guess what? No Frankie.

"Frankie?" I whispered. *Where'd he go?*

I checked each hallway. No Frankie. Panic filled me, and my heart thumped so hard and fast it felt like a drum being played by a hyperactive troll. I raced back to find him, but as I passed a dark crevice, someone put a hand over my mouth and pulled me into the shadows.

Another hand grabbed my flashlight, switching it off.

"It's me. Pismo," he whispered. "Frankie's right behind us. Someone's following you."

"Pis—"

"Shh. Wait here."

He edged around me, out of the alcove, and into the hall. I couldn't see anything, but I felt Frankie ease up next to me. At least, I hoped it was Frankie. I reached for his neck and felt the familiar bolts to make sure.

I didn't know whether to trust Pismo. He was an obnoxious little transfer student with a bad attitude. But when we noticed a light swooping around the tunnel, Frankie and I leaned back into the darkness.

"Whoa! Watch it," Pismo said to the flashlight-wielding follower. "You'll blind someone."

"Pismo," Rufus said. "Beat it, punk. What're you doing down here?"

"I take an evening swim in the grotto," Pismo said. "Care to join me?"

"You *do* know there's a flesh-eating fish monster in there?"

"Clarence? Sure, he's a hoot. Come on, I'll introduce you."

"No thanks, weirdo," Rufus said. "You see anyone else down here? A couple annoying little dorks?"

"Yeah," Pismo said. "They went toward Frankenhammer's lab."

We waited in silence.

Finally, Pismo came back to the alcove.

"He's gone," he said, running a hand through his long bangs to lift them off his face. "So spill. Whatcha two doing down here, and why was Rufus following you?"

"I'm—uh . . . we're—um—exploring?"

"Yeah, right. You're the worst liar in the history of forever." He swished his towel at me. "What's going on? I want in."

I looked at Frankie. Frankie looked back at me. Pismo draped an arm over my shoulder. "Runt," he said, "some people are more equipped for delinquency than others. I'm your man."

It was true. Pismo didn't care about rules, and I felt I could trust him. After all, I knew his secret. Pismo was a merman—that was why he needed the nightly swim. He didn't want anyone to know, mostly because people thought mermaids were stupid. You couldn't get through a day without hearing a "dumb mermaid" joke, thanks to the sirens, who hated mermaids.

"What's the plan?" Pismo said.

"We're breaking someone out of a holding cell," I said.

"Goody," Pismo said, hopping up and down. "I love a good prison break. Who're we springing, and what'd he do?"

"It's a she. The Girl Explorer who showed up after Dr. Critchlore's assembly."

Pismo stopped hopping.

"Are you crazy?" he asked. "That thing was . . . it had those teeth . . . and claws . . . Are you crazy?"

"I've talked to her. She called me family. I know she can help me find out where I come from."

Pismo shrugged. "Okay. Let's go."

CHAPTER 6

*It's like an underground city down there. Not only does it
have classrooms and offices, but there are also stores, a museum,
a spa, and a bowling alley.*

—SOMEONE DESCRIBING THE CRITCHLORE CASTLE DUNGEON

W e reached the entrance to the holding cell hall. The guards
were gone, but when we opened the door, we saw an ogre-
man sitting in a chair in front of the last cell. I closed the
door and looked at Frankie.

Up until now, I hadn't done anything wrong. I hadn't broken
any rules. But as soon as we entered that hallway, I would become
something new—a rule breaker.

I took a deep breath to calm myself. "Okay, Frankie, what was
Darthin's plan?"

"I don't know. I thought you knew."

Oh no. All this time, as nervous as I was, I still had a certain
confidence that Darthin's plan would lead to a quick getaway. Now
we were doomed.

"Go on," Pismo said, pushing me forward. "We'll improvise."

I opened the door, and we dashed into a dark, doorless cell

hidden from the guard's view. He was playing a video game on a handheld device and didn't look up.

"Sounds like *Monster Blaster Four*," Pismo whispered. "He's at level thirteen, right before the troll shows up and stomps the villagers."

"How are we going to get past him?" Frankie asked.

"You guys stay here. I'll lure him out," Pismo said.

Before I could ask him what he was going to do, he left. He walked straight down the hallway, like he wasn't even trying to hide from the guard. Frankie and I watched from the shadows, knowing we couldn't be seen.

"Level thirteen is a beast," Pismo said.

The guard startled. "Hey, kid. You're not supposed to be down here."

"I know. I heard the roar of the bellicose troll and had to see you beat him. I've done it fourteen times. It never gets old."

"You've beaten the bellicose troll?"

"Sure," Pismo said. "Want me to show you?"

"Yes! I've been stuck on this level forever."

"There's just one thing," Pismo said. "See, I'm a merman—please don't tell anyone—and I've got to get in the water soon or my legs will turn into a fish tail. Can we go down the hall to the grotto?"

Smart thinking, Pismo. I smiled at Frankie, and he nodded.

"You don't need to go that far," the guard said. "See that cell over there? The underground river comes up in the corner. You can put your legs in there."

Oops. There went Pismo's plan.

"Really? Okay."

Frankie and I listened while Pismo defeated the bellicose troll. He gave us a running commentary on his moves. The guard laughed and kept saying, "No way!" I looked at Frankie and pointed to my wrist, as if I had a watch there. We didn't have much time.

"Dude," Pismo said. "Looks like your battery is almost dead. Hand me your charger."

"Charger?"

"Yeah. If we plug this in quickly, you won't lose your spot."

"Plug it in where?" the guard asked. There weren't any electrical outlets in the dungeon.

"Uh-oh," Pismo said. "We didn't save the game at the last checkpoint. We'll lose everything if you don't get this plugged in."

"My charger's in the office. Upstairs."

"I'll stay here and watch your prisoner. You go plug it in."

The guard was silent.

"You can trust me," Pismo said. "I told you my secret, after all. Plus I'm taking Professor Dungely's Prisoner-Watching Seminar. Go."

"I had to take that twice," the guard said. "I kept failing the practical exam."

"It's difficult," Pismo said. "I think you're doing an awesome job. Go on. It will only be a few minutes."

"Okay, I'll be right back."

Frankie and I ducked back into the shadows as the guard raced by. Then we ran to Pismo, who was drying himself off with his towel.

"That was too easy," Pismo said. "No wonder he failed the practical."

"Prisoner-Watching Seminar?" I asked.

Pismo smiled and nodded. "I need the extra credit. You guys have three minutes, maybe two."

The metal door had a small window I could look through if I stood on tiptoes. I saw the Girl Explorer huddled in the corner of the cell, lit by a dull lightbulb hanging from the ceiling. Holding my medallion, I saw her monster form. Dung beetles, I'd never seen a more frightening beast, with those jagged teeth, powerful horns, and sharp, sharp claws. I felt the scrapes on my chest and knew that if she'd closed her fist, her claws would've dug out half my torso.

I tried to swallow over the lump of fear stuck in my throat.

"Hello?" I said. She looked up. "We're here to rescue you." I turned to Frankie. "Can you pull this door open?"

Frankie grabbed the door and pulled. The metal squeaked and screamed as it was pried off the hinges. The monster ran out.

"Just shove it back in the doorway," I told Frankie. It looked a little bent, but hopefully the guard wouldn't notice. "Let's go."

"Take her to the grotto," Pismo said. "I'll meet you there."

Running next to the most fearsome monster I'd ever seen was terrifying, but her glamour worked as long as I didn't touch my medallion with my hand. I told myself I was just running with a little girl.

We reached the grotto, a deep underground cave that opened up off the hallway. A string of dim lightbulbs circled a subterranean lake, each one hanging above a sign that warned of the danger of stepping too close to the water. The cave was eerily quiet, except for the echoing pings of water dripping from the stalactites covering the ceiling.

36

"What's your name?" I asked the monster.

"Saradakbecoveltorpiclowin," she said. She leaned over the water and took a sip, sending out ripples.

"Can I call you Sara?"

"Yes, little one of the fameely."

"Where is the broken place you said you're from?" I whispered.

"Far away. Eet beautiful. Lots of trees and mountains. We leeved in forest. Not many trees at new home."

Trees and mountains. "Is it near the Etarne Cliffs?"

"Don't know that place. We want to go home. Don't leek Pravus."

Frankie took a step toward the water. "Something's moving down there," he said.

"Step back," I told him. To Sara, I said, "Why can't you leave Pravus?"

"Have to obey Pravus. He defeated the fameely." She approached me, grabbing my arm. *She's just a girl*, I told myself, heart racing. *Just a girl*. "Eef you come for us, we can leave. The spell says obey the fameely feerst, captor second. Pravus not fameely. Says fameely dead. He ees master now. But you have medallion. You smell right. Fameely. You weel save us."

Interesting. I'd never been told that I smelled right before. Still, I didn't understand what she meant.

I was about to ask another question when Frankie screamed. In the stillness of the cave, his scream was as startling as a crack of thunder. I turned to see him on his back, a thick tentacle wrapped around his leg, dragging him into the water.

I grabbed him, but I knew I wasn't going to win a tug-of-war against the flesh-eating fish monster. "Sara! Help!"

Sara hopped over, landing on the tentacle. In a flash, it flew back into the water. Frankie scooched away as fast as he could. We both crouched against the wall, trying to get as far away from the water as we could.

"Thanks, Sara," Frankie said.

"Is Clarence trying to make friends again?" Pismo had entered the grotto, smiling wide. "I told him not to grab people."

The fish monster's clammy head popped out of the water. A low growl filled the dark cavern, echoing off the rocky walls.

Sara growled back, edging closer to the water, which made me nervous.

Something flew out of the water and hit her with a splat. She reared back and then looked down at a huge, dead fish, as big as an ogre's foot, lying on the gravel. She bent over it, made some growling, gurgling sounds, and when she stood back, the fish was nothing but bones.

"Land piranha," I whispered, remembering the nickname for Sara's kind.

"There you go, Clarence!" Pismo shouted. To us, he said, "I think he likes her."

"Runt, we need to get back to the movie," Frankie said.

"Tell your monster friend to hide in the cave at the far end of this wall," Pismo said. "She'll be safe there."

"Sara?" I asked.

"I stay in cave," Sara said. "Thank you, young one."

"In the morning, we'll figure out what to do."

With that, Frankie and I raced back to the movie. I waited in the hall while Frankie ran inside to get Boris so we could switch places. When they came out, I grabbed my hat from Boris's head. It was wet and smelled like soda.

"Sorry," he said. "Scary movie." He leaned toward me and whispered, "There was kissing." Then he shivered.

I went inside and took my seat next to Syke, who was soaked with soda and had popcorn stuck in her hair.

"The movie frightened him," Syke whispered. "Many times."

"Sorry," I said, stifling a laugh.

I felt someone's gaze and turned around. Rufus sat glaring at me. If suspicion had a face, he was wearing it.

CHAPTER 7

Welcome to Skelterdam! If you're human, like me,
you'll be dead before you finish reading this sen—
—WELCOME SIGN IN SKELTERDAM,
WHERE NO HUMAN CAN SURVIVE

The next morning, I crossed "Save the Monster" off my to-do list. That felt both good and scary. I remembered Rufus's angry glare and wondered if he'd snitch on me when the Girl Explorer couldn't be found.

I had to stick to the plan. We'd decided that I should make a plea for Sara's release, so it would look like I didn't know she'd already escaped. I went to see Dr. Critchlore before breakfast. The secretary's desk was empty, which made me think Professor Vodum had been reassigned to yet another job.

I walked right into Dr. Critchlore's office.

"Dr. Critchlore, I—"

I stopped because it wasn't Dr. Critchlore standing in front of his desk, eyeing *The Top Secret Book of Minions* through its glass case. It was Dr. Thiago Pravus, headmaster of the Pravus Academy, and Dr. Critchlore's worst enemy.

Dr. Pravus looked like he'd just stepped out of a commercial for stuff that rich people buy. Everything about him looked expensive, from his blue suit and silk tie to his neatly trimmed black-and-gray hair and perfect tan. He seemed to exude power, and I took a step back before realizing what I was doing.

"Knowledge is power," he said, tapping the glass case that held Dr. Critchlore's prized book. "But wisdom is knowing what you don't know."

He turned and looked at me with an eyebrow cocked, a lip twitching to sneer at me.

"Get out," he said.

I backed up another step before realizing that I wasn't the trespasser here—he was. Why was he standing there, acting like he owned the place? Where was Dr. Critchlore?

"Dr. Pravus." I gulped. "I don't think you should be in here."

He stepped toward me. I wanted to run, but I'd been told over and over that a minion doesn't run.

"You don't think so? And since when does your opinion count, minion?" He spit out the word *minion* as if it tasted disgusting. It sucked the confidence right out of me.

"Wh-wh-what are you doing here?" I asked. I couldn't think of anything else to say. I just wanted to stall him until someone else arrived. Someone more adulty.

"Who do you think you are?" I noticed he wore black gloves, and the reason I noticed this was because one of his hands was reaching for my throat. "You have the audacity to speak to me, to question me? Is this how Critchlore trains his minions? Outrageous."

He had been moving slowly, talking slowly, but all at once

he lunged at me, grabbing me by the throat. I couldn't breathe, couldn't scream. He yanked me forward so he could whisper in my ear. "I could kill you for that. I could kill you and the Evil Overlord Council would allow it. They do not appreciate acts of insubordination."

I grabbed his arm, but he was so strong. His expression changed from outrage to pleasure. He was squeezing the life out of me and enjoying it. His scrutiny of me was intense, as if he was trying to record every bit of fear and pain I was experiencing.

My vision grew spotty and the room spun. But then he threw me to the ground. I grabbed my neck, gasping. Air, sweet air, filled my lungs.

"But then I'd owe Critchlore a minion in recompense," he said. "And each of mine is worth ten of you. Get out."

I got up and ran.

I told myself that running was smart because I could find a teacher or a security guard. But I knew I was running because I was scared out of my mind. That man was not sane. Every molecule in my body quivered frantically in complete terror.

As I ran, my brain finally showed up to the battle, telling me all the things that I could have done. I could have screamed for help. I could have lured him to the trapdoor and then activated it. I could have fought.

But I knew I wasn't brave enough to do any of those things, and that made me feel worthless.

I found Dr. Critchlore in the dungeon, meeting with the market-ing department in the conference room. I told Betsy, the dungeon administrator, what had happened, and she went in and told Dr. Critchlore. He ran past me, straight for his private elevator, looking furious.

I felt sick. I tried to convince myself that I'd done a good job. I had discovered the intruder and ran for help. That was the right thing to do. Dr. Critchlore would be happy with me, maybe even call me into his office to thank me.

He did call me into his office a few hours later, but it wasn't to thank me.

"You left him in here? Alone? Are you an idiot?" It was Dr. Critchlore's turn to rage at me.

"He choked me," I said. "He said he could kill me and the Evil Overlord Council would allow it."

"That's true," Dr. Critchlore said. "The EOC deals harshly with anything reeking of an uprising. Whether it's an entire populace or a single minion."

"Why was he here? Isn't that against the Minion School Directives?"

"No. He's very clever. He said he came for his minion, who wasn't here to attack us but to return our Minion Saboteur. Minion kidnapping is strictly forbidden between minion schools and punishable with fines, imprisonment, and the loss of four teeth and a thumb. Banishment to Skelterdam, if it's a repeated offense."

I wondered how it was okay for Dr. Frankenhammer to send a Minion Saboteur to Pravus's school, but Pravus's sabotage of *our* school had been a violation of the code, according to Dr. Critchlore. "Isn't using a Minion Saboteur a breach of some law?"

"Actually, no, if it's done in accordance with the Spying Guidelines." He waved his hand in the air. "Evil Overlords want their minions trained to detect saboteurs and spies. It's complicated. Plus having contradictory laws allows the overlords to arrest anyone, anytime they want."

"What happened when he couldn't find her?" I asked.

"Who? His minion? He found her."

"What?" Oh no. No, no, no.

"Pravus makes his minions wear tracking bracelets." Dr. Critchlore snorted. "That's a bit desperate, if you ask me. But in this case, helpful, because she escaped somehow. We found her in the grotto. Seems to have gotten on well with the flesh-eating fish monster. It's a pity. Dr. Frankenhammer would've liked a closer look at her anatomy."

Okay, maybe her going back with Pravus was a good thing. Except I still needed answers. There had to be some way to free her.

"That scoundrel," Dr. Critchlore went on. "I'm sure he was up to something, but nothing seems out of place. My bug-detectors have detected no listening devices. No explosives, no poisons, no obscene graffiti. What was he up to?"

"He said 'Knowledge is power, but wisdom is knowing what you don't know.' He was standing by *The Top Secret Book of Minions* when I came in." We both looked at the book, sealed in its locked glass container.

Dr. Critchlore went over to his bookshelves, moved some books aside to reveal a safe, and opened it. He removed a key and unlocked the glass case. Carefully, he lifted the book from its perch and set it on his desk. When he opened the book, we saw what Dr. Pravus had been up to.

The pages were blank. Dr. Pravus had stolen *The Top Secret Book of Minions* and replaced it with a phony.

Dr. Critchlore didn't scream. He didn't throw anything, or yell, or hit me. He just looked at me and pushed a button on his desk, and I was sucked out of the room by gravity as the trapdoor I was standing on was activated.

CHAPTER 8

Tackle three-ball: a ball-and-bat sport played by two teams of eleven on a hexagon-shaped field. Teams take turns trying to score by touching five bases and crossing a goalpost without being tackled by the opposing team. Bonus points are awarded for beaning a runner while he's off base.

—*OFFICIAL GUIDE TO SPORTS*

I had never been trapdoored before, and it was the worst. The fall wasn't bad. I landed on a soft pile of straw. It was what the journey did to my insides that hurt the most. I had done something terrible. My gut was so screwed up with worry and humiliation that I felt shaky and weak.

The Top Secret Book of Minions was gone because of me. If only I'd stood up to Dr. Pravus. If only I hadn't run away. If only, if only, if only.

I left the trapdoor pit, climbed the stairs, and ran out of the castle. I kept running, heading down the main road toward the entrance. I ran and ran; trying to distance myself from the queasy feeling in my stomach that told me I was in so much trouble.

The gravel crunched beneath my feet. I wanted to howl, to scream.

At the entrance, the gates were closed, so I leaned against them, resting my head between two bars, and looked out. Outside was scary. The thought of being on the other side of the gate, alone, terrified me. I belonged inside.

I turned around. Every time I saw the castle, sitting majestically at the end of the long, tree-lined drive, I felt amazed that I was here, that I'd lived here most of my life. I'd always felt so lucky. Maybe that was my problem. Maybe I'd been given too much good luck, and now the powers that be were balancing it out with some bad luck.

A lot of bad luck.

I pushed off the gate and walked back up the main road. I could see the tips of buildings peeking out among the trees. So many trees. Sara would have liked it here. Poor Sara.

I took the first road on the right and headed for the dorms. Stevie, a second-year giant, sat between two oaks, practicing "sitting still so nobody notices you until it's too late." The giants took a class called Stealth Techniques and Strategies for Minions of Impressive Size and had to practice on the rest of the student body. Poor Stevie wasn't very good at sitting still. I felt bad for the guy, so I tried not to notice him. As I got closer, he shook with silent giggles. I kept my gaze forward and braced myself for what was coming.

"GOTCHA!" he said as he scooped me up. He squeezed me hard around the middle, crushing my ribs.

"Stevie!" I yelled. "Not so tight."

"Oops, sorry." He pulled me up to his face. "I got you."

"Yes, you did," I said. "Good job."

He placed me on a branch at his eye level, about two stories above the ground. "You look sad," he said. "What's the matter?"

I sighed. "Stevie, did you ever run away from something because you were scared?"

He thought about it for less than a second. "No."

"I think I might get expelled," I said. I felt a new wave of despair when I said those words out loud.

"Why?" he asked.

I shook my head because I didn't want to talk about it. "I don't want to leave this place."

"You don't have to!" Stevie said, looking excited. "I'll keep you in my room, with my pet alligator, Teethy. I hardly ever forget to feed him." His eyes went wide for a second, which made me think he probably had a hungry alligator in his room.

"Thanks, Stevie," I said. "It's a really great offer, but I think I'll wait and see what happens with Dr. Critchlore."

"Okay."

I noticed movement in the distance and saw the school gates open. A large bus entered the campus, "Vilnix Academy" written on its side. Giant breath! I'd forgotten about our tackle three-ball game.

"Stevie, let me down. I've got a game to get to."

This was perfect timing. Playing a sport where you get to tackle people is the cure for when life gets you down. I think a famous philosopher said that.

Professor Zaida, the Literature teacher, was our faculty coach. She didn't really know much about tackle three-ball. She never came to practice and often read a book during the games, only looking up every once in a while to make sure everyone got a chance to play. But every team needed a faculty coach, and she was ours.

"Runt Higgins," she said, marching up to me. She wore a Critchlore hat with a brim, but other than that, she didn't look very coachy. "What is the meaning of this?" She pointed at the imps, who were decked out in their brand-new tackle three-ball uniforms.

"I promised them they could play. They helped me escape from Miss Merrybench."

"Runt, I admit I don't understand the rules or pay much attention to the games. I still don't know what the blazes it means when you all yell 'Flipit!'—"

"I've explained this to you five times," I said, using my patient voice. "When there are three runners on base, and it's third down, the batter can switch-hit and if the runners yell 'Flipit!' they can run in the opposite direction to score."

"Regardless"—she shook her head like that was nonsense—"this is a very violent sport. Those imps are smaller than me!" Professor Zaida was a little person and very protective of the smaller minions in general. "I really don't think they should be out here."

"We've been practicing, Professor Zaida. They're tougher than they look." We watched as Uhoh and Fingers ran at Eloni, who was playing catch with Boris. Eloni caught the ball with one hand and swatted the imps away without even looking at them. They went flying, but they bounced up laughing.

"Make sure they don't get hurt," she said.

"I'll put them in one at a time. As right-field linebacker or something."

She nodded and patted me on the arm, because she's nice like that. "Good luck."

I started at first bag, Eloni pitched, Boris caught, and Syke played left field. Other students took the remaining positions. Frankie wasn't allowed to play in league games because of his enhancements, and Darthin didn't like sports, so he read a book while watching from the stands.

It felt good to lose myself in the game. The hitting, the beaning, and the craziness that followed shouts of "Flipit!" The imps played with so much enthusiasm it was hard not to smile, especially when two of them tried to take down Vilnix's biggest player, Huge Alfred.

We lost, 5–4, but it was fun. After the game, the players who hadn't gone to the infirmary enjoyed Cook's postgame lunch in the shade of an oak tree.

I always enjoyed hanging out with the Vilnix players. Vilnix Academy's motto was "Arts and Warcraft." They trained humans in painting, sculpture, music, and literature, because EOs love to be celebrated in the arts. They also trained monsters for war, like everyone else.

I stood in line for cheeseburgers behind a Vilnix player named Lance. "We almost didn't make it here today," he said.

"Really, why?"

"Last night someone released battle termites in our practice siege area—they ate up the walls and everything." He pointed to the table of condiments. "That isn't ogre jelly, is it?"

"No, chunky peanut butter. Eloni likes it on his burger. That's terrible about the termites."

Lance nodded. "Coach wanted to cancel the game, so we could

help rebuild the practice area before the recruiters come to see our graduating monsters in action."

Everyone in line started talking about the random acts of sabotage that both schools had experienced lately.

"We thought it might be Critchlore, because you guys need the business," Lance went on. "But we heard he was out of it last week."

"Yeah, we were dealing with our own sabotage," I said. "Thanks to Dr. Pravus."

"Pravus," he said. "It was probably him. Did you hear he just bagged a sweet recruiting deal from Cera Bacculus? She'd been set to go with the Minion Preparatory's graduating Troll Mob, but then they got lost in the Caves of Doom on a field trip."

"It happens," I said. "It took us three hours to get out of there once."

"They were lost for five days. They claim they were given a false map at the site, and—get this—the school that was there before them was the Pravus Academy."

Interesting. We'd all thought that Dr. Pravus had sabotaged us because he hated Dr. Critchlore. But if he was sabotaging other schools, maybe he was up to something bigger. And how was he getting away with it? The Minion School Directives said that sabotage was punishable with the loss of license and banishment to Skelterdam.

We ate and talked about the great and not-so-great plays of the game, and how much we hated the team from the Pravus Academy. I lost myself in the camaraderie until clouds rolled in and extinguished the warmth of the sun, which reminded me that I was doomed and had better do something about it.

CHAPTER 9

There are two kinds of artists:
those who make their overlords look more noble and attractive
than they are, and those who are in prison for being accurate.
—FIRST THING TAUGHT AT THE VILNIX ACADEMY

I pulled out my to-do list and wrote "1. Redeem myself for losing the *TSBM*" on the bottom. I circled it and drew an arrow that pointed it to first place, ahead of "Save the Monster," which had been crossed out, erased, and then rewritten. I had no idea how I was going to do those two. In the meantime, there were the other items: finding out where I came from and who cursed me.

Fortunately, I wasn't the only person working on this problem. Now that I had some free time, I decided to go see what Uncle Ludwig had found out.

Uncle Ludwig was the school librarian. He wasn't really my uncle; he was Dr. Critchlore's uncle. He also wasn't much of a librarian, because he rarely opened the library. Having kids around tended to interfere with his research, which, I'd just learned, was focused on finding out where I came from and who had cursed me. I felt special, knowing that someone would sacrifice all his time and talent for me.

The library was located on the first floor of the castle. I tapped on one of the glass inserts of the library doors, which were locked, as usual.

"Go away. I'm working," he yelled. "Go outside and play!"

"It's me, Runt," I said.

I heard footsteps, and then the door burst open. "Fantastic!" he said.

I smiled and followed him inside. Uncle Ludwig was a mess, as musty and tattered as an old book. His clothes were yellowed and worn, and he hadn't shaved. A pair of glasses sat on his scraggly hair, and another pair hung from a necklace. He mumbled to himself as he headed back to his desk.

I couldn't wait for him to share his research with me. He was probably excited too, after having to keep it a secret from me. Cook hadn't wanted me to know I was cursed.

We reached his desk, which was piled with books. Four library carts jammed with more books blocked the front.

"You can start reshelving these"—he pointed to the carts—"and then I have some carts in the back you can get to."

"Um, Uncle Ludwig, I'm not here to reshelve books."

"What?"

"No. I'm here to talk about my curse."

"What curse?"

My heart did that flippy thing, where it speeds up and then

seems to collapse all at once. "Haven't you been researching my curse? I'm going to die on my sixteenth birthday unless I find out who cursed me and get him or her to take it back. Cook told me you were researching where I came from."

"Right!" he said. "Of course. The curse. Cook. Where you came from. It's all related, you know."

"Huh?"

He rummaged through piles on his desk. "Your medallion," he said, motioning with his hand. I took it off and handed it to him. He squinted through his glasses, turning the medallion as he tried to read the strange writing along the edges. "Yes, just as I suspected."

"What? You know where it comes from?"

"No. I have no idea," he said. "See, that's how it all ties together."

I tried not to look exasperated, but it was difficult.

"Your medallion," he explained, "that strange beast who attacked us yesterday, where Evil Overlord Dungbeetle gets his minions."

"They all have something in common?"

"I don't know!" he shouted. "They're mysteries. How do you make caffeinated moon biscuits? I don't know. Where do giant sloth beasts hibernate? I don't know. Why would anybody curse you? I don't know!"

"But . . . haven't you been trying to find out? Cook told me that's what you've been doing in here, when you lock the students out."

"Yes! I've been collecting clues, sending out researchers to follow leads. I'm close; I know I am. I will find it if it's the last thing I do."

"Find it? The curser, you mean?"

"No. The fountain of all knowledge. The great repository of

forbidden and forgotten things." He gazed over my shoulder, as if something was lurking right behind me.

"What are you talking about?"

"The Great Library, my boy." He smiled. "All the answers are in the Great Library. I just have to find it."

I reshelved some books while listening to him mumble about a librarian order and its complex system of secrecy. He said things like, "You have to know your ABCs," and "The poem, the poem," and "I wish I had more carts."

I felt a sluggish doom engulf me. I'd been hoping Uncle Ludwig would have some clues about where I came from, but he had nothing. It made me mad, and I left without reshelving the books on the last cart. That would show him how angry I was.

"It's a fairy tale," Darthin said later in our dorm room.

I collapsed onto my bed, pushed down by my new companion—Complete and Utter Doom. Frankie sat at his desk, feeding his pet turtle. He'd saved the turtle from Dr. Frankenhammer, who'd been using its DNA to create a shelled minion. Frankie's side of the room was filled with saved creatures, mostly small things like mice and rats. There were also two frogs, a snake, and a dead jellyfish.

"The Great Library is a myth," Darthin said.

"But Uncle Ludwig says it's real," I told him. "He's been researching it for years. Years!"

"I'm sorry."

I sat up. "Tell me what you know."

Darthin sighed and sat down next to me. "The myth goes like this: Hundreds of years ago there was a Realm of Enlightenment.

In some retellings, it's called Erudyten, because *erudite* means 'having great knowledge.' Erudyten was ruled by a benevolent king, called King Wellread. Early in his rule, he often despaired when he walked among his people. He found it frustrating that so few of his subjects could converse intelligently about the latest novels or news of the day. 'My people are stupid!' he lamented."

"Lamented?"

"Cried. Seriously, you haven't heard this story?"

"Nope," I said. "Frankie?"

Frankie shook his head.

"Wow. He decided to educate his people because he felt that, more than natural resources or scenic beauty, his realm's most valuable asset was its people. They were hardworking and honest and supportive of one another. He loved his stupid people. So he passed a royal decree that children had to attend school. He built libraries and set up book clubs. His people collected knowledge from all corners of the world. The rewards of his program went well beyond improving sidewalk conversations. The people grew smarter. They created amazing inventions and sold them all over the world. Erudyten became very rich and more advanced than ever."

"Sounds great. What happened?"

"Smart people from other countries began to travel to Erudyten, to visit its libraries and study at its universities. Many decided to stay. Other countries suffered from this 'brain drain'—losing their best minds to Erudyten. Those countries were jealous of Erudyten's wealth but didn't want to put in the same effort into creating it themselves. They preferred to use their countries' money to make weapons and armies. And palaces for their rulers. Lots of palaces.

"These other rulers knew that something had to be done about Erudyten. So they got together and decided to use their weapons and their armies to destroy it. Erudyten, being a pacifist realm, thought it could appease its enemies with gifts of money and technology. But for all its knowledge, it was unable to foresee the anger and resentment toward it, and it was destroyed."

"Darthin, what does this have to do with the Great Library?"

"The capital city was under siege for months before it fell. During that time, the myth tells of a band of librarians who secretly collected every book from every library, and there were millions— tens of millions—of books. They snuck them out of the city to a safe location far away, where the evil usurpers would never be able to destroy them. The royal family vowed to create a new society to share its knowledge."

"So why do you think this is just a fairy tale?"

"C'mon, Higgins. A secret band of librarians, sworn to hide all those books until a kingdom capable of protecting that knowledge arises? Someone would have found something by now. Nobody can keep a secret that long."

I wasn't so sure. Nobody knew that Cook used a mix for her "homemade" ogre cakes.

"I'm sorry, Runt," Darthin said. "I'm sure it's disappointing, knowing that Uncle Ludwig hasn't been trying to find out where you came from."

"That's not even the worst thing that happened to me today." I told them about my confrontation with Dr. Pravus and the lost book.

"You couldn't have done anything differently," Frankie said. "Pravus would have killed you. The man's a psycho."

"Critchlore will forgive you," Darthin said. "He's just mad about losing the book."

"The most valuable book in the school," I said. "The one that contains the secret for creating an undefeatable minion."

"It doesn't matter," Darthin added. "Nobody can decipher that book. Dr. Frankenhammer said that the hieroglyphics are impossible to read. Unless we find some bit of writing that has a translation on it, it won't be decoded."

"You know where a translation might be found?" I asked Darthin.

"Don't say it."

"In the Great Library. Along with all the other forgotten knowledge of the world."

"I said, 'Don't say it.' The Great Library is a myth."

"But what if it isn't?" I asked. "What if it does hold clues to where I'm from and what my medallion means. What if it has a new secret book of minions I can give Dr. Critchlore so he doesn't hate me? Finding the Great Library could solve all my problems."

Darthin's desk alarm blared, and he jumped up to shut it off. Frankie and I watched as he walked over to the window and raised his arms in the air.

"All hail the omniscient Irma Trackno," he said. "Benevolent ruler and friend to all who support her."

"He doesn't believe in the Great Library," I said to Frankie, nodding at Darthin. "But he believes his evil overlord has the power to see him do his nightly tribute."

"All hail Irma Trackno," Frankie whispered. I shot him a look, and he said, "What? She might."

58

CHAPTER 10

All overlords demand proof of loyalty, whether it's
Elvira Cutter's Seven Labors, or Tankotto's weekly Tribute Day,
or Irma Trackno's nightly pledge of fidelity.
—PROFESSOR GALBRAITH, IN KNOW YOUR OVERLORD CLASS

Weekend over, the next morning I reported to my first class, which was helping Mistress Moira in her tower. Since I was a junior henchman trainee, she was my mentor. She was also the school seamstress and chocolatier, and maybe the Fourth Fate from mythology. Nobody could confirm that last part, but she did look somewhat goddess-like, wearing a gold-trimmed white robe.

I climbed the steps to the top of the tall tower, my legs burning because there were so many of them. As I climbed, I thought about my to-do list:

1. Redeem myself for losing the *TSBM*.
2. Save Sara and her family.
3. Find out where I'm from.
4. Find out who cursed me.
5. Beg him/her to lift the curse.

I needed to put something easy on there, like climb the steps of the tall tower, just so I could cross something off as done.

At last I reached Mistress Moira's quarters. Her door was open, and I heard voices inside.

"Moira, they have to be done a week from Saturday." It was Dr. Critchlore. I stepped away from the door because I didn't want to face his anger again.

"Derek, it's unreasonable," Mistress Moira said. "Twenty dresses in two weeks?"

"Not just twenty dresses. They have to be the height of fashion. No! Higher than the height of fashion. They have to be the clouds of fashion, the sky of fashion. The outer universe of fashion. Way, way up there in the fashion sense."

"I'll do my best. That's all I can do."

"Moira, we're talking about the Siren Syndicate here." He shivered. "They control all river trade. It's the only decent trade route. Roads are sabotaged regularly. Dragon shipping is fantastically expensive. Not to mention unreliable. If a dragon spots a sheep or something shiny on the ground, he forgets all about his delivery and you have to send a search party out for him.

"If the Siren Syndicate is dissatisfied, I'll never get another shipment of anything. That means no minion supply business, no training equipment, no anything. This school will fail and my ridiculous family will vote me out at the next meeting. Moira, please," he said, his voice low and urgent. "It's important."

"I shall do everything in my power to complete the dresses."

"Thank you."

He turned to leave and I froze where I stood, my chest exploding with thumps of panic.

"You," he said, stopping in front of me. "Higgins." He shook his head like he was disgusted, then brushed past me, nudging me on the shoulder. I fell backward a little bit, and a huge lump expanded in my throat as I realized that Dr. Critchlore hated me. I saw it in his eyes.

Mistress Moira noticed me standing there. "Good morning, Runt," she said, smiling brightly.

"Good morning," I said, my voice cracking a little. I blinked away the tears that were forming. "That was . . . an interesting conversation."

"That man." She waved a hand. "He wants the impossible. Dresses for the girls, in two weeks."

I sat down next to her on the couch, startling a squirrel, who ran to the tree in the corner. With her wide windows and all the foliage, including a grass carpet, Mistress Moira's room felt like a meadow in the sky. "I guess this would be a bad time to ask you to make me a crush-proof jacket."

"A what?"

"A jacket I could wear so that when a giant grabs me, he doesn't break my ribs."

She laughed her booming, infectious laugh. "Oh, Higgins, you slay me. A crush-proof jacket."

She reached for a piece of paper on the side table, wrote a quick list, and handed it to me. "This is a list of supplies I'll need from the dungeon," she said. "I've got to get to work, so I'll need these as soon as possible."

I looked at the list. It would take me twenty to thirty trips to get all that stuff. I would collapse after one trip.

"Frankie could do this a hundred times faster than me," I thought out loud.

"That's a splendid idea," Mistress Moira said. "Why don't you get him to help?"

"Okay. I'll do one trip now, before second period, and then I'll tell Frankie to check in with you during free period."

I was exhausted after that, but I managed to make it to my History of Henchmen class on time. I'd been desperate to get into the Junior Henchman Training Program, thinking that being a henchman was the best chance I had of finding my werewolf family. Now that I knew I wasn't a werewolf, being a henchman was even more vital to my quest to find my family. I would need every advantage I could get, since I was nothing but a scrawny human.

There were only five kids in the class now, so it was much easier to find a seat. Frieda the ogre took up two seats in the back row. Janet Desmarais, the most perfect person ever created, came in holding hands with Rufus Spaniel. They took the two seats behind me, next to Jud, another werewolf.

A part of me was hoping that Rufus and I would become friends, now that I'd proved myself worthy of being a junior henchman trainee. Maybe our relationship would move beyond insults.

"Hey, Runt," Rufus said. He scooched his chair forward and leaned toward me. "How many werewolves does it take to bring down a dragon?"

"I don't know." I smiled at him, waiting for the punch line.

"Of course you don't. You're not a werewolf." He laughed hysterically at his joke.

Professor Murphy, our stumpy teacher, entered the room, followed by a slim, dark-eyed, dark-haired kid I'd never seen before. Professor Murphy dropped his briefcase on his desk. The new kid took a seat next to me, keeping his gaze forward.

"This is much better, eh?" Professor Murphy said. The class had gone from twenty-seven students to five. It would probably go down further before graduation. Typically, there were only one or two junior henchman graduates each year.

Professor Murphy nodded at the new kid. "We have a new addition to our class. Please welcome Meztli . . ." He paused and looked at his paper, then mumbled something that sounded like "Shocoyosin." We all said hi. Meztli turned and waved at us.

"Meztli is a were-jaguar. He's an exchange student from a country called Galarza, which is located in the southern continent of Orgal, just below the isthmus of Skelterdam. He's working on mastering our language and tells me that he understands more than he speaks. I'm told he possesses the qualities necessary for this special track, and he's up to speed on his homework."

"*Sí*," Meztli said.

Were-jaguar! Man, that sounded cool.

"Okay, to work. You five—er—now six were selected after we evaluated your performance on a series of tests. As you know, a henchman needs to possess certain skills—strength, the ability to perform under pressure, and bravery. You all"—he looked at each of us, stopping at me—"well, most of you, proved that you possess these qualities. In this term we will expand on those attributes and learn about problem-solving for your EO, getting a diverse team of minions to work together, and taking on your EO's enemies. These are must-have skills. No Evil Overlord will hire a henchman who isn't able to perform these basic, although difficult, tasks. Now, then, you've all read the first case study in your History of Henchmen textbook, right?"

A chorus of mumbles answered him. If the others were like me, they hadn't. I mean, why do the homework if you didn't think you were going to be selected for the class? Being picked had been a complete surprise to me. Still, I should have written "Do my homework" on my to-do list.

"Let's have a quick quiz." Professor Murphy leaned against the edge of the desk facing us.

Oh, cryptids, I'm doomed.

"Thirty-five years ago, a revolution in the realm of Riggen overthrew EO Egmont Luticus," Professor Murphy said. "An evil overlord can only oppress his people so much before they revolt. In this case, the revolution was triggered by what famous event . . . Meztli?"

Meztli looked up from his notes. He tapped his forehead like he was thinking. He tapped it again and again, and then said something in his own language. He nodded when he was done.

"Um . . . okay," Professor Murphy said. "I assume you're referring to the Great Headache Uprising. That's correct." Then he addressed the class. "As you all know, aspirin and other drugs were manufactured and sold by the Elixir Syndicate, which controlled the supply of medicine. That's what a syndicate does. Instead of competing against one another, companies band together to control prices and supply. The Elixir Syndicate kept raising the price of aspirin, and Luticus didn't like it. He threatened them with attacks from his undead army if they didn't lower their prices.

"The Elixir Syndicate responded by cutting off all aspirin to Riggen. Without aspirin, the people grew very angry, because if there's one thing that will give a person a headache, it's living under an overlord as cruel as Egmont Luticus.

"The revolution began. Luticus went to the EO Council to ask for help from the other overlords. This is standard procedure; the EOs tend to protect one another. But in this case, he was turned down. By whom . . . Janet?"

"Oh, I know this," she said, crinkling her brow in a really cute way. "It was one of the big ones?"

Professor Murphy hadn't stopped smiling at her. "That's correct. It was Wexmir Smarvy, Luticus's northern neighbor. Unfortunately for Luticus, Smarvy wanted him to fall. He had his eye on the port city of Balti, where he wanted to build a vacation palace.

"Without support, Luticus was overthrown by rebels led by a chicken farmer. That chicken farmer is now . . . Rufus?"

"Fraze Coldheart," Rufus said.

Rufus always got the easy questions.

"That's right. And his first act as overlord was . . . Frieda?"

Frieda had been watching a bug crawl across her desk. She smashed it with her fist, then looked up at Professor Murphy.

"Correct," Professor Murphy said. "He got the overlords together to squash the Elixir Syndicate, which had clearly grown too powerful. The overlords installed their own thug, Fat Pharmo, to take over medicine production. Fat Pharmo split the company into smaller pieces, and the EOs left them alone after that. Jud, can you name another organization that has power equal to the EOs?"

"The Pravus Academy," Jud said. "Pravus has those EOs eating out of his hand, they're so desperate to get his giant gorillas."

"That's true, but the Minion School Directives keep minion schools from gaining too much power. Nothing frightens the EOs more than the thought of a minion school syndicate. Imagine, one person controlling the supply of minions! The EOs would destroy Stull before letting that happen.

"No, I was thinking of a group even more powerful than Dr. Pravus—the Siren Syndicate. Runt, tell us how the Siren Syndicate has avoided the fate that befell the Elixir Syndicate."

"Um, bribes?" I said, because that answer worked most of the time for questions about EOs.

Professor Murphy shook his head. "You didn't do the assigned reading, did you?"

"Well . . . no." But neither had the others, I was sure. They'd just gotten away with lame answers.

"That's one strike, Mr. Higgins. Three strikes and you're out." He picked up his notebook and made a vicious check mark in it. I felt like I'd been stabbed in the chest.

He addressed us all. "I take great pride in the henchmen who graduate from my program. They are a reflection of my teaching skills. If you do not measure up to my standards, I won't allow you to continue in this class, headmaster interference or not." He glared at me again before turning to the board.

As he wrote the names of the major evil overlords and the kingdoms they ruled, he answered the question I couldn't. "The Siren Syndicate has a cozier relationship with the EOs than the Elixir Syndicate had. They ask permission before raising rates on shipping, and they've allowed the EOs to have a say in who is elected Grand Sirenness."

He finished his list and turned to us. "Tomorrow we're going on a field trip to the capital to watch a session of the Evil Overlord Council. The trip will take all day, so please notify your other teachers that you'll be gone."

He looked at me, then added, "Let's see if we can get through the day without anyone being demoted back to regular minion status."

CHAPTER 11

In Bluetorch, all books are banned except for two:
Dark Victor's autobiography and his collection of soufflé recipes.
—TRUE FACT

During third-period study hall, I met Syke outside. She was eating something that looked like a tulip. Inside the flower were a bunch of plump pink seeds.

"What *is* that?" I asked.

She tried to get another seed, but the flower's mouth snapped at her fingers as they got close to the fruit.

"I got it from Tootles," she said. "It's part Venus flytrap, part pomegranate." Her fingers darted inside the flower but came out empty. "Because that's the problem with eating fruit—it's just not enough of a challenge."

"Is that from his secret greenhouse?"

She nodded.

I used to think I knew this school better than anyone, but apparently not. I had no idea where his secret greenhouse was.

"Tootles has a secret greenhouse," I said. "Dr. Frankenhammer has a secret lab. Remember when I said everyone has a secret something?"

She nodded, smiling in victory as she freed a seed.

"I bet Uncle Ludwig has a secret library," I said. "Want to go check?"

"Actually, I have some math homework I'd like to get started on."

"Really?"

"No, not really," she said with an eye roll. "We have time before Literature. Let's go."

"Uncle Ludwig?" I tapped on one of the locked doors' windows. "It's me, Higgins. I'm here to reshelve books."

The door opened in a flash.

"Syke said she'd help," I said, explaining her presence next to me.

"Good, good. Come this way."

He led us to his desk, through the usual maze of carts loaded with books.

"We'll sort them first," I suggested. Uncle Ludwig nodded and sat back down to his work. I'd filled Syke in on my plan as we walked to the library—that we'd ask Uncle Ludwig some questions while we worked, and then, maybe close to the end of free period, we'd spring the big question on him. Real subtle-like.

Syke held a book called *Social Struggles in Euripidam and Why We Don't Have Any*. I nodded at her to ask the question I'd prompted her with—did he know of any books on Skelterdam?

Syke nodded back. "So, Uncle Ludwig," she said loudly. "Where's your secret library?"

I threw a paperback at her leg. She was the opposite of subtle.

"What's that?" he asked, looking up from his book.

"Your secret library? We know you have one. Where is it?"

"Well . . . now what makes you think . . . I'm sure I don't know what you're talking about."

He had one. That was obvious.

"Uncle Ludwig," I said, "these can't be the only books you're working with."

"Yeah," Syke said. "It's strange that you studied at the prestigious Amlick University, and now you're stuck in this dust hole, with the most ridiculous books." She picked up another one and read its title. "'*Maya Tupo's Miraculous Cures for Everything.*' That's got to be true, right? Not just something someone wrote to suck up to Maya Tupo.

"We know you're better than this." She waved her arm to include the whole library. "And we know there's an order of librarians who dream of a day when knowledge can be freely shared and not hidden. Who protect that knowledge in the Great Library. That seems more like you than this place.

"C'mon, Uncle Ludwig. Where's the secret entrance? Is it behind that bookshelf?" She walked behind his desk. "Do I pull out a special book, and the whole wall swings open?"

"That's a bit of a cliché," Uncle Ludwig said. "I'm hurt you think I'd be so unoriginal. If I had such a thing."

"No? Then it probably isn't the fireplace either. I bet it's underneath this room," Syke said. "Maybe one of these bookshelves pushes to the side." She stood next to one and motioned for me to help her try to move it.

"The thing about a secret entrance," Uncle Ludwig said, "is that you want to be able to use it quickly, and then cover it up just as quickly, so nobody can follow."

"Maybe you have a special key that goes somewhere?" Syke said.

We hadn't budged the bookshelf, so we bent down to look for seams on the floor instead. "Or a switch by your desk?"

Uncle Ludwig didn't say anything. We looked over and saw that the reason he didn't say anything was because he was gone.

"What the wyvern?" I said. We rushed over to the desk. "Where'd he go?"

"To his secret library," Syke said. She ran her hands under and around his desk. She moved to his chair. "Look, the chair's base is solid, like a pedestal. Weird."

A muffled voice called from under the floor. "Sit on the chair."

"You do it," Syke said to me. So I did. The chair was wide and padded. All of a sudden the seat dropped, like a trapdoor, and I fell onto an air mattress. Uncle Ludwig stood next to the mattress in a chamber only a little bigger than an elevator. Above me, the chair opening had already snapped shut.

"It's fine, Syke!" I yelled.

"Okay!"

Uncle Ludwig pushed a lever, and Syke dropped down. She rolled off the mattress and stood up beside us. "So this is it? Your secret closet? I'm a little underwhelmed."

Uncle Ludwig smiled. He put his finger to his lips, and then said, loud and clear, "*If books were food, I'd eat a feast, and savor every taste.*" At these words, the door opened, and Uncle Ludwig led us out onto a narrow balcony with a wooden banister. "*The tangy tales and pepp'ry myths, not one would go to waste,*" he said, and the door closed behind us. I recognized the lines from a poem he recited all the time. But those thoughts quickly left my head when the lights came on and I saw the most amazing library spread out below me.

The school's main library, the one all students used, was depressing, dim, and uninviting; the books placed on rusty metal shelves. Here, I felt like I'd walked into an oil painting; it was radiant. Amber lighting lit up rows and rows of rich wooden shelves. Every detail was stunning, from the marble floor to the frescoes painted on the stucco ceiling. It smelled of old books: a little musty, leathery, and papery.

We stood on a balcony at one end of the two-story space. The narrow walkway circled the room, with aisles leading off into the second-floor stacks. Below, wooden columns with decorative golden tops held up the balcony.

"It's amazing," I said. I couldn't stop staring. Everywhere I looked, there were beautiful details. I felt like I was floating through all the beauty, the view swirling through my brain and lifting my soul. I was sure a boys' choir would start singing soon. It was the most amazing room I'd ever seen, and I wanted to stay forever.

"It's . . . wow . . . ," Syke said.

Uncle Ludwig beamed. "It is my treasure. And when a cloud comes to visit, I will show him this room, and he will invite me to join them."

"A cloud?"

"Covert Librarian Order Until Death," he said. "The secret society that collects books and takes them to the Great Library. When I find a CLOUD, I'll find the library."

We climbed down a spiral staircase in the corner. Uncle Ludwig showed us his book-restoration area, his cozy reading nook, his section on picture books. "This one is banned in fourteen countries,"

he said. The book had a cartoon monkey and a man with a big yellow hat on the cover. "It's considered very subversive."

The stacks were organized with a section for each of the seven Greater Realms of the Porvian Continent. The thirteen Lesser Realms were grouped together, as were the Island Realms. The Dismantled Realm was split into three sections, and there was a dark, forgotten section in the corner.

"Look at this," Syke said, coming out of one row. "*The History of Worb.*"

"Upper Worb or Lower Worb?" I asked.

"It just says 'Worb.' That's what's funny."

"It used to be a single country," a familiar voice said.

We looked over and saw Professor Zaida standing on a step stool as she pulled a book from the stacks.

"Professor Zaida, what are you doing here?" I asked.

"I'm the Literature professor," she said. "And these are books." She looked at us like it was obvious. "Plus I've lost my third-period zombie class." That was true. After word of their work on Miss Merrybench got out, they'd been quickly recruited by Fraze Cold-heart, who had a fondness for undead minions.

Syke thumbed through the book. "I can't imagine a complete Worb. Irma Trackno and Wexmir Smarvy despise each other."

"Which is why that history book is banned," Professor Zaida said. "Smarvy would destroy this castle if he knew that book was here. He does not want any talk of reunification of the Worbs. Please forget you saw it."

"Uncle Ludwig?" I asked. "This is dangerous, isn't it?"

Uncle Ludwig nodded. "Dr. Critchlore wanted to shut it down, but then I presented him with *The Top Secret Book of Minions*, and he allowed me to continue as long as I added safety measures. I also had to promise to side with him whenever a family vote comes up."

"So you won't vote 'no confidence' in Dr. Critchlore?" I asked, remembering what Vodum had said about the family vote.

"Heard the rumors, have you?" Uncle Ludwig said. "*I* won't vote against him, but the rest of the family is already looking for someone to replace him. There's been talk of bringing in a more successful minion school headmaster to oversee operations here and get us back on top."

I gasped. "Not Dr. Pravus?" I said.

"Some in the family think so, yes. He's obviously brilliant. And quite charming. Derek is the only Critchlore who despises him."

That couldn't be true. The man was a monster, and I mean that in the "mean and evil" sort of way, not the "cool and powerful" way.

I stood there, stunned, unable to comprehend what he was suggesting—that the Critchlore family would fire one of their own and bring in Dr. Critchlore's worst enemy. It was unthinkable.

"What are the safety measures?" Syke asked, still holding that illegal book.

"See that button by the fireplace?" Uncle Ludwig said. "It's a self-destruct button. In the event of an EO finding out about this library, that button will destroy all the evidence."

I shuddered at the thought of all this beauty being destroyed by the push of a button.

Professor Zaida shook her head as she stepped down from her perch. "Ludwig, I'm going to borrow these books on myths of the Plutharic Realm, if you don't mind."

"By all means, Professor Zaida," he said. "Just remember to return them this time, eh? I'd hate to lose more books to that paper-eating pooch of yours."

"I'm so sorry about that," she said. "Runt, Syke." She winked at us. "I'll see you in class. Today is doughnut day, so don't be late." She disappeared behind the stacks.

"Yes," Syke said, pumping her fist in the air. "Doughnut day. I love Professor Zaida."

"There's another exit over there," Uncle Ludwig said, nodding at the spot where Professor Zaida had left. "It comes out of a rock wall in the dungeon, near the grotto. Don't use it. The grotto is very unsafe."

"Because of Clarence?" I asked.

"If that is the name of the flesh-eating fish monster, then yes. Those tentacles come out of nowhere."

I looked at all the books that Uncle Ludwig had collected. I'd never seen so many in one place.

"Uncle Ludwig?" I asked. "Where'd you get *The Top Secret Book of Minions*? Can you get another one?"

"The *TSBM*?" he said. "It took years to track that down. I finally found it in the shady region of Corovilla. It was fantastically expensive but worth it. Dr. Critchlore let me continue my work here, and now we own a priceless piece of history."

"Right," I said. "So finding another copy?"

"Would be impossible."

The number one item on my to-do list—redeeming myself for losing the book—just got a whole lot harder.

CHAPTER 12

The fable of Little Red Riding Cap teaches us to share,
because if she'd shared her basket of food with the wolf, he wouldn't
have eaten her grandma. You can't blame a wolf for being hungry.
—RUNT HIGGINS'S LITERATURE ESSAY

The number one item on my to-do list was impossible, but the number three item on my list, finding out where I came from, just got a little more interesting. Sara had said, "We are Ohtee." Now I had a real library to find out what that meant.

Uncle Ludwig had never heard of anything called Ohtee. He suggested I start looking in the Cyclop-edia, which was a whole row of books about everything. I found the "O–N" book, but when I opened it, I saw that large sections had been blacked out.

"That set came from Bluetorch," Uncle Ludwig said, sitting beside me at a table. "When Dark Victor came to power, he censored books but soon decided it would be easier to burn them."

I didn't find an entry for *Ohtee*, or *Otee*, or *O/T*, but there was one for *Oti*. It read:

The Oti tribe hails from the western slope and foothills of the SMUDGE
mountains in SMUDGE.

It didn't say "SMUDGE"—that's just what it looked like.

The Oti were hunter-gatherers who lived in small bands without centralized political leadership. They were peaceful, but bound together to defend their territory from invaders. Known for their fierce fighting and SMUDGE.

All the rest was blacked out.

"Do you have another Cyclop-edia?" I asked Uncle Ludwig.

"Encyclopedia. No, and my set is incomplete," he said. "I don't have an *M*. Do you see now how important it is to find the Great Library? Who can live in a world with no knowledge of things starting with *M*?"

Syke had been exploring the stacks, but she returned to the table where Uncle Ludwig sat. "So where are your files on Runt?" she asked. "You must have collected lots of clues about where he came from, right?"

"Er . . . files?"

"Cook said you've been researching where Runt came from," Syke continued. "For years. So what have you found out about him?" She sat down opposite him and leaned over the desk, capturing him in her glare.

"I . . . um . . . that is . . . my files are upstairs, but I remember . . . Runt arrived here a few years ago—"

"Eight years ago," I corrected.

"Right. Cook took him in, gave him her last name . . ." He looked around the room, then at his watch. "Goodness, look at the time. I must be off."

Syke shook her head.

"You two must leave as well." He stood up and shooed us out.

Syke's brow was furrowed, and she walked like she was punishing the ground.

"What's wrong?" I asked. I pulled her to a stop in the castle's foyer. We were still a few minutes early for Literature.

"Uncle Ludwig. Heck, everyone here is so self-centered. Critchlore, Vodum, Frankenhammer, every one of them. They only care about their own stuff."

"What about Mistress Moira, Professor Zaida, Tootles and Riga . . . ?" I said.

"Okay, fine, not them. But Uncle Ludwig is just like Dr. Critchlore—so wrapped up in his own work that he ignores everyone else. Which just reminds me of the fact that all my hamadryad relatives hate Dr. Critchlore, but they won't tell me why."

"Really?"

This conversation was making me nervous because I knew why the hamadryads hated Dr. Critchlore, why oak trees regularly pelted him with acorns when he passed near. I'd just found out from Dr. Frankenhammer that Dr. Critchlore had destroyed the forest where Syke had lived, killing her mother. He told everyone that he'd saved Syke from the fire, but it was a fire he'd caused on purpose. I didn't want to tell Syke the truth, because then she would hate him, and if she hated him, she would leave the school.

The sudden realization of what a huge hypocrite I was made me feel heavy with guilt, so I stepped away from Syke and sat down on the staircase.

"They despise him," Syke said, sitting next to me. "So I asked—*why would you let me be raised by someone you hate?*"

I didn't really understand that either. I knew she couldn't live in the trees like regular hamadryads. I'd assumed Dr. Critchlore was their only option. Still, it made me wonder. "What did they say?"

"They said I was too young to understand. I'm thirteen; I'm not a baby. I don't know why they won't tell me why they hate him. It must be something terrible."

It was. And I had to tell her. He'd killed her mother! But there had to be an explanation. Why hadn't Critchlore known it was a hamadryad-protected forest? His family had lived in the castle for generations. I told myself that I needed more information before I could tell Syke the truth, but I knew I was stalling.

"Syke," I said, "I'm not mad at you anymore for not telling me I'm not a werewolf."

"Thanks, Runt."

"Even though it really hurt my feelings, because I felt like everyone was laughing at me, I know you just didn't want me to be hurt."

"Exactly."

That said, I felt better. I was still hurt that she'd let me make a fool of myself for so long, but not as much since I realized I was doing the exact same thing. Keeping secrets.

The bell rang, and we headed up one of the winding staircases that led from the foyer to the second floor.

"What am I going to do now?" I said. "I have no idea how to find out where Sara and I come from."

"You go find your own CLOUD," Syke said. "With this." She showed me a book. It was *The History of Worb.*

"Syke, are you crazy? You stole this book."

"Serves him right," she said. "He's had years to research your curse, and all he's done is look for that stupid library. You take this illegal book on your field trip tomorrow, sneak off to the capital library and ask if anyone is interested in it. Find a CLOUD yourself. But be careful."

She stuffed it into my bag.

That night, after dinner, I went to see Cook in the kitchen.

"Hi, everybody," I said, waving to the dishwashers, the food preparers, and Pierre, my foster brother, who was setting out lunch bags for our field trip.

They all nodded hello. Cook sat at a table, checking a printout of her menus, still wearing her apron and hairnet, and the cat-eye glasses she loved.

"Hi, Mom," I said, sitting next to her.

"Runt," she said. "Great game yesterday."

"Thanks. We should have won." I thought about telling her that I'd lost *The Top Secret Book of Minions,* but I shrugged that idea away. There was nothing she could say to make me feel better about that. She might be able to help me with my Uncle Ludwig problem, though. "Hey, you know what?"

"Hmm?" She raised her eyebrows as she scratched off something on her list.

"I went to see Uncle Ludwig after the game, to see what he's found out about me?"

"Yes?" She looked up at that. "What's he found out?"

"Nothing," I said. My stomach got all twisty when I said that, like it only now realized the danger I was in. "He has been . . . working on something else. He has no clue where I'm from."

"That can't be right," Cook said. "He's told me over and over that he's getting close."

I shook my head. "He thought I'd been left here a few years ago. I've been here eight years."

Cook slammed her pen on the table. Anger seemed to inflate her, like bread rising. "That man promised me he would work on nothing else! I gave him everything you had with you. Except your medallion, of course, because you cried whenever I tried to take it off. I told him, 'You find out where he's from.' And he told me he would make it his top priority." Cook slapped the table, hard. "That man lied to my face, and after I gave him my family's treasured book collection!"

"What am I going to do?" I felt tears pool in my eyes and then burst free. In a flash, I was sobbing. All at once, my impending death seemed to be rushing at me like a flood I couldn't dodge.

Cook got up and squeezed me in a hug. "I'll talk to Dr. Critch-lore. He owes you."

I slumped. The last thing I wanted was for Cook to tattle on Uncle Ludwig for me, especially since Dr. Critchlore was already mad at me for losing the book.

"No, don't," I said, wiping my face with my sleeve. "Uncle Ludwig thinks he can find the answer to my problem if he solves his own problem. Let's give him some more time."

She let go of me and stood up. "Really? Because I have a mind to—"

"Don't say anything yet," I said. "What exactly did you give him?"

Cook sat back down. "You were a mess when they brought you to me. Like you'd been rolled in mud. You wore a loose dog collar around your neck, and you howled at me when I tried to take it off." She chuckled at that. "I managed to clean you up and wash your clothes. You wore an undershirt, a silky shirt with a fluffy collar that peeked out over a jacket that was probably once a very pretty shade of blue. Your pants matched and had a gold stripe down the side. It was like you'd been playing dress-up in a medieval play."

"I'll ask Uncle Ludwig if he still has them," I said. "Hey, what are you packing in our lunch tomorrow?"

"The usual: sandwich, fruit, cookie for most of you. Something disgusting and crunchy for Frieda." She smiled at me. "Your first trip to the capital, Runt. It's going to be so exciting!"

I smiled back. It was exciting. I wasn't just going to see the capital for the first time; I was going to take Uncle Ludwig's book and find a CLOUD. Tomorrow was the day I took matters into my own hands.

CHAPTER 13

*The purpose of the United Nations of Overlords is to allow
for a consensus in resolving disputes between countries.
Also, we like to gang up on the weak and bully them.*

—CERA BACCULUS ON THE UNO

I could barely sleep; I was so excited about visiting the United
Nations of Overlords. The UNO! Plus I was on a secret mission.
If I could find a CLOUD (currently number one on my to-do
list), I could find the Great Library, which would have a complete
set of encyclopedias. They probably had another copy of *The Top
Secret Book of Minions* too.

I was on my way to solving all my problems.

There were thirteen junior henchmen trainees on the trip—the
six of us third-years, three fourth-years, one fifth-year, one sixth-
year giant, and two seventh-years. We had to take the jumbo van,
because Frieda and the giant didn't fit comfortably in the normal
van. I loved the jumbo van. It fit twelve minions of impressive size,
or forty-eight normal-sized minions. I had a jumbo seat to myself,
which meant I could stretch across a seat as big as a king-sized bed.

I leaned across the aisle to ask the new guy, Meztli, a question.
"Hey, Meztli?"

"*¿Sí?*"

"Have you ever heard of the 'Broken Place'?"

"*¿El Lugar Roto?*"

"Okay, sure."

He thought for a second. "*Amigo,*" he said, "*nadie va al Lugar Roto.*"

"*¿Nadie va?* Nobody goes there?"

He shook his head. "No. It is across the sea, on the *Continente Currial*. In a place where there are many shakes of the ground. *¿Cómo se dice?*" He wobbled in his seat.

"Earthquakes?"

"*Sí,* earths quake. Everything breaks. It is the broken place."

That didn't sound like what Sara had meant. She'd said it was broken by war.

"And the peoples there? They are *loco,*" Meztli went on. "Crazy. Like for instance, they no eat their meats on the bone. No. They slice the meats off the bone, and then hide the meats between two slices of bread." He threw up his hands in disgust.

"Like a sandwich?" I asked.

"*No sé.* I don't know. But this thing they do? It's *loco.* Sometimes they put a red sauce on the meats, and the red sauce—it is not blood. It is called after a baby cat . . . cats' pup, or something. I am not even lying."

"Ketchup?"

"*Sí,* it is a cat's pup. What kind of cat has a pup? *Loco.*"

Okay, so Meztli was no help. I sat back to think about what I was going to do in the capital.

"'Look at me,'" Meztli said in a high voice. He held an invisible sandwich in his hands, and he took a pretend bite. "'I no eating meats. I only eating bread. You cannot see the meats.'" He shook his head. "Who does that?"

Meztli was going to be in for a surprise when he opened the lunch bag that Cook had prepared for each of us.

It was a long drive, but at last we made it. Once in the capital, we drove down wide, perfectly paved roads lined with trees. Huge buildings flanked the road, each one looking like a castle or a palace of some kind. Every Evil Overlord kept a residence in the capital for when they traveled here on business. I got goose bumps when I realized that we were driving by the palaces of Lord Vengecrypt, Fraze Coldheart, maybe even Maya Tupo.

At the end of the road, we could see the main Evil Overlord Council Building, a long, modern building fronted by flagpoles hoisting the flags of the seven Greater Realms, the thirteen Lesser Realms, the Island Realms, and the ripped flag of the Dismantled Realm. One flagpole was empty, as if they had forgotten a realm.

The road split in two as it hit the expansive park in front, the right side passing by the Stull National Government buildings. On the left side of the park I saw the Stull National Library, the Stull Museum, and the Stull Performing Arts Center.

Professor Murphy suggested that we eat lunch in the park before entering the EO Council building, so we grabbed our bags and sat at benches to eat. We were near the library, so I ate in a hurry and then asked Professor Murphy if I could go inside to use the bathroom.

"Take a buddy," he said.

"Meztli?" I asked. He was sitting next to me on a bench, holding his ham sandwich like it was something disgusting. He pulled the ham out and tried to wrap it around the bread.

"Want to go to the library?" I asked.

He shook his head, pointing to his sandwich. "At least put the meats on the outside." He added in a deep voice, "'Look at me! I eat huge slab of meats. I tremendously hungry beast!' That's better, no?"

"I'll go," Janet said. This earned me a hard stare from Rufus when he saw us leaving together. He was playing catch with Frieda and Jud.

We climbed up marble steps to enter the arched doorway. Inside the lobby, a series of archways led to different sections for each realm. The sections were large, mostly empty spaces. Rooms that used to hold bookshelves now held displays that proclaimed each realm's greatest achievements. Apparently, Maya Tupo invented trees. Sure she did, and I was a swamp monster.

No sign of an encyclopedia anywhere.

"I'm going to the ladies' room," Janet said. "Be right back."

"Okay." I stepped up to the information desk.

I looked to the left and then the right, making sure nobody was within hearing distance. The librarian, a woman with graying hair and a friendly face, waited patiently for me to ask my question.

"Excuse me," I said. "I have this book—um—that I found. It seems odd to me, and I wondered if you were interested in it?"

I carefully eased the book out of my pack and showed it to her.

She leaned over to look and then gasped. "Put it back. Put it back," she whispered, waving her hands at me. "That's an illegal book. You could be—" She stopped talking as an elderly woman walked by behind us. Wrapped in a torn and dirty shawl, the old lady stumbled and reached for the counter next to me. She peeked down at my bag, so I quickly covered up the book.

"Xena, are you okay?" the librarian asked.

"Dizzy," she said. "Lately I've been feeling dizzy. And numb." She took a deep breath and then walked away, out the front door.

The librarian looked sympathetic. "Poor, old homeless lady," she said. She returned her attention to me. "Don't let anyone see that book. Destroy it. And get out of here. Please. This is not a place to ask questions."

It was a library. What else did you do there?

Janet came back wearing a black scarf around her head, dark glasses, and a fake mole on her cheek.

"What's with the getup?" I asked. "You look shifty."

"Shifty is in," she said. "I don't want to look like a dorky little kid on a field trip." She looked me up and down. "No offense."

I tried another librarian in the Upper Worb section and got the same horrified response to the banned book. Janet slapped my shoulder and said, "You're going to get us arrested. I'll wait for you in the lobby."

I tried two more librarians before thinking I had better get back to Professor Murphy. Dejected, I went to find Janet and saw her talking to a very tall man in a corner of the entryway. The man stood hunched over, like a crane, so that their heads were close enough to whisper in each other's ear.

"Who was that?" I asked when she walked over to me.

"Nobody," she said, heading for the front door. I didn't follow, which made her turn around and look at me. "Okay, here's the deal.

You don't mention that man, and I won't say anything about the book you're flashing around that could get our school shut down."

"Deal."

Going down the steps in front, we passed the disheveled woman from earlier. "Spare change for food?" she asked.

I pulled out an apple from my backpack. She took it with stiff hands, as if she couldn't bend her fingers. "My thanks," she said. She put a hand on my shoulder, and then let it fall to the Critchlore patch on my jacket. She gasped when she saw my medallion. "Your coin."

"Excuse me?"

"Sorry, I feel so weak." She nodded to the library. "If books were food, I'd eat a feast."

"And savor every taste," I replied, recognizing the opening line of the poem Uncle Ludwig loved.

She smiled and continued:

"The tangy tales
and pepp'ry myths,
not one would go to waste.

A story soup,
a side of plays,
the sweet, sweet songs of yore.

I'd eat them all.
I'd never fill,
and then I'd ask for more."

She took a bite of the apple, so I finished the poem:

"Alas, my friend,
there'll be no taste,
no wordy banquet waits.

The books are gone,
the tables bare,
the tales of yore erased."

I knew that poem by heart because I'd heard Uncle Ludwig recite it many times while I reshelved books.

The old lady nodded. "What a clever boy," she said. "You know the poem." She struggled for breath. "You . . . have the coin." She patted my Critchlore patch. "The Archivist sent you. You must warn . . . something's happened. Warn the Archivist." She sat down.

"I'm sorry, do you need a doctor?"

"No." She waved a hand to dismiss that suggestion. "A doctor cannot help. I was tricked. I'm so ashamed. Tell the Archivist. The chameleon is coming."

"I don't know who the Archivist is." I pointed to the building. "Is the Archivist in the library?"

"*Z* is an *A*, *Y* is a *B*, *X* is a *C*," she said. "You have to know your ABCs."

"Runt Higgins!" Professor Murphy was gathering everyone up from lunch.

"I have to go," I told the lady. "I'm sorry. I hope you feel better soon."

She didn't answer.

Janet pulled my sleeve, and we jogged back toward the grassy area where the rest of the class waited.

"Did you see that, Janet?" I said. "She recognized my medallion."

"She called it a coin," Janet said. "And I wouldn't put too much faith in her recognizing it. Did you see her eyes? They looked bleary."

"But what if she did?"

"Then I guess you've solved your mystery," she said. "You're not a werewolf; you come from a family of crazy homeless beggars with bad teeth."

We entered the United Nations of Overlords building. The atrium was enormous, with a high ceiling and giant lettering on the far wall that read, "The Evil Overlord Council . . . In Us We Trust." Balconies ran along the walls at the sides and across the facing wall of the room.

Janet rejoined Rufus as his field trip buddy. Everyone had a buddy except me. I was on my way to stand with Professor Murphy, who was getting our visitor badges, when a hand grabbed my shoulder and spun me around. I looked up and up and up into the face of a vicious-looking ogre-man who must have weighed eight hundred pounds. "Come with me," he said, the words rolling out of his mouth like an avalanche, crushing the air around me.

"Uh . . . I'm here with my school group . . ."

He picked me up around my middle (again, a crush-proof jacket would've come in handy here) and carried me like a briefcase through the atrium. I passed Rufus, who has holding his gut, laughing. In a flash, he turned serious, pointed to Janet, pointed to me, and then slit his throat with his hand. Oh, dung beetles, what had he told this guy?

"Sir, there's been a mistake," I said. Then I remembered the book. What if they found that book in my possession? I'd be arrested. Uncle Ludwig would be arrested. Dr. Critchlore's School for Minions would be shut down, all because of me and my stupid, selfish quest.

The guard opened the door to a ground-floor office, threw me into a chair, and left the room.

Great. And me with no buddy to tell Professor Murphy where I'd been taken.

CHAPTER 14

*Irma Trackno came to power thirty years ago, promising
to reunite the Worbs under her rule. Wexmir Smarvy told her to
stay in her frozen wasteland and stop pretending to be an overlord.*
—ADDENDUM TO *THE HISTORY OF WORB*, BY ANONYMOUS

At first I thought I was shaking with fear, but I was actually shivering because the temperature in the room was several notches below freezing. I could see my breath, which was weird because it had been very pleasant in the atrium. I felt like I was in a freezer decorated as an office, with a large desk, some chairs facing it, and file cabinets along a wall. Above them hung a picture of an iceberg.

The longer I sat, the more worried I got. Why had I brought the illegal book? Why did I think I could just wave it around and find a CLOUD, when Uncle Ludwig had been looking for years and hadn't found one? If Dr. Critchlore hated me for losing *The Top Secret Book of Minions*, imagine what he'd do if I brought the Evil Overlord Council down on us for illegal book possession.

As I looked for a place to hide the book, the back door burst open and a man—no, a creature—stepped inside. He was unlike anything I'd ever seen. He stood like a man but looked like a seal—bald, with dark eyebrow-less eyes and rubbery gray skin. A long nose jutted out from his face, topped with jowly cheeks speckled with whiskers.

Another seal-faced man came in and stood on the other side of the door. This one held a spear. When he got into position, they both bowed their heads.

A tall woman walked in carrying a bucket of fish in her white-gloved hands. She wore an anorak, white and soft, with a big fur-lined hood and an embroidered belt. She wore this over black pants and boots. She had white hair that flowed to her shoulders, and she seemed to command the room with her presence. I expected the furniture to bow down too.

She put the bucket on the desk and sat opposite me. She pointed to my jacket. "You attend Critchlore's School for Minions," she said.

"Yes."

"I have some questions." She tossed a fish over her shoulder, and one of the guards caught it in his mouth. He slurped and crunched until the fish was gone. A second fish went to the other guard.

"I've heard rumors." She leaned forward now. "The cowardly minions video, Dr. Critchlore's near death, his new fondness for"—she made a disgusted face, like she couldn't bear to utter the next words—"recreational activities."

It was true; in the past week I'd seen him take up rock climbing, television watching, and art. It wasn't his fault. His secretary, Miss Merrybench, had been drugging him, to make him fall in love with her.

"Is this true?" she said. She leaned back, her hands together, fingers tapping each other lightly. Her stare was cold and hard, like that iceberg in the picture.

"We were sabotaged," I said. "Dr. Critchlore was drugged."

"Weakness," she said, waving a hand in the air. "The strong cannot be sabotaged."

"Dr. Critchlore knew about the plot, of course," I said. I could reiterate the ridiculous explanation he had given everyone. "He decided to play along, which would allow him to catch the culprit, and—"

"Stage a bit of countersabotage?" she interrupted. "Yes. That's what I would do," she said, nodding. And then she smiled for the first time. It was a scary smile. The kind you think predators have when they happen across easy prey.

"Yes. He's brilliant."

"So I've heard." She tossed two more fish. "And is he still single?"

"Huh?"

"Is he romantically attached to anyone?"

"Um, I don't think so. He's kind of heartbroken right now because he lost his secretary, who was the saboteur. She died before he realized how sinister she was, and now he calls her The One Who Got Away."

"Interesting." She smiled again. Honestly, I thought she was too old for him, but I wasn't going to say anything. I didn't want her to throw that bucket of fish at me.

"Is that all?" I asked. "I should get back to my group."

"Yes. If anyone asks, tell them you were suspected of spying for Egmont Luticus, the banished overlord of Riggen."

I nodded. At the door, I turned and asked, "Have you heard of a realm called the Broken Place?"

She laughed. "I'm fairly certain all the realms could be called that."

"There you are, Higgins," Professor Murphy said, handing me a visitor's badge. "Don't wander off. There's no telling what could happen to you in this place."

"Really?" I said, looking right at Rufus. He laughed.

"Let's go inside," Professor Murphy said, leading the way.

I held my breath as we entered the General Council Chamber.

Through these doors I might catch a glimpse of a real evil overlord, like Lord Vengecrypt from Carkley. Legend had it that he defeated four lesser realms in one massive land-and-sea assault. Or Wexmir Smarvy, overlord of Lower Worb, a realm that grew bigger every day. I was going to pee my pants; this was so huge.

A long table stretched across the stage. The chairs were empty, but the viewing area was packed. People filled the wide aisles and huddled in groups on the floor in front of the stage. Professor Murphy led us to a row of seating near the back.

We sat down and waited. Professor Murphy pointed out important people in the audience—the vice premier of the neutral region of Stull; the coaches of the championship boulderball team, who were getting an award from the overlords; and the different operatives of the EOs, feeling one another out over treaties and alliances.

"Ah, the Critchlore minions," a voice behind us said. We turned into the smirking gaze of Dr. Pravus. I slunk lower in my chair because he scared me. He also reminded me of what a loser I had been, letting him steal Dr. Critchlore's book.

"I see that Dr. Critchlore is branching out," he said. His entourage, who clung to him like warts on an ogre, laughed. "A school for minions *and* models? We all know your minion business is struggling, but what an inappropriate choice of a side business."

"Ballroom dancing is becoming popular with the EOs," Professor Murphy said. "As usual, Dr. Critchlore will be ready to fulfill a need you haven't even discovered yet. Once again, he will have something that you don't."

A dark anger flashed across Dr. Pravus's face. "Listen, you grub," he hissed. Professor Murphy looked frightened all of a sudden, like the kid who'd thought he could go up against the school bully, only to be smacked down. Pravus was right in his face. "Critchlore is going down, and I'm going to be the one who finishes him off. He's got nothing." He smiled and said louder, to everyone, "All Critchlore has is cowardly ogre-men, a dwindling recruiting class, and no sports teams of note." He laughed as he moved down the aisle.

With a shaky hand, Professor Murphy reached out to grab the arm of a woman following Pravus. She held a clipboard and wore an official-looking badge.

"Mrs. Collins," Professor Murphy said. "What is Dr. Pravus doing here?"

Mrs. Collins consulted her clipboard. "He's here to petition the overlords to allow him to take over another minion school."

Professor Murphy's brow furrowed in anger. "Impossible! That's against the Directives!" He turned to us to explain. "The EOs don't want fewer suppliers—it raises the cost of recruiting minions. They do not allow mergers or acquisitions."

"I've seen the petition," Collins said. "Pravus says the high demand for his minions is already raising costs. If he could take over a struggling school, he'd be able to increase the number of excellently trained minions, which would decrease recruiting costs for the overlords. Plus he's offered to privately fund a new school run independently from his academy. A specialist school of some sort. It's a win-win, really."

So it was true! Pravus *was* after Dr. Critchlore's school. It all made sense now. He'd spent the last few months sabotaging our school and making us look bad. We'd lost recruits and customers, and now Pravus was ready to swoop in and take over.

Why couldn't the Critchlore family see through his schemes? Or maybe they did, and they admired his tactics.

We watched Pravus as he reached the open floor in front of the stage. He was courted by many people, probably underlings of overlords hoping to secure Pravus minions for their bosses. He was a rock star here, for sure, and by rock star, I mean he was like a really spectacular boulderball player. We called them rock stars.

Professor Murphy wrote down the names of everyone Pravus talked to. When Pravus left, Professor Murphy stood up. "Time to go."

"What?" I said. "We just got here."

"We've gotten what we came for."

"But we haven't seen anything yet! The evil overlords haven't even arrived."

"We could wait for hours, and they still might not show up. They each want to be the one who keeps the others waiting. Most of the work is done in private chambers anyway."

This was turning into the worst field trip ever. I was disappointed and angry, and I felt like a failure.

As we walked through the atrium, I spotted the mysterious white-haired lady on the second floor. She stood against the balcony, flanked by her seal-like guards. I pointed her out to Professor Murphy.

"Who is that?" I asked.

"Well, look who made it down from the frozen north," he said. "The Strong and Wonderful Irma Trackno."

Irma Trackno? I'd just had a private meeting with an evil overlord? My jaw dropped faster than Dr. Critchlore's trapdoor.

"You will never meet a more ruthless or power-hungry overlord," he whispered to me. "She'll attack anyone at any time, sometimes losing half her armies in the process." To everyone else, he said, "Each EO has a suite on the second floor. They conduct their private business in those chambers. No one is allowed up there except EOs and their henchmen."

As he said this, Dr. Pravus exited the elevator next to her.

"He shouldn't be up there," Professor Murphy said. "That man is getting too bold."

We watched as Dr. Pravus strode confidently down the corridor away from Irma Trackno. He knocked on a door decorated with two crossed fists, and a human stepped outside, closing the door behind him. He was an average-looking guy wearing a shiny baby-blue suit over a red shirt and black tie.

"Interesting," Professor Murphy said, nodding at the henchman.

"What he's doing there is actually the first lesson in my Stealth Techniques for Henchmen Seminar. If you're up to no good, wear something flashy, and that's all witnesses will remember. Not your height or the shape of your nose. They'll remember the odd color combination you wore, or the strange flower in your lapel. What you need to focus on are the things that do not change—height and weight, the shape of the ears. He has very odd, small ears."

"That's not an evil overlord?" I asked.

"No, that's Tankotto's man," Professor Murphy said. "Tankotto is the fourth-most powerful EO, but he recently lost a chunk of Burkeve, which he claims is rightfully his, to Cera Bacculus. He's thought to be allied with Elvira Cutter, with side alliances with the Island Realms and General Nix." He rattled off facts like an uncensored encyclopedia. "Tankotto isn't loyal to any one minion school; he recruits from anyone."

We couldn't hear what they were saying, but the conversation soon turned angry. Dr. Pravus wanted to see Tankotto, but the henchman kept shaking his head. Pravus tried to push his way past, but the henchman stood firm.

"I trained you!" Dr. Pravus said, loud enough for the whole atrium to hear.

"You trained me to obey my EO," the henchman replied, just as loudly. "And that's what I'm doing. He does not want to be disturbed."

Dr. Pravus stepped back. He pointed his finger at the henchman and spun around to leave. Just as he reached the elevator, one of Irma Trackno's seal-men approached him. They spoke briefly, and then Dr. Pravus shook his head. He tried to enter the elevator, but the seal-man grabbed him and pulled him toward his master, who stood glaring at Dr. Pravus.

"Interesting," Professor Murphy said. "Irma Trackno has never recruited minions before. Her army is completely homegrown and trained."

She had asked about Dr. Critchlore too. What if she had been checking me out, to see if she wanted to recruit Critchlore minions? What if I hadn't impressed her, and that was why she was seeing Dr. Pravus? My heart sank as I realized I had probably just failed Dr. Critchlore. Again.

CHAPTER 15

Do you ever get the feeling that nobody knows you exist?
—WHAT'S-HIS-NAME,

FROM THAT FORGOTTEN REALM IN THE CORNER OF THE MAP

We made it back to school in time for dinner. I loaded up my tray and headed for the corner. As I edged between tables, I heard someone say, "Runt Higgins."

I turned. It was Rufus, wearing a wicked smile. I told myself to keep walking, to not stick around for what was certain to be a new humiliation. But something about Rufus made me stop.

"I saw you reciting poetry with a beggar woman in the capital," he said.

His friends laughed.

"What's the matter, Runt? Can't find a girl your own age?"

Laughter charged at me from all sides, so I fled. I made it to my table and sat alone, waiting for my friends with my head down over my tray.

Pismo slid in next to me.

"Dude," he said with so much pity I winced.

"What?"

"That was pathetic." He shook his head.

"I know."

"You gotta zing him back," Pismo said.

"How do I zing Rufus?" I asked. "He's bigger, stronger, smarter, more popular, super handsome, and, oh yeah, he's a WERE-WOLF!"

"Man, do you need my help. Okay, listen." Pismo stood up and started pacing. "He taunts you for talking to an old beggar woman. You say, 'That's right, Rufus, your mom told me to remind you to change your underwear, because you always forget to do it at home.' Zing!"

I laughed. "I can't do that. I can't think up insults on the fly."

"It's easy. Here's another example. You take whatever embarrassing thing he taunts you with and turn it around on him. Rufus says, 'Hey, Runt, I hear you got first place in the Loser Games.' You say, 'Thanks, Rufus, I never would have won if you hadn't been eliminated for cheating on the Stupid Test.'"

I laughed. Pismo was good.

"He'll beat me up."

"Better a broken nose than a broken spirit," Pismo said. "But to be safe, keep it light. You're agreeing with his insult, and then pulling him down with you. If he gets mad, it will look like he can dish it out but can't take it."

"I guess," I said.

"We'll practice tomorrow." He patted my back. "Half an hour, three times a day, for a couple of weeks. You'll get there."

The next morning, I received a message on my DPS that Mistress Moira wanted me to meet her in the ballroom instead of her quarters at the top of the tower. I looked to the sky and said, "Thank you!"

The ballroom was filled with workers and noise. Tootles was working on the runway while other workers brought in folding chairs and propped them up against the walls. The stage was filled with set designers and Mistress Moira's dressmaking operation. She sat behind a sewing machine perched on a long table covered with bolts of fabric. Behind her, two racks held dresses in progress. Dr. Critchlore stood next to her, a fashion magazine in his hand.

I hesitated, not sure I could take another blast of Critchlore hate. I wanted so badly to do something right in his eyes. I considered telling him about Irma Trackno. Maybe this piece of information would redeem me a little bit.

"We're going to need programs, music, ushers," he told Mistress Moira. "A backstage crew to keep things moving. Someone to announce the girls, a photographer, a lighting crew. I'll do the seating chart. The girls will need makeup and hair stylists. Maybe they should do a dance number? I'll ask the dance instructor. What's her name? Witherspoon? Willoughby? Worthington?"

"His name is Chaz," Mistress Moira said. "You're thinking of the music instructor you fired four years ago—Norma Wilkinson."

"Right. She was always snapping her fingers. Drove me crazy. Anyway, according to this article, we also need gift bags for the guests. Are you writing this down?"

"No."

"Moira!"

She stopped sewing and looked up. "I am not your fashion show coordinator. I'm a seamstress and I'm making the dresses. Do you want to try to make a dress, Derek? You need to find someone to direct the show if you don't want to do it yourself."

"A director," Dr. Critchlore said, nodding. "Yes. That should be me, shouldn't it? But on the other hand, if this whole thing is a bomb, I might not want to be too closely associated with it."

"Thank you for that vote of confidence." She continued sewing.

"It's not you, Moira. It's the sirens. Who knows what they're expecting?"

"You should. You're the one who made promises."

Dr. Critchlore waved his hand. "Vodum can direct."

"Good grief, no."

"You're right. He's awful. Okay, I'll do it." He took a deep breath, nodded to Mistress Moira. "Thank you, Moira." As he turned to leave, I stepped in front of him.

"Dr. Critchlore?"

"Not now. I'm very busy."

"I know, it's just . . . something happened at the EOC building yesterday I thought you should know about."

"Professor Murphy has briefed me—" He brushed by me, leaving.

"This happened earlier," I said to his back. "An evil overlord asked me questions about you."

He turned around. "What sort of questions?"

I gulped. "Mostly about the sabotage. I told her you were playing along and staging some countersabotage, and she seemed impressed."

"You told . . . her?"

"It was Irma Trackno."

"I see." He looked down and shook his head.

"And then I saw her talking to Pravus. I think she might be looking to recruit some minions. Maybe if you contacted—"

He held up his hand to stop me. "Thank you for that information."

"But if she's looking to recruit minions—"

"I would not send a single student of mine to Irma Trackno. Not one single minion. Not ever."

He left.

That wasn't the reaction I'd been expecting, but he did thank me. In all honesty, I felt a little relieved. He knew that Irma Trackno was reckless with her minions, and he cared about how we were treated. He might act demanding and indifferent, but I knew he cared.

I turned to Mistress Moira. "Do you need me to fetch anything?" I asked. Her table was covered with piles of fabric and lace, boxes of jewelry, buttons, hair thingies, and other girly stuff. I felt myself gripped with a really strong impulse to run away and roll in some mud.

"Yes, I have a list right here," she said. She riffled through piles of stuff on her table and finally came up with the piece of paper. "Just give this to Betsy. She'll know how to find them. Bring them back up here as soon as you can."

"Okay," I said.

Deliveries completed, I snuck away from the ballroom to go to Uncle Ludwig's secret library and return the book I'd "borrowed."

On my way out, I passed the siren girls, who were waiting at the end of the runway to practice their walks. I decided to ask them something that had been bugging me: Did they know this wasn't a modeling school when they came here?

I hadn't directed the question at anyone in particular, but Bianca answered, which didn't surprise me. She was the kind of kid who had to say something in class every day. "Of course we knew this wasn't a modeling school," she said. "But it's so much better! Look, the school we were supposed to go to is awful—no boys, strict rules, they treat us like we're delicate little flowers. Here, we get to take interesting classes and meet interesting creatures. Sure, it's not for every siren, but we like it and we want to stay." She took a step toward me. "Our moms can't find out otherwise, understand?"

I nodded. Once in the foyer, I pulled out my to-do list and added, "Make sure siren mothers don't find out this isn't a modeling school." Then I felt silly because that wasn't something I'd forget to do. Maybe that was the problem with my to-do list. I added things I wouldn't forget, and I forgot to add things I needed to remember.

CHAPTER 16

It's always darkest before the dawn,
or if you're in Fraze Coldheart's dungeon.
—A JOKE SHARED BY EVIL OVERLORDS

The regular library door was locked, so I went down to the dungeon. I sprinted around the grotto, watching out for flying tentacles, and eased myself inside the secret door. I took the book out of my backpack and headed for the stacks.

Uncle Ludwig was nowhere to be seen, but Professor Zaida sat at a table near the fireplace. She had a large book open and was taking notes on a pad.

"Hello, Runt," she said.

"Hi," I said. I stuffed the book into my backpack when she wasn't looking. I didn't want her to know I'd taken it. "Is Uncle Ludwig around?"

"Upstairs," she said.

I walked over to her and leaned against the table. "Professor Zaida, do you think he's a good librarian?"

"Well, he got his master's degree in library science from Amlick University in the capital, where he learned how to sort books by evil overlord, how to properly censor a book, and the best techniques for public book burning."

"Those don't sound like librarian skills. What about researching stuff? Do you think he'll be able to find out where I'm from? Do you think he'll find the Great Library?"

She tilted her head, like she hadn't heard right. "The Great Library?"

"Yes, he says all the answers are there. But I'm not so sure. Darthin says it's a myth. What if it is? What if Uncle Ludwig's been wasting all this time, and he never finds out where I'm from?"

"You're trying to find out where you're from?" she asked.

"I have to."

She closed her book and put her hands on top of it. "Runt, you don't need to know where you're from to know who you are. The past doesn't define us. Look at me. I was born in West Chambor to a family that already had twelve children. We lived in crowded, poor, miserable conditions, and if I could forget those years, I would. What I mean to say is—don't fixate on where you came from. You have a home and family here, and a bright future ahead of you. Don't take those things for granted by being obsessed with the past."

"I know," I said. "I'm grateful for all I have, really. It's just that Mistress Moira says I came here with a curse, and if I don't find who did it and get it removed, I'll die on my sixteenth birthday."

Professor Zaida's eyes widened, and then I got the uncomfortable pity face that people made whenever I mentioned my curse. She couldn't help it; she was so nice.

Uncle Ludwig's steps clanged down the spiral staircase in the corner. He carried a large stack of books, so I jumped up to help him. He nodded to the nearest table, and once sitting, he opened a notebook, turning to a blank page. I put the books down and sat opposite him.

"This is terrible news," he muttered. "Terrible."

"What happened?"

He looked up, surprised that I was still there. "Runt, I'm very busy."

I was still angry, and I wasn't going to let him brush me off. He'd been doing that for eight years, apparently. I reached over and put my hand on his notebook. "Uncle Ludwig. I need to know what you've found out. I was talking to Cook—"

"You told Cook about my research?" He looked nervous now, and I caught him glancing over to a section of books by the circular staircase.

"I told Cook about your lack of research. You told her that you're close to finding out where I'm from."

"I am," he said.

"What have you found out?"

Uncle Ludwig looked over at Professor Zaida, still taking notes at her table.

"I'll tell you everything," he whispered, "but you must assure Cook that I'm being completely open with you. Promise me."

"Okay. I promise." Geez, how valuable were Cook's books?

He nodded. "I *am* close to finding the Great Library. The CLOUDs know I am, which is why I can't leave this castle. If I did, their assassins would—" He slit his throat with his finger. "It's a very ruthless organization. They have to be, obviously, to protect something that important."

"If you can't leave the castle, how will you find a CLOUD?"

"I have operatives who feed me information. These operatives have contacts throughout the realms. I've been collecting information for years—rumors, myths, and hearsay mostly, but also suspicious disappearances of books and whole libraries as realms change rulers. Whenever there's a regime change, I make sure my men are there, and I tell them: 'Watch the books! Follow the books.'"

He stood up and motioned me over to another table. Spread out on top of it was a map of the Porvian Continent. He motioned for me to sit and then pointed to the map. "We know the Great Library is somewhere in the Porvian Continent, probably in a mountain fortress. Unfortunately, mountain fortresses are everywhere. There's not a single realm that doesn't have six or seven of them. Some EOs are searching too." He tapped on two countries: Voran and Razik. "Tankotto and Cera Bacculus are racing to find the library."

"Why?"

"They both border the country to the north of us, Burkeve. Tankotto claims that Burkeve and parts of Razik rightfully belong to him. Cera Bacculus disagrees. Right now, many EOs support Cera's claim to Burkeve, mostly because she's the second-most powerful EO. But they all suspect that the proof of Tankotto's claim may lie in the Great Library's historical documents. If those documents were to surface, Cera would lose her supporters. To make sure that doesn't happen, she will destroy the library."

"You have to find it before she does," I said. "And warn them."

"I'm sure they know," he said. "Those librarians know everything. Their business is information, and they're good at collecting it. It's like they have ears everywhere. They're also good at hiding."

"If they're so good at hiding, how are you ever going to find one?"

"Ha! They can't outsmart me forever. I'm a Critchlore! And I'm getting close. Last week I tracked down a CLOUD in Urlichaven. I sent a man to meet him, but the CLOUD didn't show. I just learned that he'd been poisoned. I wasn't the only one to have found him out, apparently."

"Cera Bacculus poisoned him?" I asked.

"Of course not. You don't poison someone if you want information from him, Runt. Think! How does a dead informant help you find answers?"

I shrugged.

"I believe he was killed by another covert librarian."

"Why?"

"Why do you think?"

I had no idea why a librarian would kill someone. "Because he had too many overdue library books?"

"No! To keep him from talking to me, obviously! Runt Higgins, are you really this dense? Good grief."

Well, now I felt stupid. I slumped in my chair.

"Listen: The CLOUDs will kill to keep their secrets. They will even kill their own. Any whiff of betrayal or ineptitude, and you're gone. Believe me, I know how their organization works. They protect themselves with many layers of operatives, each one only knowing what he needs to know. They're spread out throughout the continent; they never meet with more than two other CLOUDs at a time."

"It's amazing that you got so close to one."

"No, it's not." He shook his head, disappointed again. "They may be smart and secretive, but they can't hide from me forever. I've known for quite a while that they use the 'If Books Were Food' poem to identify themselves to each other."

"Everyone knows that poem," I said.

"No," Uncle Ludwig said. "It's their secret poem. I learned it long ago when one of my men followed a CLOUD to his drop-off point and recorded it."

"But there was an old lady at the capital. She recited it when I gave her an apple."

Uncle Ludwig grabbed my arm. "Who was she? What did she look like? Where exactly did you see her?"

"On the capital library steps. You think she's a CLOUD? But she didn't work in the library."

"They are covert librarians, Runt," he said. "Covert. That means they're librarians in secret."

I mentally slapped my forehead. I should have known that. *Gah!* Could I say anything that wouldn't make Uncle Ludwig think I was an idiot?

"She said some other stuff too," I said. "It sounded crazy at the time."

"What? What did she say?" He leaned close to me. "Tell me!"

"She said I was a clever boy—"

"Ha! Not likely."

"She looked at my jacket, at the Critchlore crest, and then she said I should warn the Archivist. She said that she'd been tricked. I had to tell the Archivist that the chameleon was coming." I winced because that sounded ridiculous, but I was sure that was what she'd said.

"Why would she think you know an Archivist?" Uncle Ludwig said, looking off into the distance while rubbing his chin. "That's the highest rank of CLOUD, aside from the director."

"Do you think—?" I asked, hoping he'd fill in the rest because I had no idea what to think, and I really didn't want him to think I was stupid. Well, stupider.

"It's possible," he said.

"I agree."

"Imagine, a CLOUD right here at Dr. Critchlore's," he said. "And not just any CLOUD, but an Archivist."

Wow, really?

"There's more than one?" I asked.

"Oh, yes. There are four, if my research is correct. They are the only CLOUD operatives working outside of the Great Library who actually know where it is located."

"Who could it be?" I nodded to Professor Zaida. "She likes books. A lot."

"It could be anyone. The CLOUDs are cunning and smart, and stay hidden at all times. It could even be Jake, the stable master."

"He can't remember his last sentence," I said.

"The perfect ruse! Pretend you're an idiot, and nobody will suspect you. It's got to be someone who leaves the school on business, which would allow him to collect books and take them to the Great Library. Moldy manuscripts, it's probably Dr. Critchlore himself! And if it is, I'll kill him. He knows I've been searching for a CLOUD."

My DPS beeped. I pulled it out and checked my message. "Mistress Moira wants something for her backache," I said. "I've got to get her a pillow."

"Tell her to stretch every twenty minutes," Professor Zaida said from across the room. "And, Runt, I'm not going to be at practice this afternoon. My uncle is ill and I need to check on him."

"Okay," I said. "Don't worry about us. We'll be fine."

"That's the third sick relative she's had to tend to this month," Uncle Ludwig whispered. "The members of that family have terrible immune systems."

I left. I didn't realize it until later, but I'd forgotten to replace the book.

CHAPTER 17

Ask not what your EO can do for you, because he'll laugh in your face.
—DR. CRITCHLORE, IN A COMMENCEMENT SPEECH

I headed to my History of Henchmen class, wondering who at the school could be a CLOUD, and how I could find him or her. I arrived at the same time as Professor Murphy, who carried a stack of glossy magazines.

On a hunch, I tried the poem, which Uncle Ludwig said the CLOUDs use to identify one another. I nodded to the magazines. "If books were food . . ."

"These are magazines, not books," he said with a scowl. "Now, take a seat, Runt. We have a lot to cover today."

The extra desks had been removed from the classroom. The remaining six were arranged in a semicircle facing the front of the room, with a large one on the right. All the seats were taken except the one on the far left, so I sat there, next to Meztli.

Professor Murphy wrote on the board: "Problem Solving for Your Evil Overlord."

He turned to face us. "I had planned to present our next case study, about how one of Maya Tupo's henchmen rid her realm of an infestation of battle locusts by bargaining for the use of another realm's giant toads."

"Titanatoad," Meztli said with a shiver. "*Ranas gigantes*. One ate my *tío*."

"That's right. Giant toads. And I'm sorry about your uncle," Professor Murphy said. "They are indiscriminate eaters. In addition to clearing the land of locusts, they ate most of the country's crops, cows, and even some farmers.

"Sometimes the cure is worse than the disease." Professor Murphy sighed. "It's a great lesson in unintended consequences, but, unfortunately, a more practical application has come up, and the locust lesson must wait. Just this morning, Dr. Critchlore appointed me fashion show manager. My assignment came in a DPS mail."

He pulled out his DPS and read, "'M—We need to put on the best fashion show ever seen by anyone in the history of all time. I want you to take the job of fashion show manager. We have eleven days, so get cracking. I will check your progress daily.—DC.'"

Professor Murphy as fashion show manager? He was wearing a blazer he'd worn every first and third day of the week for the last five years. Whatever the opposite of the height of fashion was, that blazer was it. The color might once have been rich and vibrant, but now it looked like an old couch that had been spilled on a few hundred times and then shredded by cats.

"Since we are learning about problem solving for your EO," Professor Murphy went on, "we shall apply those lessons to this practical case. Imagine I am your EO, and this is the problem you will help me solve—how to put on a fashion show." He shook his head, like he just realized how ridiculous that sounded.

"The first task is to understand the problem." He wrote that on the board. "In this case, as I've said, the problem is putting on a fashion show. Step two: Identify what is unknown." He wrote that on the board too. "In this case, that would be everything. I know nothing about putting on a fashion show. It is a subject in which I have neither interest nor experience. Which brings us to step three: When in doubt, delegate. I have nothing but doubts, so I have decided to pass this assignment down to you students. You will each be in charge of one of the duties of a fashion show manager. Janet and Frieda are participants, so they are exempt from the assignment and will get full marks."

Janet and Frieda high-fived each other. Well, it was a high five for Janet.

"Given the importance of this event," he went on, "I will be available to assist. Now I am going to start you boys off with a research assignment." He rested a hand on his stack of magazines.

"It says here," he held up a magazine called *Fashion Times*, "that we need a backstage manager during the show. This is a job that needs a person who has a good relationship with the models—"

"That's me," Rufus said, raising his hand. "Girls love me."

Janet scowled at him.

"But I only have eyes for you, Janet, I swear."

"Fine," Professor Murphy said. "Read up on the duties of the backstage manager. Recruit helpers from the general school population if you need to." Professor Murphy plopped the magazine on Rufus's desk.

"Chaz, the choreographer, has asked for someone to oversee the nonmodel participants in the show. He is planning on having escorts for some of the girls as they walk down the runway, and some dance numbers."

"That should be Jud," Rufus said. "Dog has moves!" He held out his fist, and Jud bumped it.

"Fine. Next, set design. Obviously, this is a job for Riga, who is quite artistic. Meztli, why don't you work with her, make sure she has what she needs."

"Claro que sí," Meztli said. *"¿Quien es Riga?"*

"She's married to Tootles," I said. "They live in the tree house by the lake."

"Gracias."

"Is that everybody?" Professor Murphy asked. I raised my hand because he hadn't given me a job yet.

"Nobody else, then?" he asked again, ignoring me.

"Professor Murphy?" I said. "I don't have a job."

"Right, Higgins," he sighed. Then he looked down at his list. "Let's find something for you. Hmm. Photography, no." He began mumbling. "I'm not really getting an artistic vibe from you." He flipped the page over. "Programs? That needs a keen eye for detail, so . . . no. Entertainment manager? Good heavens, no. Stylist?" I fluffed my hair and smiled at him. "Again, no."

"There has to be something I can do."

Professor Murphy thumbed through his magazines. "Okay, here. This one talks about having gift bags for the guests. You fill decorative bags with free samples of beauty supplies. Simple. Why don't you be in charge of that?"

"Okay."

"You know who he should work with?" Rufus said. "The mole people in the Supply Station."

"Great idea. That is excellent problem solving, Rufus," Professor Murphy said. The mole people were the meanest, dirtiest, cruelest beasts in the castle. I turned to glare at Rufus, and he smirked at me.

"I'll be checking your progress daily," Professor Murphy said.

We spent the class period taking notes on how to do our tasks. After class, as we left, I overheard Rufus talking to Janet. "This is full lunar, man," he said. "I feel like I'm gonna morph and eat someone. How am I gonna get recruited if Dr. Critchlore doesn't get this school together? A fashion show? You have got to be kidding me."

"Relax, Rufus," Janet said, laughing. "Just think how great this will look on your transcript—an A in Fashion Show."

"You laugh, but this is serious. I've always been a lock for a major EO. If this school continues to tank, I'll be lucky if I'm picked up by some loser EO near Skelterdam."

Janet patted his arm with a sad face that made me want to hug her.

I went to find Syke for free period. As I veered around the fountain in front of the castle, I heard a roar coming from the hedge maze. I was used to hearing sounds coming from the maze, usually cries of frustration. I don't think I'd ever heard a roar, though, so I went to investigate.

Jake, the stable master, stood near the entrance, an empty dragon collar dangling from one hand, a bloody sack in the other.

"Hi, Jake," I said. "Did you lose something?"

"Hi, Higgins," he said. He went back to staring at the maze entrance. Jake had a very short attention span because of the many concussions he'd suffered in his years of caring for dangerous animals. He was also scarred with burns across his face and hands.

"Jake?" I said.

He looked at me. "Hi, Higgins."

I nodded to the collar. "Is there a dragon loose in the maze?"

"I was told to bring Plopper over, with his wings bound so he couldn't fly out. Plopper don't like to have his wings bound. He's real mad."

We heard another roar, proving Jake's point. A blast of fire shot up from the middle of the maze, followed by a human scream.

Great screaming banshees!

"There's someone in there with him!" I cried.

Who would be dumb enough to enter a maze with an angry dragon?

CHAPTER 18

*Just like smooth seas do not make skillful sailors,
soft training methods don't make strong minions.*

—DR. PRAVUS, EXPLAINING HIS MINION-TRAINING PHILOSOPHY

Jake!" I screamed. "You've got to get Plopper out of there!"

Jake nodded and ran into the maze, blowing a whistle that he used to call the wyverns to eat. "Come here, Binky!"

"It's Plopper!" I yelled at him.

"Right!" he yelled back.

I pulled out my DPS and sent a quick alert to Mrs. Gomes. A thump shook the leaves on the hedge, followed by another scream. Smoke rose from inside.

Jake stumbled back out of the maze. "Higgins, how'd you get to the middle so fast?" He looked around. "Oh. This ain't the middle."

"Come on," I said, answering my own question about who was stupid enough to go into a maze with an angry dragon. "I'll get you to Plopper, and you can unbind him so he can get out."

"Good idea."

I raced down the narrow pathways of the maze, Jake following. The maze was huge, and Tootles used lots of tricks to make it difficult.

There were loops, one-way doors, and false exits. Some of the hedges were realistic fakes, hiding secret passages.

I ran forward, took the first left, then a right, jumping around Plopper's little land mines as I went. Suddenly, my leg hit something and I fell forward, hard.

I looked back and saw that I'd stumbled over a trip wire, which had lifted a section of fake hedge. A mass of spiders streamed out of the gap, each as big as my hand. I screamed. Jake bounded between the spiders and me, and threw something bloody to the ground in front of them. The spiders went right for it.

"What's going on?" I asked as Jake lifted me up and away. There was no way Tootles would do that to a kid. Frustrate us with a difficult maze, yes. Frighten us with spiders? No way.

"Vodum said some guy wanted to see if the maze would make a good training arena. A way to weed out the weak."

Vodum? "What guy?"

"A guy who's looking to take Dr. Critchlore's place as headmaster."

Pravus? This did seem like something he'd do to kids.

We raced through a curving bit and reached a secret latch that opened a trick door. Once through, we sprinted forward. Screams filled the air. I raced around a corner, only to come face-to-face with a swamp creature, who hissed at me.

More screams rang out. This time they were mine. I turned around, crashing into Jake, and we ran. I lost track of where I was; I just took turn after turn to get away from frog face.

We'd gone to the far side and then back toward the middle, dodging tricks and traps as we went. A giant, automatic fist tried to knock us down. We had to jump over some black tar that would have held our feet tight. I was losing my breath, and my legs felt weak, but raging panic helped keep me going.

Fires dotted the hedges and the air turned smoky. As we rounded a corner, one whole side had flames licking out of the middle in a straight line, about waist high. The green hedge crackled with anger.

I saw a scaly, spiked tail swish around a corner. I skidded to a halt and turned around to let Jake go ahead, but guess what. No Jake.

I noticed scaffolding in the center of the maze. Two men were watching Plopper's progress, and the person he was chasing.

"Hey!" I yelled. One of them was Professor Vodum. "He'll destroy the maze!"

"Runt!" Professor Vodum yelled. "Get out of there! You'll ruin the test!"

I was about to ask what was going on when I noticed that Plopper had turned around and was coming straight for me.

Plopper was a small dragon, a little bigger than a unicorn. Like most dragons, he could move very quickly in the open, but his body had trouble with the tight turns of the maze. He made up for his lack of speed in the maze with the ability to chase me down with a ball of fire.

He roared. I got one look at his pre-fireball-spitting face and knew I had to get out of the way, fast. I ducked around a corner and watched the ball of fire hit the hedge behind me. Plopper didn't follow, so I edged back and peeked around the corner.

Plopper had turned away from me. I noticed another form curled into a ball farther up the path, wearing a light green second-year jacket. Plopper thumped right by him, which surprised me because I'd never seen the "curl up in a ball and hope nobody notices you" technique work before. I ran over and put a hand on his shoulder.

He looked up, trembling. "Vodum said that man wanted to see how fast I could reach the center, and then they sent the dragon after me!"

"Come on. We've gotta get out of here," I said, pulling him up. We couldn't go back—the whole pathway was on fire. We had to get away from the flames, which were everywhere now.

Plopper was panicking too. I heard his frantic roars. This might sound crazy, but I ran toward them. I couldn't let him be trapped in here with his wings bound, unable to get away from the fires he'd started.

"What are you doing?" Second-year said.

"Up may be the only way out," I said.

We ran into Plopper as he reached a dead end. He spun around, eyes wide with panic. I approached him, arms up.

"It's okay, boy," I said. Second-year clung to my back like a tick. I could feel his hands burrowing into my jacket, using me as a shield. "Let's get you out of here."

Plopper clawed at the ground with his front foot.

I'd had a lot more confidence for this sort of thing back when I thought I was a werewolf. Knowing I was human made me realize how fragile I was. How easily the dragon could rip me to shreds.

"C'mon, Plopper." I slowly stepped toward him. He huddled back into the dead end, head turning from side to side, looking for an escape. He was as afraid as we were.

"Easy, now." I was within reach. "Let me unhook your harness."

I made the clicking noises I'd heard Jake make when leading the dragons out of their stalls. I slipped past his head, hot nostril air blowing out at me. I reached up with one hand and undid the belt-like latch of the thick leather strap that held down his wings. My other hand scratched him behind the ear, because I knew he liked that.

The belt swung free. I jumped on his back, Second-year swinging up behind me.

"Up, up!" I yelled, squeezing Plopper with my legs. He took a few fast steps, but couldn't get his wings wide enough for liftoff. He ran straight for a hedge wall, climbed up it enough to get his wings clear, and we rose.

Once in the air, Plopper circled until he spotted Jake holding a bloody rabbit, then swooped right for him. He landed and nuzzled into Jake, clearly distraught and needing comfort. Second-year and I swung down.

I looked up and saw Mrs. Gomes riding Puddles. Puddles did his name proud, and the fires were extinguished as he peed on them. Tootles ran up, his white hair escaping from his ponytail as he put his hands to his head in shock and anger. "My hedges! What's happened to my hedges?"

Vodum and his guest had disappeared. I headed for the castle to tell Dr. Critchlore about this insanity.

Vodum's desk was empty, so I knocked on Dr. Critchlore's open door and said, "Excuse me, Dr. Critchlore?"

Dr. Critchlore sat behind his giant desk. He looked up. "Vodum!" he screamed. "I told you I'm not to be disturbed!"

"He's not there," I said. "In fact, he nearly destroyed the hedge maze by—"

At that moment, Vodum walked in, shoving me out of the way.

"Dr. Critchlore," he said, "your eleven fifteen appointment is here." He turned to whisper in my ear. "Tattletale."

"My what?" Dr. Critchlore asked.

"Your eleven fifteen appointment with Mr. Peabody," Vodum said. "The family wants to make sure they have a replacement in case they decide to get rid of you with a vote of no confidence. Mr. Peabody represents a candidate who has a few questions about operations."

"Operations?" I asked.

"He wants to see if the grounds are compatible with what his boss has in mind—"

"And that involves a dragon chasing a second-year through a hedge maze?" I asked.

"Well, since we don't have a detention pit, Mr. Peabody was checking out other possible opportunities for student discipline."

"Tell him I'm busy," Dr. Critchlore said.

"You have to see him," Vodum replied. "The school charter says that if the family calls for a vote of no confidence in the leader-ship—"

Dr. Critchlore slammed down his pen. "Fine. I'll meet with him. Harris, get back to class. Vodum, you are the worst secretary I've ever had, and that includes the one who poisoned me. Send the man in and get me some coffee."

"I'm on a break."

Mr. Peabody was a large man, wearing an ill-fitting suit that was too tight for his muscular frame. Vodum only came up to the man's broad shoulders.

He sat down opposite Dr. Critchlore and opened his notebook. "My boss would like to know if you've ranked your students based on their ability to tolerate pain," he said.

I tiptoed out, right behind Vodum, who left the door open and stood next to it, listening in.

CHAPTER 19

Dragons will not be used for student discipline without the prior approval of the security team.

—ALL-POINTS SAFETY BULLETIN NO. 58, FROM MRS. GOMES

At lunch I tried to recruit some helpers for my gift bag project.

"I'm helping Meztli with the scenery," Eloni said, flexing his large biceps. "That little dude is so cool. He told me in his country there's a monster called a Cherufe that lives in the molten lava of volcanoes and makes the earth shake when he's angry. So awesome!"

Frankie was helping Mistress Moira. Darthin had been snagged by an upperclassman to help with logistics. Syke was supposed to be practicing with the girls, but instead, she was helping Tootles mend his torched maze. That left only Boris, so the two of us went to find Pismo, who was returning from the lake.

"Sure, I'll help," he said, surprising me with his quick response. "A fashion show project will get me out of PE. Since the zombies left, I'm the only one in Coach Foley's class, and I do *not* need one-on-one attention from that psycho."

"Great," I said. We headed back to the castle through the Memorial Courtyard. "I have a tackle three-ball game this afternoon at the Pravus Academy, so we can have our first meeting after dinner."

"You're going to the Pravus Academy? Today?" Pismo asked.

"Yes. Why?"

"I wouldn't go there if you paid me my weight in pearls."

"Why not?" Boris asked.

Pismo sighed. "The Pravus Academy isn't like this school. I was there for three months, and if my dad was trying to show me what jail would be like, it worked."

"What do you mean?" I asked.

"Dr. Pravus doesn't treat his minions like we're treated here," Pismo went on as we walked back to the castle. "He has a detention pit, and sometimes they forget that you're down there.

"He makes scrawny kids fight huge monsters, and they get crushed, and everyone thinks it's funny. 'We must weed out the weak,' he says. 'If you're not strong enough to take it, then you shouldn't be here.' He is entirely without compassion, and so are his minions."

The Critchlore family wanted Pravus to run this school. And now his man was checking to see if our benign hedge maze could be turned into a trial of terrors. Dr. Critchlore had to stop him. He had to convince the EO Council, and his own family, that Pravus shouldn't run our school.

But right now, all everyone could see was that the Pravus Academy was soaring, and Dr. Critchlore's School was floundering. It looked like the only people against a Pravus takeover would be us kids, and nobody cared what we thought.

"Be careful, guys," Pismo said. "They won't ease up, even if they're winning thirty to zero. Once they have a lead, Pravus tells his athletes to play dirty, just to see what they can get away with.

"We should probably meet in the morning," Pismo added. "You're going to need time to recover."

As nervous as I was after Pismo's little pep talk, I was still excited to go to the Pravus Academy for the first time.

I'd seen the Pravus Academy campus in ads, and it looked like a prison. Most of the buildings were massive concrete structures with precise angles and rough textures. Someone told me it was the Brutalist style of architecture, and I thought that was a good name for it. Cold and brutal. By contrast, Dr. Critchlore's School was picturesque and tree-filled. I shuddered to think of Pravus taking over my school and imposing his harsh environment on us.

I sat next to Syke on the bus and told her what Pismo had said about Pravus's teams playing dirty.

"Maybe we should play Frankie," she said.

Frankie, sitting in front of us, turned around to join our conversation. "Daddy—er—Dr. Frankenhammer says I can't play."

"We'd have to forfeit if they found out he's enhanced," I said. "The rules say that genetically modified individuals can only play if the other team gives permission."

"Don't you want to play?" Syke asked Frankie. She flipped her hair out of her face, and I noticed for the first time that it wasn't tied back in a ponytail. Her lips were shiny, and she smelled nice too. She put her hand on Frankie's arm, but he pulled it away.

"I'd love to play," he said. "I can hit an imp at three hundred feet."

That was true; he'd done it on a dare once, after Uhoh had taken one of our balls and was using it to bowl down unsuspecting first-years. Uhoh had just knocked a kid into a puddle and was laughing hysterically when Frankie's hit nailed him in the back. It was hilarious.

"You should put your hair back, so it doesn't get in your face," Frankie said.

Syke slumped back in her seat. "I will."

"Maybe we'll see Sara," I said, mostly to change the subject. "Maybe I can rescue her from Dr. Pravus."

"Not likely," Syke said. "Don't you think it's weird that nobody knows he has them? I mean, if Critchlore had a beast that powerful, he'd be advertising it and waiting for the EOs to start a bidding war. Pravus is up to something with them. They're probably hidden away."

It made me sad to think of Sara locked away, far from the trees she loved.

We approached an intimidating wrought-iron gate that was nearly two stories high. A pair of giant gorillas flanked the gate, and by *giant* I don't mean really big, I mean GIANT. They each stood taller than the gate.

No wonder everyone wanted to recruit Pravus's minions. They were completely terrifying.

After unloading our gear, Professor Zaida told us to head for the field and warm up while she found the other coach. "Should have been here to greet us," she said, shaking her head.

I walked with Syke and Frankie, following the rest of the team down a road scarred with potholes. We passed windowless barracks and listened to the muffled screeches and howls of minions fighting to get out. A training arena pitted four human kids against a giant swamp creature. Two kids lay crumpled on the ground, out cold.

Lots of monsters, but no sign of a Girl Explorer anywhere.

Near the field were some empty buildings that looked like practice siege targets. Some of the concrete structures had been reduced to rubble; others were empty shell buildings with metal supporting rods sticking out of the blasted-off tops. It was like walking through a war zone.

Suddenly, a giant gorilla stomped out from behind a building and blocked our way. I jumped back, my heart rate racing like a scared bunny.

He huffed, pounded his chest, and roared. He had the biggest teeth I'd seen since last winter, when I'd been on dragon flossing duty.

We huddled together, scared out of our minds.

"Frankie, go shove it off," I said.

"No, thank you," he said. "Let's just wait for Professor Zaida."

The gorilla charged right at us, and we screamed. He stopped before he touched us, and backed up, as if he'd made his point. This was his road.

"Don't look it in the eye," Eloni whispered. "That makes them crazy."

"Minions can't attack another school's minions. It's in the Directives," I said.

"Tell that to him," Eloni said. "Go on, we'll wait here."

Syke rolled her eyes and then strode toward the beast.

"Syke, don't!" I called, but she just waved her hand at me.

Looking at her, with her hair neatly brushed, and her face all glowy, it hit me. She had tried to look pretty for Frankie, and Frankie hadn't noticed. And now Syke was mad. She was ready to take out her anger on that gorilla. I kind of felt sorry for the gorilla.

"Move it, fuzzball," she said, standing right below him with her hands on her hips.

The gorilla roared and pounded his chest.

"I said, MOVE IT!" Syke pointed toward the side of the road. He didn't move. She walked forward and pushed his foot. He jumped back. He seemed shocked, as if nobody had ever confronted him before.

In a swift movement, he reached forward and swept up Syke in his paw. He brought her close to his face and made a sound like a soft grunt. He tilted his head sideways to get a look at her from that angle. I knew that look. It was the "Wow, you're kind of cute" head tilt. Syke didn't struggle; she gritted her teeth and said, very calmly, "Put me down. Now."

The gorilla put her down. He slowly backed away, nestling himself between two buildings, never taking his eyes off Syke.

Syke turned and waved us forward. "C'mon, let's go."

Everyone passed her, heading for the field.

"Did you see that, Frankie?" I said. "Syke's beauty tamed a wild beast."

Syke smiled, but then Frankie said, "You are one tough dude," and the smile faded.

It was the last smiling any of us did that afternoon. The game was a disaster. The Pravus team played dirty from the first pitch, which nailed me in the head. Their tacklers piled on our runners, even after the play had ended. And I'm pretty sure one of them was at least part swamp monster, and monsters aren't allowed to play unless they can maintain their human form. This guy had a green complexion ("he's just a little ill"), webbed hands ("those are gloves"), and was stronger than an ogre ("good diet and exercise"). Twice he picked up Boris and, instead of tackling him, threw him across the field and back into the dugout.

The only one of us who could match these guys was Eloni, but here's the thing about Eloni—he's the happiest guy I know, with a huge smile that could light up a moonless night, and a booming laugh that makes everything more fun. He could get creamed by a fair hit, and he'd just laugh and tell his tackler, "Great hit." But if someone plays dirty against him, or, worse, cheap-shots his teammates, it's good-bye joyous affection of the islanders, and hello angry volcano god.

Our angry volcano god was ejected in the first inning for head-butting their first bagman, who'd fouled Boris after Eloni had warned him to cut it out. Without Eloni, we were doomed.

And then Professor Zaida was ejected when she ran onto the field to pry some Pravus kids off Boris while screaming, "Leave my kids alone!" That left Frankie to be our coach.

Poor Frankie. He watched, twitching with the desire to jump in and help us, but held back by the inner voice of Dr. Frankenhammer telling him he couldn't. It was painful to watch him struggle on the sideline, holding his head to keep it from popping off. The other team would do mean things just to laugh at Frankie's spastic response.

We rode the bus home in silence, bruised and battered.

"I really don't think it should be legal to sit on someone's face when they're on the bottom of a pileup," Boris said, holding an ice pack to his chin.

I can't express how much we hated the Pravus team.

CHAPTER 20

Keep your friends close, but your enemies closer. Unless your enemy is a mole person, because his body odor will make you cry.

—ANONYMOUS

We didn't want to go to the cafeteria after our humiliating loss. But hunger won out over pride, and we snuck in, hoping nobody would notice us.

Nobody did. Everyone was watching the newsfeed on the giant screen at the end of the room. There was a story about Pravus's giant gorillas.

"They really are unstoppable," Pravus said to the interviewer. "It's remarkable to see them in action. Ogres, trolls, giants—they don't have anywhere near the strength and speed of my gorillas. When you add a few years of my special training, well . . ."

"Unstoppable," the reporter finished for him.

Pravus smiled.

"Tell that to Syke," I said.

The reporter went on. "Dr. Pravus is a very busy man, and it looks like he's about to get busier. Rumor has it that Lord Vengecrypt has pledged to recruit a good portion of his graduating class. And there are rumors about a possible expansion in the works."

"I do need more room if I'm to keep up with demand," Pravus said.

"Dr. Critchlore's has five times the area of the Pravus Academy," Darthin said.

"Forget that," Eloni said. "Lord Vengecrypt has always gotten his minions from Critchlore. Always."

"Always," I echoed. "You know what? Maybe that's why Pravus was sabotaging us—so he could steal Critchlore's best customers."

"Probably," Darthin said. "And now, when Dr. Critchlore should be fixing this school, he's planning a fashion show. It's insane."

The newsfeed blinked out, replaced by a headshot of our leader. Dr. Critchlore's serious expression silenced everyone. "Students, faculty, staff, and the Useless Hanger-on, yes, I mean you, Vodum. I have an announcement. I've just received word that the Siren Syndicate"—he shivered—"will be here a day early. I am hereby suspending all classes while we all work to prepare for their visit.

"In addition, I've heard rumors that I want to put to rest. I have no plans to install a gauntlet of pain. What a ridiculous notion! Please do not worry that my training methods have stooped to that level.

"That man testing one in our hedge maze works for someone who might replace me as headmaster. I'm mostly sure this won't happen. Well, maybe forty percent sure. So, everyone, just calm down.

"That is all."

‡‡‡

The next morning, Boris, Pismo, and I headed to the dungeon. Mole people (MP), underground creatures with scaly green skin, red eyes, and hot tempers, ran the Supply Station.

"Pismo, please remember to be respectful," I said. The last time we were here, they gave him a leaky hazmat suit because he was rude.

"Don't worry, Runt," he said. "I'm pals with these guys now. They love me."

I rolled my eyes.

With classes canceled, I thought the place would be quiet, but it was busier than ever. Mole people raced around filling orders, driving forklifts through the tall aisles, and unpacking boxes.

We stood at the counter. I rang the bell, but there was so much beeping and shouting that even I couldn't hear it. I waved my arms in the air, trying to get someone's attention, but they all ignored me.

Pismo put a hand on my shoulder just as I was about to hop over the counter. "I got this," he said. "You might want to cover your ears."

"Why?" I asked, but before I could cover my ears, my question was answered.

Pismo opened his mouth, and out came the most ear-aching screech I'd ever heard in my life, and I used to feed hungry banshees in the Aviary.

All activity ceased. The mole people turned toward us. I thought they'd be mad at that horrible sound, but one walked over and said, "Yeah, Your Royal Deepness, what do you want?"

Pismo pointed at me.

"Um, thank you, Magnificent Inventory Master," I said. "Uh, we're here on official fashion show business—"

"So are we all," he said. "Get to the point."

"We need to assemble gift bags for a couple hundred guests. That means we need bags, and—um—gifts to put into the bags."

"Professor Murphy said you'd be coming. Conference room, over there." He lifted a panel in the counter, and we followed him to a large room. He directed us to sit, and then disappeared into the long stacks of supplies.

We took seats and I dropped my magazines on the table.

"Pismo, what the heck was that?" I asked.

"My screech?" he said, leaning back in his chair. "Powerful, isn't it?"

"It's still ringing in my ears." I had a feeling it was a mermaid thing, and I didn't want to say anything else, because Pismo didn't want people to know he was a mermaid.

Boris reached for a magazine. He took one look at the cover (girls in dresses) and shoved it back at me. "Maybe you're part banshee," he said to Pismo.

"I am," Pismo said. "It's clever of you to notice."

Boris smiled. He wasn't called "clever" very often.

"Okay," I said, getting to business. I opened the magazine to the gift bag article. "It says here that gift bags are usually filled with things like lipstick and perfume. I wonder if they have any of that down here?"

"Doubtful," Pismo said. "Judging by the mole people. Unless the lipstick is brown and lumpy, and the perfume smells like a garbage dump."

The mole person returned with an armful of bags. "Pick one," he said, dropping them onto the table.

We sorted through the pile. There were simple paper bags, colored bags, ones with handles, others without, and all kinds of materials.

"I like this velvety one with the drawstring," Pismo said. He turned it upside down to empty it, and out fell a plastic bag filled with eyeballs. "Ooh, but not that, I would think."

"We have lots of those bags," the MP said. "In the empty version."

"Great," I said. "They look elegant. Do you have any with the school's logo stitched on them?"

"Can be done," he said.

Two more MPs came in carrying boxes as the first one swept the bags back in his box.

"Pick out the items you want for the bag," the first MP said. "And we got another box from your father, Prince Pismodor. Do you want it?"

He was looking at Pismo.

"No. But I'll take it," Pismo said. The MP nodded and left.

"Prince Pismodor?" I asked.

Pismo closed his eyes and shook his head. "My ridiculous father has been sending me photophore stuff. It's one of the things we—uh—banshees . . . manufacture—er—in our nests. He wants me to get Dr. Critchlore to sell them as part of his minion supply business. But who wants photophore stuff, unless you're going underwater?"

"What's a photophore?" I asked. Boris wasn't really paying

attention. He was searching through the other box. The remaining MPs left with the box of bags, and took their body odor with them, thank goodness, because I felt like I'd been holding my breath for five minutes.

Pismo reached into his box and handed me a black dress. "In the depths of the ocean, it's very dark. A lot of animals make their own light with light-producing organs called photophores. This material mimics that kind of bioluminescence. It senses when you need light and it lights up. Here, watch."

He pulled the long-sleeved dress on over his head. It fell to midthigh on him.

"Nice dress," Boris said.

"It's not a dress. It's a tunic. All the men in my family wear them, since we don't have . . ."

He wanted to say "legs," I was sure. I decided to help him out. "Dignity?"

He scowled at me. "We make gloves too," he said, throwing us each a pair. Then he turned off the lights.

His tunic lit up with bright ocean-blue dots. The light was powerful and beautiful.

I put on the gloves. The black material felt light and silky, like I was wearing water. "Wow," Boris said. "My hand is like the sky. It has stars!" He turned his hand over. "Oooh, look at my fingers!" Each fingertip blasted out light like a flashlight.

"That's so cool," I said. "Why haven't you shown them to Critchlore?"

"Everyone knows these are made by . . . banshees, so nobody will buy them. Nobody wants to go against the Siren Syndicate. The

144

sirens hate us and they're much too powerful. So why bother? I've got about twenty boxes of these things."

He closed the box and stuffed it under the table.

"Sirens hate banshees?" Boris asked.

"Sirens hate everyone," Pismo said.

We got back to work, searching through boxes for appropriate things to put in the gift bags. We rejected anything that looked like it belonged in Dr. Frankenhammer's lab—eyeballs, tongues, feet with claws, those sorts of things. It took a while, but we managed to fill our example bag with stuff we thought was cool. I pulled the gold drawstring shut, and it looked great.

Boris ran off, late for his emergency ogre-man seminar on personal hygiene. The sirens were coming, and Dr. Critchlore wanted to see some improvement in this area.

"I'll give this to Professor Murphy and see what he thinks. Thanks for your help, Prince Pismodor."

"Shut up."

"Will you be king someday?" I asked as I pushed my chair in.

"Not likely. I'm the youngest of fourteen. Besides, who wants to be king of the mermaids? That's like the punch line for a joke about being stupid."

That was true. "It's not fair," I said.

Pismo shrugged. "Things are changing. Lord Vengecrypt just recruited a bunch of mermaids for his coastal attacks. People will see we're not stupid. It's just not happening fast enough for me."

We packed up our stuff to leave. "Can I keep these gloves?"

"Sure," he said. "Just don't tell anyone where you got them, okay?"

"Okay," I said.

We walked out of the conference room. Just as we were about to lift the section of the counter that would let us leave, a mole person's clawed hand grabbed Pismo. When Pismo looked at him, the mole person just shook his head.

"Can't blame a guy for trying," Pismo said as he emptied his pockets of all the stuff he'd tried to steal.

CHAPTER 21

The early bird catches the worm. But if you sleep in, you can catch the early bird, and I bet he tastes better.

—TEENAGE WEREWOLF, TO HIS DAD

The next day, I sat beside Mistress Moira onstage, picking green sequins out of a multicolored pile. Professor Murphy charged up the runway, heading right for us with a look on his face I hadn't seen since someone put an eyeball in his coffee.

"Higgins, what the blazes is this?" he said. He held my gift bag.

"Um . . . a gift bag?"

"This is what you came up with?" he said. He dumped the contents on a table next to Mistress Moira, calling out each item as he lined them up. "A jar of gourmet ogre jelly? You do realize that only ogres believe this to be gourmet? It's made from something nobody would consider a fruit, and it's infused with cockroaches."

"I don't read Ogre. I just thought the jar looked cool."

"One Dr. Critchlore's Tornado in a Can™—"

"Some of the bags could have Earthquake in a Can™, or Flood in a Can™," I interrupted. "They're fun at parties."

Mistress Moira chuckled softly.

"A ring that looks like it came as a free prize in a box of cereal?"

"It's a slingshot. That little ball on top of the ring shoots up to fifty feet," I explained. "The mole person said that Dr. Critchlore uses them when meetings get boring." Professor Murphy's hand went to his neck. He had a small red scar just below his ear. He frowned at me and picked up the next item.

"So we have disgusting jelly, a cheap weapon, and a natural disaster. And we are planning to give this out to our elegant and sophisticated guests. Brilliant."

"Thank you?"

Mistress Moira laughed again and then covered her mouth.

"I was being sarcastic. That's another strike for you, Mr. Higgins. I'm giving this job to someone else." He looked around the room.

"No, please, give me another chance," I begged. "Did you like the bag? I told them to stitch the Critchlore crest on that."

He looked at the bag, feeling its velvety softness. "The bag is fine. But you have to understand how important this is. The future of this school depends on us making a good impression with these ladies."

"I know," I said. "I'll find better stuff. I'll get a girl to help this time." I guessed I didn't really understand this task. Honestly, I still can't imagine why anyone wouldn't want a Tornado in a Can™.

"You have one more chance," he said. He turned around and left.

I put the items back in the bag and pulled the drawstring closed. It was such a beautiful bag, but I had no idea what should go inside. It had to be something that represented the school while also pleasing the sirens. Professor Murphy had called them "elegant" and "sophisticated."

"I wish I could put in Pismo's gloves," I said to myself. "They look elegant, which the sirens will like, but they also have a surprise, which is just like Dr. Critchlore. He's always doing surprising things."

Mistress Moira stopped sewing and sighed. "You got that right," she said, nodding at the room. "What's surprising about the gloves?"

Uh-oh. I didn't want to reveal Pismo's secret. But on the other hand, Mistress Moira seemed to know everything about everybody. "Pismo's dad sent him some gloves, but Pismo doesn't want to show them to anybody. He's embarrassed about them."

"Because they're made by mermaids?" Yep. Mistress Moira knew everything.

I nodded. "The gloves light up in the dark. They give off this really beautiful pale blue light." I reached into my bag and pulled out the pair that Pismo had given me.

Moira held them, feeling the waterproof, soft-as-silk material. "They're lovely."

I sighed. "Why do the sirens hate the mermaids?"

"It's a senseless hatred," she said. "Built on jealousy and greed and the thirst for power."

"Thirst for power?"

"Yes. Many leaders, especially the bad ones, use hatred and bigotry to control their own people. They blame all their problems on some other group, in the hope that their people won't see that it's their own leaders causing the problems. Didn't you take Dr. Critchlore's Tools of the Tyrant class?"

"Next year," I said.

"Well, when the sirens are unhappy, the Grand Sirenness points her finger at the mermaids. 'It's their fault! Those stupid, greedy mermaids have trespassed into our rightful realm! They hate everything that lives on land, especially us, and they want to destroy our way of life.' Then her people rally with her against this made-up mermaid threat."

"I was going to give these gloves to you," I said. "I thought maybe you could use them to make the show more amazing. But the sirens will know where they came from, won't they?"

She nodded. "The sirens will destroy Dr. Critchlore if there's as much as a whiff of something mermaid in this school."

Over the next few days, the mood around campus was gloomy. Our boulderball team, our stealthball team, even our previously undefeated waterdragon polo team all suffered defeats, mostly at the hands, fins, and claws of Pravus teams.

Morale was low. Nobody wanted to work on a fashion show when there were important minion lessons to be learned.

I wasn't having any luck finding the Archivist either. I kept trying the opening to the *If Books Were Food* poem, hoping that someone would reply with the next line. But I never got the response I was looking for.

Me: "If books were food . . ."

Betsy, the dungeon administrator: A sigh, then, "Dieting would be so much easier."

Mr. Griphold, detention dean: "Libraries would be more crowded."

Pierre, my foster brother: "We wouldn't have to eat Cook's seafood tetrazzini."

Mr. Everest, dean of students: "Food fights would be more painful."

Professor Chowding: "Darthin would be obese."

I went to check in with Uncle Ludwig and found him in his secret library, huddled over a table with Professor Zaida as they examined a pile of old, leather-bound books. I stood by the staircase, and when he saw me, he came over to see if I had news. I shook my head before he could ask.

"Who could it be?" I lamented.

"Don't give up. Of course the Archivist will be hard to discover," Uncle Ludwig explained. "Remember, this person is a high-level operative, so he's going to be extremely cunning and stealthy. He might show no interest in books whatsoever. And he's probably a highly trained fighter too. And strong. Keep your eyes open for someone who leaves campus at times carrying a large load."

Professor Zaida swept a few books into a bag and stood up to go. "I'll leave you those books, Ludwig," she said, pointing to the pile left on the table. "I'm going to take a few of these on my camping trip this weekend."

"Okay, Valerie," Ludwig said. "And please thank your sister for sending those books here."

"Gentlemen." She nodded at us and left.

With a bag of books.

To go on a camping trip.

I felt a sudden jolt. "Do you think—" I started, doing a double take to look back at Professor Zaida.

"Hmm?" Uncle Ludwig said.

"—that she'll pack more than just books? The forest is filled with dangers, and she's so small."

‡‡‡

As depressed as I was about my lack of progress, it made me happy to see the girls having so much fun with the show. They modeled for one another and laughed and made up dances and different walks. Jud was doing a good job with the imps, who would be acting as ushers until the show started.

Syke and Janet were still unhappy about the whole thing. Syke, I could understand—she wasn't exactly the fashion show type. But Janet? She could walk down a runway in Professor Murphy's Monday/Wednesday coat and still look amazing.

As I made yet another delivery, I passed the group of girls, huddled around the end of the runway, looking at pictures.

"Bianca, you look really good in maroon," Verduccia said. "I think when Mistress Moira finishes that, you are going to look stunning."

"Thanks. I love how that dress drapes on you," Bianca said. "And Frieda, yellow really brings out your eyes."

They oohed and aahed over one another's shots. Even Frieda managed to say something nice about someone else.

"You look too pretty to eat," she told Meika in her husky voice. "Like a delicate little flower I don't want to stomp on, even."

"Thanks, Frieda."

Dr. Critchlore stood on the stage, Professor Vodum next to him. I wanted to try the poem out on Dr. Critchlore, so I waited in the eaves.

"We've lost recruits," Vodum said. "And now customers. On top of that, our sports teams are tanking, and the Siren Syndicate is coming tomorrow. Derek! Stop looking so calm. What are you going to do?"

"I'm going to put on a fashion show," he said.

"Your cousin and I could help you!" Vodum whined. "You know everyone in the family loves Greta. She and I could persuade the rest of the family to not vote 'no confidence.' We could save your job. All you have to do is meet my demands."

"If I met your demands, then I would have to vote myself out, because I would have no confidence in anybody who would make you second-in-command."

He turned his back on Vodum and headed for Mistress Moira, but I intercepted him.

"If books were food—" I started, looking at him expectantly.

"My students would starve, because Uncle Ludwig never opens the library," he said. "What do you want, Hogwarth?"

Rats. Time for my backup plan. "We have a game in Yancy on Friday, and I think we can actually beat them. It's not going to be canceled, is it? Because of the arrival of the Siren Syndicate?"

"Huh? Yancy? What?"

"Tackle three-ball game. Day after tomorrow. It's still on, right?"

"Sure, why not?" He shook his head like it was a ridiculous question.

Mistress Moira got up to help fit Joelle in her dress behind a screen. Dr. Critchlore stood waiting for her, so I asked him another question.

"How long will the Siren Syndicate be here?"

"Just through the weekend, thank goodness," he said. "But everything has to run smoothly. You have no idea how fearsome these women are. One perceived slight, one misstep, and they *will* destroy us."

"Do they have monster powers?"

"I didn't mean that literally, Hunter. Although I imagine they could give Pravus's giant gorillas a good thrashing, ha!"

"Right," I said. "Like Syke."

He'd been watching for Mistress Moira to come back, but he looked over at the mention of his ward. "What?"

"Syke. When we went to the Pravus Academy, one of the gorillas tried to block our path. Syke told it to back off, and it did. It was amazing."

"Syke did that? Why didn't anyone tell me?"

I shrugged.

"Interesting," he said. "I had thought it was a myth, but perhaps, like all myths, there's some truth to it."

"To what?"

"Music soothes the savage beast. We've tried music, of course, but what if it's something else? What if it's beauty? Imagine . . . we could be sitting right on the one thing that can stop those monsters. Stop Pravus." He pointed at the girls, smiling. "And it's so simple."

"That gorilla was just a kid, not a full-grown adult," I said. "It probably hadn't had Pravus's special training yet either."

"Special training, my butt. Those gorillas don't need special training. Honestly, if Pravus tripped over a log, he would take credit for inventing wood."

"Still, you can't be thinking of sending Syke against another one," I said. "The hamadryads will destroy you."

"No, not Syke. You're right. We'll have to find another one. The prettiest one. Jessica. No, Jane. No . . . what's her name?"

Uh-oh. What had I done? Was he really going to send one of the siren girls to go up against a giant gorilla? That was crazy.

I had to warn Janet, so I left.

I passed Vodum in the foyer. On a hunch, I stopped and said, "If books were food—"

He looked up at me. "Blech, books taste terrible."

Not a surprise, that one.

I left the castle, heading for the girls' dorm. Once outside I ran into Janet, who was bundled up in a blanket.

"Janet, you look terrible," I said, which wasn't exactly true. Even sickly, she looked great. She made a greenish complexion look like a mossy forest in the early-morning light. Breathtaking.

"I feel so sick. I'm not going to be able to greet the sirens tomorrow. I'm on my way to tell Dr. Critchlore, but I don't think I can make it up the stairs. Can you tell him for me?"

"Actually, I wanted to warn you about something," I said. "I think Dr. Critchlore is going to be looking for you. I told him about Syke standing up to the giant gorilla at Pravus's, and he thinks that beauty might be their soft spot. He wants to test his theory out with you. But don't do it, Janet. It's too dangerous."

"He wants me to go on a secret mission?"

"Yes, but like I said, it's really dangerous. You should just wait for the siren mothers to get here tomorrow."

"I'm good," she said, throwing off the blanket and bundling it in her arms. Suddenly she seemed in perfect health. She bounded up the castle steps.

CHAPTER 22

Wherever there's trade, the sirens are there, taking a cut.
They are a greedy, evil, cunning, bloodthirsty organization.
—DR. CRITCHLORE, SPEAKING WITH ADMIRATION
ABOUT THE SIREN SYNDICATE

The next morning, we were in full dress uniform: black slacks, button-down shirts, and double-breasted military jackets. We lined the long drive up to the castle, with the larger minions closest to the entrance. Next to them were the ogre-men, the monster minions in their monster forms, then the skeletons and other undead minions, and finally, the human-sized kids like me. The imps and other small minions circled the fountain in the middle of the drive.

On the steps of the castle, the teachers stood on one side, the siren daughters on the other. Dr. Critchlore, in his full military-style uniform, stood at the top.

My chest swelled with pride to be a part of this incredible display.

But then I felt a sharp poke in my back. I turned around into the angry glare of Rufus, flanked on either side by his werewolf buddies, Lapso and Jud, who should have been down the road with the other werewolves.

"I know what you did, Runt," he said, spitting out my name like it was something disgusting.

"What?"

"You told Critchlore about the gorilla and Syke. He wants to see if it's true, but did he send his precious tree nymph? No. He sent Janet. To take on a giant gorilla."

He was whispering in my ear, and I could feel the heat and spit of his words. Mostly the spit.

"If anything happens to her, you're dead," he said. "I'll maim you myself. I don't even care if they kick me out of this school."

I shook. I couldn't speak. Nobody had threatened to kill me before. Well, except for that person who'd cursed me. And Miss Merrybench. And Dr. Pravus when he was choking me. So, technically, this was the fourth time my life had been threatened, and it was still extremely unnerving.

"Even if she comes back fine, you're still gonna pay," he went on. "I'm gonna get your pathetic butt thrown out of this school for good. You weak little loser, it makes me sick to see you wearing the same uniform as me."

I felt like running away, or collapsing into a ball. How was I still standing? My legs felt like jelly.

Rufus backed off as the limousines approached. They drove slowly, like panthers slinking through the jungle looking for prey. One by one they unloaded their guests, and the siren women stood on the gravel, waiting for the last limousine. It was larger than the other ones, and decorated with fancy flags. When it stopped, four attendants took up positions at the corners of the car, and another two stood ready at the door.

From my position near the sirens, I was able to see Grand Sirenness Marissa as she exited the car. An attendant reached down, offering a hand, and she emerged. She was stunningly beautiful, wearing a sheer blue dress that seemed to swish around her. She had silky blond hair and a golden tan, just like her daughter, Bianca. Her blue eyes sparkled.

She looked up at the castle and then took in everybody standing at attention. She smiled and we all smiled back, she was that powerful.

"Bianca, darling," she said, stretching her arms for a hug. Bianca floated to her mother, and the Grand Sirenness held her daughter gently, so as not to smudge or wrinkle or otherwise disrupt her appearance. "You look lovely."

"Thank you, Mother. So do you," Bianca said.

"This castle is very impressive." She looked up again and nodded.

Dr. Critchlore approached, took the offered hand, and kissed it with a bow. "Grand Sirenness," he said. "Welcome. Welcome to you all," he added to the others. "If you'll follow me, we have a reception waiting in the rear courtyard."

Cook asked me to help Pierre serve at the reception. I tried to steer clear of Rufus while I took a tray of hors d'oeuvres to the group of sirens and their mothers standing by the gazebo, looking out on the lawn, and beyond it, Mount Curiosity.

"Tell me, girls," Grand Sirenness Marissa said, "what have you been learning here?" She waved her hand in dismissal of my offered plate.

Bianca looked at her friends for help. "Um. Modeling stuff, mostly."

"'Modeling stuff'?" Marissa said. "What do you mean?"

Bianca's face turned pink. She looked cute, and I stood watching with my head cocked to one side. "Um," she said.

"Um?" her mother said. "It appears that poise and decorum are not part of the curriculum."

"I apologize, Mother. We have learned so much it's hard to know where to start. We learned how to march—er—walk, with grace. And that . . . models . . . work best . . . when they work together?"

"Really?"

"The difference between the impossible and the possible is a team of models," added Grace.

"Even small models can do great things, if you have enough of them," put in Meika.

I was pretty sure those were all quotes from Dr. Critchlore's book, and the girls were just substituting *models* for *minions*. The siren mothers did not look impressed.

"Pi is the ratio of a circle's circumference to its diameter," said Verduccia, who really liked math.

"This is upsetting," the Grand Sirenness said. "If I had known how sketchy the curriculum is at this academy, I would have thought twice before sending you here."

Dr. Critchlore walked up carrying two glasses of champagne. He handed one to the Grand Sirenness.

"I am not impressed, Dr. Critchlore," she said. "You are teaching them teamwork? Mathematics?"

"Yes, yes, of course," he said. "It's the latest thinking in the—er—institute of higher modeling theory."

Not one person had taken an hors d'oeuvre from my tray. I couldn't bring a full plate back, or Cook would kill me. So I ate one myself. It was really good. I ate another. I didn't want to miss out on this conversation. I wanted to hear what else Dr. Critchlore was going to make up.

"And—er—the advanced theories of effective modeling, really, enhancing the individual's self-style and inner confidence—"

At this point, another siren mother strode into the group. "Excuse me, Your Elegance," she said. "I must interrupt. Look who I found by the seafood platter." She yanked on the arm of the person behind her, who turned out to be Pismo.

"You!" Grand Sirenness Marissa said. She slammed her champagne glass to the ground. The look of hatred on her face was so intense I thought Pismo might spontaneously burst into flames. "What are you doing here? And wearing a school uniform." She turned back to Dr. Critchlore, rage face still at maximum power. "Dr. Critchlore, explain to me why you have a mermaid in your school. With my daughter!"

Dr. Critchlore opened his mouth, but no words came out.

The Grand Sirenness turned to her daughter. "Bianca, were you aware of this?"

"Yes, Mother," she said. "We all know he's a mermaid, but he didn't want anyone to know, so we didn't say anything."

Pismo looked stunned. "You knew?"

"Of course," Bianca said. "You're kind of famous back home, Prince Pismodor. I've seen your likeness on more than fifteen bounty posters. You destroyed our sea pool by breaking the restraining wall, you covered our rocks with goop so we couldn't sit on them to lure sailors to their death, you were caught stuffing poisonous puffer fish into our nets . . . I could go on."

Pismo almost smiled, then he turned serious. "I was reckless in my youth," he said.

"Don't tell me you've changed," Marissa said.

"I have," Pismo said. "My father wants peace. We all want peace."

She scowled at him, not believing it. "I want him taken care of."

WANTED

PISMO AQUOVA
for:
DESTROYING OUR SEA-POOL!
COVERING OUR ROCKS WITH GOOP!
STUFFING POISONOUS FISH INTO
OUR NETS! (WE COULD GO ON)
$1,000,000,000

Dr. Critchlore took Pismo by the arm. "Come," he said. "She's right. You shouldn't be here."

He rushed Pismo over to Professor Twilk and pointed to the back entrance of the castle. Then he returned. "Your Grand Elegance, I apologize. As you know, minion schools, uh, and modeling schools—especially modeling schools—are constantly trying to further our understanding of all races, and mermaids have always been a mystery to me. I shall send him home immediately. In addition—"

Grand Sirenness Marissa held up her hand to stop him. "I would leave right now if it weren't for my daughter. I do not want to diminish her moment of glory. The show will run as scheduled. After that, we will take our daughters home, and they will not return. In addition, I will make sure that you never get another shipment on our rivers for as long as you live."

Dr. Critchlore paled. This was exactly what he'd feared.

The Grand Sirenness swept past him. Then she turned around. "Oh, I forgot to mention. I have taken the liberty of inviting a few guests. Make sure you have room for them at the show."

"Of course," Dr. Critchlore said. "Any guests of yours are welcome. How many extra seats will we need?"

"Let's see," she said. "There's Lord Vengecrypt's wife and daughters, Irma Trackno is sending her assistants, Wexmir Smarvy's wife and daughters are coming—they'll need to be seated away from Lord Vengecrypt's wife as they despise each other. Cera Bacculus's daughters and entourage. Goodness, it seems like there will be hundreds!"

"Hundreds?"

"Yes, the Society of Evil Overlords' Offspring. Current membership is close to one hundred."

"The daughters and wives of evil overlords are coming here?" Dr. Critchlore managed to whisper. "To our little fashion show?"

"I just said that."

I positioned myself behind Dr. Critchlore because he looked like he was going to faint.

CHAPTER 23

Minion school rankings are determined by evil overlord customer reviews, recruit retention rates, percentage of students who complete the program, and bribes.

—*STULL NEWS*, THE ANNUAL MINION SCHOOL RANKING EDITION

The atmosphere was tense. The fashion show wasn't until the day after tomorrow, and the siren mothers were enraged after discovering that a mermaid attended the same school as their daughters.

Fortunately, a little rest in their guest quarters in the West Wing of the castle managed to ease their anger a bit. They came down for the official school tour looking more interested than angry, and Dr. Critchlore decided to act as if nothing had happened.

We met in front of the castle: the siren girls, their mothers, Dr. Critchlore, and the junior henchman trainees, who'd been asked to serve as escorts. Tootles had fancied up the grounds, and everything sparkled—the Wall of Heroes, the statues in the Memorial Courtyard, even the dragons' scales.

I was paired with Bianca, and as we walked, the two of us listened to Dr. Critchlore and the Grand Sirenness discuss the challenges of leadership.

"And don't get me started on family interference," Dr. Critchlore said. "Everyone's an expert."

"Try keeping a feud going when everyone starts begging for peace," the Grand Sirenness said. "You have seriously damaged my hard work, Critchlore."

"Maybe it's time to end the feud," Dr. Critchlore said. "I've heard that King Aquova has been trying to broker a diplomatic truce. You know they're not stupid. And they are not a threat to your business. You could help each other. You could become so much more working together than fighting. Why not end this war?"

The Grand Sirenness looked furious. "You know as well as I do that that will never happen," she whispered. "Those mermaids act like they own the ocean. We hate them. They hate us. It is a hatred that unites my people."

Hatred is the tool of the tyrant. Mistress Moira was right.

"And *you* know that things *are* changing," Dr. Critchlore said. "EOs are taking an interest in mermaids, for coastal attacks and defense. Instead of being the last bigot, you could be the one who gets the credit for changing things. You know the first rule of leadership—find out where people are heading, then jump in front of them and say, 'Follow me!'"

The Grand Sirenness didn't laugh at Dr. Critchlore's joke.

"Mother," Bianca said, "the mermaids aren't evil. They're really nice. I've met three of them—"

She stopped abruptly when the Grand Sirenness clamped a hand over her daughter's mouth and hustled her away.

As I followed the group, Rufus bumped into me from behind, knocking me to the ground.

"Hey, watch where you're standing, doofus," he said. "Geez, my four-year-old sister is bigger than you." He stomped on my calf before walking away.

I stood up and limped behind everyone toward the dormitories. After a few seconds, I said, "Oh, yeah? Well, my sister's bigger than you too."

I shook my head. That was lame. "Oh, yeah? I may be small, but at least—" I couldn't finish the sentence. I felt like such a loser.

"Psst."

I turned around. Pismo's head peeked out of the bushes. "Fish sticks, Runt! You haven't learned anything. Come with me. I'm going for a swim in my secret spot."

"You're supposed to be hiding from the sirens," I said.

"They won't see me," he said. "Come on, I know what will help you."

"I'm supposed to be on the tour." I pointed at the group, which had stopped in front of the dormitory for minions of diminutive size.

"Do you really think they'll miss you?" Pismo asked.

"No," I said. It was true. They wouldn't.

We walked down the service road, heading for the isolated beach where Pismo had saved me from the imps' trap not long ago. Its nearness to the swamp kept most people away, so we were safe from siren eyes.

"I can't imagine this place without the sirens," I said.

"It's crazy, but I'll miss them too," Pismo said. "They've been so nice to me. Every one of them. They should hate me. Sirens hate mermaids. They hate that we can breathe underwater, and we hate their stupid singing power. It's a rivalry as old as water."

"But you don't hate the sirens here," I said.

"I tried to," Pismo said. We reached the lake and took the path along the shore. "I feel like a traitor for not hating them."

"Maybe others would feel the same way, if they just got to know each other. You probably have lots in common."

"Yeah," Pismo said. "We both hate submarines. And sharks. And we both love octopus ice cream."

"Yuck."

"I don't want to leave, Runt. I like my legs. If I go home, I have no idea when my father will let me leave again. Probably never, if I cause another war."

"Another war?"

"After I broke their sea wall, the sirens hurled depth charges down on our capital. Destroyed a lot of homes. After that, I was kicked out and sent to the Pravus Academy, because my father said it was rated the best, but it was pure hell, let me tell you. Actually, if Pravus takes over this school, I think I'd rather go home. That man is insane. I'm pretty sure he takes pleasure in watching people suffer."

I felt my hand go to my neck, and I remembered the evil glint on his face as he choked me.

We sat down in the sand, facing the water.

"Okay, Runt," Pismo said. "Let's get to work. I've been thinking about something that might help you with confrontation."

"Okay."

"Do you remember when I yelled at you for snitching me out to Mrs. Gomes? You told her you thought I was the saboteur, and I really let you have it."

"Yeah, I remember."

"I screamed in your face, and you shook like a baby squid. You couldn't form a complete sentence, you were so scared."

"I told you. I remember." I threw a pebble into the lake.

"Don't do that. The fish hate it."

"Sorry."

"I'm kidding. They don't care." He laughed. "And then I insulted your friends. I said they were all losers. When I did that, it was like you transformed. You actually stepped toward me, like you were ready to fight."

"They're not losers. It makes me mad when people say that."

"Don't you see? You *are* brave. You'd probably jump off a cliff to save someone else. Oh, wait, you did. You just have to channel those feelings into defending yourself. Stop thinking that you're unworthy." He stood up. "Stand up for yourself!"

"Okay, I'll try."

"No, you won't. You're just saying that to agree with me."

"I know."

"Barnacles, Runt! You're such a loser."

"I know."

"Syke's kind of a freak."

"No, she's not." I stood up to face him. "She's awesome."

"See? Now do that for yourself. I'm Rufus. 'Gee, Runt, I didn't see you there. What are you, like, seven?'"

"Yeah, a seven-year-old you had one of your friends sit on, so he wouldn't beat you in the henchmen test."

Pismo looked shocked. "Wait, really?"

"Yeah, Jud sat on me so I'd miss my turn. Rufus told him to."

"Man, that's lame. If you have to cheat to win, then you're cheating yourself out of knowing you earned a true victory. My dad says that whenever I cheat at sea chess."

I shrugged.

"You did it, Runt," Pismo said. He patted me on the shoulder. "You stood up for yourself. You've got it now."

"Thanks," I said. "Hey, look, everyone's going on the big boat. Maybe I can catch them before they leave." I turned back to Pismo. "You better hide."

He nodded. I jogged down the beach and headed for the dock, but they left without me.

CHAPTER 24

I'll admit it. I don't understand the rules of boulderball. It just looks like a bunch of giants running around, throwing huge rocks at each other.

—RUNT HIGGINS, BEING HONEST

The next day, everyone woke with a fresh dose of deadline anxiety. The dresses still weren't ready, the programs weren't ready, I was still stumped about the gift bag situation, and I hadn't found the Archivist. My to-do list had gone through the laundry in my cargo pants and was a tattered mess.

The girls stood onstage in their Critchlore uniforms—black cargo pants, black boots, and T-shirts, ready for rehearsal. Dr. Critchlore held a clipboard and split the girls into two groups, one on each side of the stage. Rufus was supposed to coordinate things, but nobody knew where he was. Frankie and I waited backstage, ready to help out as needed.

The room was filled with people working on the decorations, installing lights, painting sets, and adding seats up in the balcony. Some professors sat and watched, since they had no classes to teach.

Dr. Critchlore stepped out from the eaves holding a microphone.

"All right, girls, here's how we'll start. I'll introduce the show, the lights will dim, the music will start, and then I'll call the first model. I'm thinking we should install big screens on both sides of the stage. What do you think, Greg?"

He was talking to our chief of construction, Oscar.

"We'll talk later," Dr. Critchlore said when Oscar didn't reply, because he wasn't sure he was being asked a question. "Advisory committee? Are you ready?" He looked in turn at the three women he'd enlisted for this job. Each one had a different vantage point: Professor Chowding at the end of the runway, Professor Zaida on the left side, and Marcia, the secretary for the necromancy department, on the right. They each held a clipboard, ready to take notes. "For now, let's just have the girls do their walks. First up"—he looked at his clipboard—"Bianca!"

"Just so you know, my mother wants me to go last," Bianca said. "She says the best one always goes last."

"That's fine. We're just practicing our walks," Dr. Critchlore said.

Bianca strode to the middle of the stage, smiled, and began her walk down the runway. When she came back, Verduccia started her walk.

Frankie nudged me and pointed at Frieda, standing on the other side of the stage. She was humming, which she did when she was nervous. She looked really nervous.

"Mother thinks it's ridiculous that there's an ogre in the show," Bianca said, following our gazes. "And an imp, and Syke. They're not sirens. They're not special, like us."

"Bianca," I said, "just a few days ago you said Frieda looked great in yellow."

"But she doesn't fit in with the rest of us, don't you see?"

"Not really," I said. "Mistress Moira said that she's highlighting what makes each girl interesting. Frieda's just as interesting as the rest of you."

"Probably more interesting," Frankie said. "Since she's not letting her mother tell her what to think."

"*Hmph.*" Bianca sulked off to join the other sirens.

Frieda hummed louder, so I went over to talk to her.

"Are you ready?" I asked her.

"*Grr,*" she said. "I don't want to do this."

"Imagine it's a boulderball game. You're playing in the championship. Right before the game starts, the announcer calls out each player, and they have to walk to the middle of the field. You do that every year."

"This is different," she said. "I'm not wearing my boulderball uniform. I'm not with my team. They aren't here to psych me up."

"The girls are your team now," I said, nodding to the line behind her.

"She shouldn't do this," Bianca said. "Everyone's going to laugh at her."

The rest of the girls surrounded Frieda, offering encouragement. "You can do it, Frieda!" "You'll crush it!" "Yay, Frieda!" Frieda looked down at them and smiled.

"What do you do to psych yourself up before a game?" I asked.

"The Frieda flounce. It's my signature move. Like this." She bent over and made a body-builder pose with her arms flexing in front of her. She scrunched up her face and growled. Then she jumped in the air and pounded back down. I swear the earth shook a little.

"That is amazing," I said.

171

She smiled.

One by one, the girls went out to do their walk. And then, finally, Dr. Critchlore called Frieda's name. She stomped out to the middle of the stage, took one step onto the runway, and stopped. She looked up at the lights and squinted.

"C'mon, Frieda, you can do it!" I said in a stage whisper. "Just walk to the end and walk back. Easier than boulderball."

"Boulderball," she muttered. She seemed to gather some inner strength. Her expression turned fierce. "Boulderball!" she yelled. She flexed her arms in front of her, and then she did it again. The Frieda flounce.

Her confidence restored, Frieda walked down the runway. It started to wobble.

"Frankie!" I said. "The runway's going to collapse when she comes back. You have to get under there and hold it up." Frankie

could lift ten Friedas, he was that strong.

"I'm on it," he said. He snuck out from the eaves, dropped from the stage to the floor, and disappeared under the runway.

Frieda strode back, a huge smile on her face. When the girls came out for their final bow, Dr. Critchlore said, "Closing comments, blah, blah, blah. Good work, everyone. Let's take ten and do it again. Then we'll work on the dance number."

I looked at the list that Professor Murphy had tacked to the wall, presumably for Rufus, the backstage manager. His next task was to get water bottles for the girls, which I did. Then I went to find someone to fix the runway. I bumped into a maintenance worker who was rushing out of the ballroom.

"Hey," I said. The guy had a huge mole on his cheek. Wow, that thing was big.

"The runway took a hit of Frieda," I told him, trying not to look at that mole, but it was like a black hole, sucking me in. "It needs to be reinforced."

"Right, thanks, kid. I'll get on it," he said, and then rushed past me.

"The runway is back there!" I shouted, but he was gone.

As I turned to head back to the stage, Frankie crashed into me.

"Runt!" he yelled. "Runt, I saw something."

"Was it Syke?" I asked. "'Cause she cut practice again."

"No. I was under the runway. The girls had finished, but people were still walking on it, so I stayed to hold it up. Anyway, Professor Zaida was in the second row talking to a guy I've never seen before. Had a huge mole on his cheek."

Frankie had a photographic memory, so if he said he hadn't seen someone before, then he hadn't.

"Maybe he's new," I said. "Critchlore probably hired more helpers for the show."

Frankie shook his head. "I don't think he's a maintenance worker. He scared Professor Zaida, I could tell. I have excellent hearing, because Dr. Frankenhammer designed me that way. I don't normally listen in on conversations, but that man sounded so mean, and she looked so scared. He said he knew who she was, and if she didn't want to end up like Rathers or Demir, she'd tell him what he wanted to know."

"What? What did she say?"

"She kept shaking her head and saying 'never.' He said, 'Hoarding knowledge is tyranny, and we won't stand for it anymore,' and then he jabbed something into her leg. He told her she had two weeks to decide. If she wants the antidote, she'll give him the information."

"Antidote? He poisoned her?"

Frankie nodded.

"I have to find her. Frankie, see if you can catch that man; he just ran that way. Okay?"

"Okay." He darted out of the room so quickly he was nothing but a blur.

CHAPTER 25

Of the twenty-seven minion schools, Westvolt Academy's graduates typically score highest on the MATs, the Minion Aptitude Tests.
—*STULL NEWS*, ANNUAL MINION SCHOOL RANKING EDITION

Professor Zaida wasn't in her quarters, and she wasn't answering her DPS. On a hunch, I raced to Uncle Ludwig's library.

As I ran, everything clicked into place. Professor Zaida, poisoned, just like the CLOUD in the capital. The old lady looking at my Critchlore patch and telling me to warn the Archivist. She said, "Z is an *A*." Z—Zaida.

Why hadn't I figured it out before? I'd asked everyone but her. Was it because she was so small and harmless looking? So nice? Because Uncle Ludwig had convinced me that the CLOUDs were ruthless and that the Archivist had to be big and strong?

I raced to the dungeon and wound through hallways until I reached the grotto. Entering the library, I could see that the lights were on. A large black bag sat on one of the tables. Professor Zaida, dressed in black and with her hair pulled back in a ponytail, came out and put three books into the bag, then returned to the stacks.

I walked out and stood next to the bag. When she returned with more books, she saw me and gasped.

"Higgins," she said, putting a hand to her chest. "You startled me."

"Professor Zaida. You're a CLOUD, aren't you?"

"What are you talking about?"

"Uncle Ludwig's been looking for a covert librarian, but a covert librarian wouldn't be a librarian in real life." I walked around the table and stood right next to her. "They'd be other things in real life, and a librarian in secret."

"Don't you have a gift bag task to get to?"

"Frankie overheard your conversation with that fake maintenance man. He poisoned you, didn't he? He wants to know where the Great Library is."

"Runt, this doesn't concern you," she said, dropping books into her bag. "Please, just forget you saw me."

"Professor Zaida, I have to find it," I said. "I have to find out who I am and who cursed me."

She softened, reaching up to touch my shoulder. "Runt, I'm so sorry."

"Let me come with you."

"I'm not going anywhere," she said, but that didn't convince either of us.

"The old lady in the capital told me. 'Z is an A.' You're an Archivist. Please."

"Oh, Runt. I guess it doesn't matter if you know now. I don't have much time—two weeks, apparently—but you can't come with me. I've taken an oath. I don't mind dying to protect the library. It's what I've sworn to do. I've also pledged to keep it a secret. The protection of the Great Library is more important than our two lives."

"Why haven't you told Uncle Ludwig?"

"We rarely admit new members. Candidates have to prove themselves worthy over years and years," she said. "And that man couldn't keep a secret to save his lunch. Look how many kids roam around his 'secret library.' But what's even worse is that button over there."

"The self-destruct button?"

"He would destroy these books to save himself. These beautiful, important books. The life's work of historians and philosophers and economists. He would burn them all to save himself. That's why I'm not ashamed to take them from him. They are going to be protected at all costs."

We stood there for a moment.

"Please let me help," I said. "I don't want you to die."

She zipped up her bag. "There is something you can do. Our enemies are getting very close, and I think desperate measures are needed here. I'm going to do something I've sworn not to do. I'm going to tell you about another CLOUD. He's not an Archivist, so he doesn't know the location of the library."

"Like you do?"

"Yes. If Xena revealed me to that man, she might have told him about Yipps. Yipps is a Bundler. Collectors bring books to him, and he bundles them up and passes them to me, or another Archivist."

"'Know your ABCs,'" I said. "That's what she meant. Know your Archivists, Bundlers, and Collectors."

"We thought that having many layers of operatives, each with only their specific knowledge, would protect us from the EOs trying to find the library. We've been able to fend them off, mostly by feeding them false information. But Cera Bacculus and Tankotto have upped their game. Using this poison is just the latest proof of that. And it's working, because they found me out.

"At any rate. Yipps works at Westvolt Academy in Yancy. You have a tackle three-ball game there this afternoon. Find him and warn him about the mole-faced man. Tell him I'm going to the Great Library. It must be protected." She pulled a coin out of her pocket. "Give this to Yipps. It will assure him I sent you."

The coin had writing similar to my medallion, but with a book in the center, rather than a wolfish creature. I pulled my medallion out and showed it to her.

Her eyes went wide. "Runt, how long have you had this?"

"Since I can remember."

She stared at my medallion for a few seconds before releasing it. "Wow," she said, shaking her head. "Okay. I have more I want to tell you, but there's no time. Find Yipps and tell him that I've been compromised. Tell him I'm going to activate the safety measures before it's too late. And don't tell anyone else about this. That's vital!"

Darthin peeked out from the stacks, holding a book. "Sorry, Professor Zaida. I overheard your conversation."

Professor Zaida sighed. "Darthin, I should have known you'd be down here. Okay, both of you keep quiet."

Syke stepped out from behind him. "Um, I was hiding from the fashion show police."

Professor Zaida threw up her hands. "Anyone else in here?"

Frankie peeked out and waved. "I chased after that guy. He was driving an expensive car that was faster than me."

"Frankie? Darthin?" I asked. "How do you guys know about this place?"

"Daddy told us," Frankie said.

"Runt," Professor Zaida grabbed my arm. "You know how important this is. Make sure they understand too."

"I will."

She shouldered her bag and turned to leave.

"And, Professor Zaida?" I said. "I think you're wrong about Uncle Ludwig."

"Hmm?"

"He wouldn't destroy these books. Not ever. Look at how he cares for them. This library, it's the most beautiful room I've ever seen in my life. He treats the books like they're his children. He probably put that button in because Dr. Critchlore made him do it. I bet it doesn't even do anything."

"Runt, that's admirably loyal of you— What are you doing?"

I stood next to the button.

"Don't do it, Runt."

I pushed it. Nothing happened.

"And you know what? He can keep a secret too. He hasn't told anyone that Mr. Griphold has a voodoo doll for everyone at the school."

They all looked at me, jaws dropping to the floor.

"Oops, secrets are hard."

Professor Zaida nodded. "You're right. I've been sitting in this library for years, listening to him research the Great Library. I think I was insulted that he never imagined that I could be a CLOUD, or any woman for that matter. He's a terrible misogynist, but I guess he has his good points." She hugged me. "Take care, Runt Higgins."

"Good-bye, Professor Zaida," I said, my voice catching because I realized that this was good-bye. She wasn't ever coming back. She was going to die rather than tell that man what he wanted to know.

My friends huddled around me.

"How could you do that?" Darthin asked, pointing to the button. "What if it really was a self-destruct button?"

"I knew it wasn't. I accidentally hit it when I was reshelving books the other day. I screamed, but Uncle Ludwig told me it was fake and not to tell anyone."

I thought about what I'd just said.

"Secrets are really hard."

I started a new to-do list, partly to focus myself, and partly to deal with the mountain of anxiety that was making me shake. At the top, I wrote:

1. Warn the professor in Yancy.
2. Find the antidote for Professor Zaida.

I had no idea how to do the second one. Maybe that guy in Yancy could help. Next came:

3. Save Sara.

4. Figure out the gift bag situation.

5. Redeem myself for losing *The Top Secret Book of Minions*.

6. Find out where I came from.

7. Find out who cursed me.

8. Get him/her to lift the curse.

My to-do list looked entirely impossible. If only writing things down was the same as actually doing them, my life would be so much easier.

It's funny; I used to worry that my school would close. Now it looked like Dr. Pravus was going to take it over and turn it into a torture camp. Professor Zaida was close to death. I'd lost the one clue to my identity, and the sirens were going to destroy my school if the takeover didn't. It just goes to show you, never think that things cannot possibly get worse, because they can. They always can.

CHAPTER 26

Necessity is the mother of invention, but threats of great bodily harm work good too.

—CERA BACCULUS, SPEAKING AT THE

EVIL OVERLORDS OF TOMORROW CONFERENCE

Usually, on the bus ride to a game, we laughed and joked and sang songs. This time was different. With Professor Zaida gone, Coach Foley had taken over. On the ride to Yancy, we listened to him lecture about strategy, grittiness, and how we were going to switch our defense to a 3–4 instead of the 4–3.

We eventually made it to Yancy, home of the Westvolt Academy. Yancy is located southwest of our school, where the land turns dry and the hills are jagged, dotted intermittently with green sage bushes. Red rock pillars, etched by eons of wind, stand like giants practicing "sitting still so nobody notices you."

The Westvolt Academy trains all kinds of minions, just like Dr. Critchlore's, but they have a reputation for training the more brainy types, and for sending a lot of humanish kids to the universities in the capital.

The school was nothing much to look at, a series of clay buildings connected by gravel paths. Only the main building rose higher than a single level, at three stories tall. It faced a huge open field that they used for tackle three-ball when they weren't using it for minion drills.

As the team jogged to the field, I told Coach Foley I needed to use the bathroom. I detoured into the main building and ran right for the secretary's desk.

"I'm looking for Professor Yipps," I said. "I have an important message to give him."

"Oh dear," she said. "I'm very sorry to tell you this, but Professor Yipps is in the infirmary. They don't think he's going to make it."

Curses! I was too late. Still, he might have some information on how I could help Professor Zaida. "Please, can I see him? I think he'll want to know what I have to say."

She smiled. "He's on the third floor," she said. "Go down the hallway to room three forty-five."

"Thanks."

Professor Yipps looked gray and shrunken when I saw him lying in his bed. The room was bright; the windows opened to the front of the school. It smelled like a mixture of disinfectant and bad breath. The acrid sourness of the air made me think the Grim Reaper was hiding in the corner of the room, waiting.

"Professor Yipps?"

"Yes, son?" he whispered.

I walked closer. "My name is Runt Higgins. I'm from Dr. Critchlore's. Professor Zaida sent me." I showed him her coin. "She's been found out. A man poisoned her, so she left to protect the library. She wanted me to warn you."

"You're too late," he said. "I, too, have been poisoned. Two weeks ago to this day."

"They want you to tell them where the library is, or they won't give you the antidote," I said. He nodded. "Is there any way to find a cure?" I asked.

"No. It is a new poison. It's making me feel numb. First my toes and fingertips, then the numbness inched up my legs. Now I feel it creeping up my arms. I don't have much time." He looked out the window and sighed. From his bed, he could see the field in front, where my teammates were warming up.

"I'm so sorry," I said. "What are you going to do?"

"I'm going to die," he said. "Professor Zaida is going to die. It's what we have pledged to do. We will never betray the library. To have people such as that man who poisoned me gain control of it is unimaginable."

I knew what he meant. It was like imagining Pravus taking over Critchlore's. A complete travesty. I swallowed over a lump in my throat as anger and sadness overtook me. This wasn't right. It wasn't fair that this good man should die for someone else's greedy ambition.

We heard a commotion in the hallway outside the room. Professor Yipps seemed to recognize the voices, because his eyes went wide. "He's back," he whispered. Then he motioned for me to hide under the bed.

I dove under just as the door opened.

"Yipps," a deep voice said. "I see you're resting comfortably. Thank you, nurse. We'd like to be alone now."

"Professor?" the nurse asked.

"It's fine," Professor Yipps said. The door closed.

It was him. The murderer. His sinister presence filled the room like a cloud of fear, and it felt suffocating. I couldn't breathe, and my heart thudded. His footsteps clicked across the floor. In the silence of the room, they sounded like a timer on a bomb, ready to blow.

"You don't have much time, Yipps," the smooth voice said. "A day at most. You can feel the poison now, can't you? Filling your chest, squeezing your heart. It's getting hard to breathe, isn't it?"

It had to be Mole Face, and he talked like he was describing Professor Yipps's outfit, not his slowly progressing death. It gave me chills that a person could be so cold.

"Yes," Professor Yipps said.

"Last chance, Yipps. With one sip of this, you'll live. Just tell me what you know."

Slowly, slowly, I peeked out. It wasn't Mole Face; it was another guy. This one sported a bushy mustache. He was taunting Professor Yipps with a small vial filled with amber liquid.

"Never," Yipps said.

"We've found it, you know," he said.

"Then what do you need me for?" Yipps's voice was barely a whisper.

"The entrance. My boss is impatient, and he will start blasting soon. Tell me where the entrance is, and I'll be able to save some valuable books. It would be unfortunate if an important document got destroyed."

"I'm a Bundler—you know that," Yipps said. "I don't know where the entrance is. Why don't you tell *me* where the library is?"

"You really don't know, do you? It's much closer than you'd think."

"I've always wanted to know."

Me too! Tell him where it is. I need to know! I held my breath, waiting for the answer I'd been searching for. *Please please please please please.*

"A trade, then," the man said. "You may not know the location, but you do know something. The name of another Archivist. Not Zaida, we know about her. Or perhaps you could tell me a story, Yipps. You CLOUDs with your poems and fables. Tell me about the Great Lady of Wisdom. Tell me where she hides her children."

"Those fables are old, useless," Yipps said.

"Oh no. We've learned so much from the ones we've found." He ran a finger up Professor Yipps's arm. "You can't feel that, can you?"

"Numb."

"That's the problem," the man said. "It's not painful enough. I've adjusted the poison. I realized it would be much more effective if my victims were writhing in agony. If the pain built slowly until it felt like thousands of tiny ants were nibbling at your skin, from the inside. Yes, I think Professor Zaida should be feeling it in another few days."

"You're evil."

"You could save her. And yourself. Just tell me how to get inside. Given your age, you must know the old ways."

"Never!"

"Hoarding knowledge is tyranny, and we won't stand for it anymore," he said, and I nearly gasped out loud. That was exactly what the poisoner had said to Professor Zaida. But that guy had a mole, and this guy had a bushy mustache.

I risked another look.

The old beggar woman had been poisoned by someone she called the chameleon. This guy must be employing the stealth techniques that Professor Murphy had described while pointing out Tankotto's henchman in the capital. Wear something outrageous and that's all people will remember. Tankotto's henchman, with those small, stick-out ears and his . . .

Wait a second, not only is this guy using the stealth techniques of Tankotto's henchman. I think he is Tankotto's henchman!

It had to be him—the flashy suit, the huge mole, and now the bushy mustache. Professor Zaida said that Tankotto was desperate to find the library and the proof of his claim to Burkeve. And this guy was worried about blasting into the Great Library, because they might destroy the one thing they're after.

"We will find them all," he said. "Phillips, Niormi, Turnhook. They will all suffer. Why not save yourself, and them? You have lost. We *will* gain access to the library, but we don't want to accidentally destroy anything . . . valuable."

"You think that knowing where the library is will get you inside? You know nothing, and you will die trying," Professor Yipps said.

The man sighed. "Such a pity. Good day, Mr. Yipps."

CHAPTER 27

In tackle three-ball, the pitcher has two balls to choose from: the light breezi ball or the heavy thud ball. The third ball is carried by the base runner, and can be lateraled to his blockers if he gets tackled.

—FROM *THE TACKLE THREE-BALL RULEBOOK*

I waited for the door to close before sliding out. Mr. Yipps looked paler, and I didn't think that was possible.

"Mr. Yipps," I said, "that man works for Tankotto! If he knows where it is, others are going to figure it out too. Please, I have to help Professor Zaida."

"Young man," Yipps said. "Zaida is prepared to die, as am I. We will not break our vow. I'm sorry. I cannot help you."

"I'm sorry too," I said. He closed his eyes, telling me that this conversation was over. I left.

I ran out of the building and across the street to the field. I could see the evil poisoner talking to someone by the gate. I looked past him and saw his fancy car in the parking lot. And then I got an idea.

"Frankie!" I yelled. He raced over. "That's the same car, isn't it? And the same guy you chased?"

He squinted. "Yes, definitely."

188

"Syke, Eloni, Fingers!" I huddled with my friends and told them my plan.

"What's going on?" Coach Foley asked. "Get in the dugout, Higgins. The game's about to start."

I didn't have time to tell him everything. We had to move!

"Coach Foley, see that man there? He used to play for the Dalloid Mercenaries. Can we crush his car before we start?" Coach Foley hated the Dalloid Mercenaries. They were the biggest cheaters in all of sports.

"That's ridiculous." He frowned at me, then looked at the man. "His car is over a hundred meters away."

"Frankie can hit it," I said.

He shrugged. "Well, get to it. I'm going to act like I don't know what you're doing." He sat down and pretended to make notes on his lineup card.

Frankie grabbed the clobber. Eloni ran to the pitcher's mound. The other team was huddled up and hadn't taken the field yet.

"Which ball?" Eloni asked.

"Thud!" I said. I hoped Frankie could hit that heavy ball as far as the car.

Syke, Fingers, and I ran toward the parking lot. It was a long way away, and we needed a head start. I wasn't sure this was going to work.

I heard the crack of the clobber and looked back. The ball screamed through the air, soaring right for the man's car. It bounced on the pavement and then rocketed right into the car's front end. Frankie was amazing. The man froze; his hands went to his head in disbelief. It really was a beautiful car.

We reached him just as he swung around, trying to figure out what had happened.

"I'm so sorry," I said. "My friend didn't mean to—"

"Your beautiful car!" Syke exclaimed, touching the man on the shoulder. "Maybe we can pull this section out?"

Fingers circled the man, examining the damage to the car. I kept eyeing him, hoping he would get on with it, but he kept his distance from the henchman.

"Back off, kids," the man said, shaking off Syke's hand. "I've got it. Just . . . back off."

Syke and I kept apologizing. Syke touched him again. And Fingers stood there like a little green statue. I picked up the ball and

we turned to leave. I couldn't believe it. My plan had gone perfectly. What was wrong with Fingers? Why couldn't he help me out—just this once? I was so mad I felt like kicking him.

"Fingers," I said, once we were away from the man. "Why didn't you grab it?"

"What? This?" He held up the vial.

I reached down to hug him, but he held up a hand. "Back off, big guy. Your appreciation is noted. Just don't touch me."

Coach Foley was trying to keep a straight face and failing miserably. He had one arm around Frankie. "Frankie, that was masterful. What I could do with a team of Frankies!"

"Nice, Frankie," Syke said. "Really nice."

Frankie smiled. "Thanks."

I ran back to the main building, up the stairs, and barged right into Professor Yipps's room. I gasped because he looked dead. He lay with his head to one side, and I didn't see any sign of breathing flutter his chest.

"Professor Yipps?" I asked. I uncorked the serum and dripped a little into his mouth. I wanted to make sure to save some for Professor Zaida.

He licked his lips and blinked. I risked a couple more drops.

"I can feel it working," he said. Tears leaked out of his eyes. "I can breathe without struggling. Aaaaah, this is wonderful."

"Thank goodness it works," I said.

"Thank you," he said. Then he frowned. "I suppose you think I'm going to tell you where the entrance is, now that you saved me?"

"I didn't want you to die. I don't want Professor Zaida to die."

"I watched you, you know," he said. "I thought you might be working together, with that man. Doing a sort of good henchman–bad henchman routine, and that you might save me, thinking I'd be so grateful I'd tell you what you want to know. It's not a bad plan."

"No, it's not like that."

"I could tell. That man . . . his car . . . he was . . ." Yipps started laughing. "It was very well done."

"It was Fingers," I said. "He's very talented."

"I have begged my associates to expand our CLOUD operation to include warriors. How are we to go up against vicious men like that on our own? We need a better defense than secrecy. We need an army. But how do you tell a pacifist to use warriors? They will never agree."

"What about your team of assassins?"

He laughed at that. "No, we have no assassins. We may have started some rumors, but we are not in the business of death." Professor Yipps leaned back and closed his eyes. I watched as he moved his fingers and then smiled at them.

"They came for her children," he said without opening his eyes. "The Great Lady of Wisdom was angry. Enraged. The earth shook and exploded with her righteous anger. But it was no good; the enemy kept coming. She drew her children close, to protect them. They would be safe as long as she hid them well. Once her children were hidden, she lay down and cried herself to sleep. The tears continue to this day. A small fire burns beneath her tears, lighting the way to her children."

"That's sad."

"That is your clue to the library," he said.

I sat there thinking. "So the woman is the library, and her children are the books? It's a riddle?"

He nodded.

I hated riddles.

"So I have to figure out who this angry lady was and where she lived?"

He shrugged. "It's all I have. The elders used riddles to protect their secrets, but they discovered that it's a very unreliable method. You never know if the right people will figure them out. Still, we all know them. I've often pictured the library as being hidden in a vast underground vault, and the Great Lady as a statue in a fountain, where water flows like tears. The fire is a memorial flame of some sort, marking the secret entrance."

I sighed. "I don't have time to track down every statue with a memorial flame. There must be hundreds in Stull alone. How am I going to save Professor Zaida?"

He moved his arm and sighed. "You're right. There is no time." He seemed to come to a decision after a short pause. "I will tell you the name of my Archivist, the man who comes to collect my books. He is equal in rank to Professor Zaida, and he will know how to find her."

"Who?"

"His name is Fardaglio, and he is the headmaster of the Kobold Retraining Center. I can't risk going myself. Once Tankotto's man realizes I've been cured, I'll be watched every second. Everyone from this school will be watched. But you—you can take the antidote to Fardaglio."

"I will, Professor Yipps."

He nodded. "Go save her. Save Zaida."

CHAPTER 28

Nothing motivates a minion more than fear, and you can't instill fear unless you are willing to inflict severe trauma. It takes a strong hand to train minions this way.
—DR. PRAVUS, EXPLAINING HIS MINION-TRAINING PHILOSOPHY

Back at school, I gave the antidote to Darthin, who was working on something in our room involving a mossy substance that glowed in the dark.

"Darthin, I need a favor," I said.

He took off his safety goggles and blinked at me. "What?"

"This is the antidote to the poison someone injected into Professor Zaida. I need more. There's an old woman in the capital who's been poisoned, and maybe others too. Can you take this sample, figure out what's in it, and make more?"

"Oh, sure," Darthin said. "I'll just put it in the poison antidote serum replicator."

"Really?"

He blinked at me, and I got the sense he was being sarcastic.

"The problem with people thinking you're smart is that they expect you to do the impossible. Take Dr. Frankenhammer. He wants me to weaponize this moss. Says if we can get it to spew something, it would make a terrific surprise attack in the forest. But how am I supposed to get moss to spew? Drip, maybe, or ooze, but spew?"

"So you're saying you can't make more of this serum?"

"Dr. Frankenhammer probably could, and he's looking for an excuse to avoid helping with the fashion show. I'll ask him."

"Thanks, Darthin," I said. "Just make sure you save enough for Professor Zaida. Yipps drank about a third of it, so there are two doses left. I hope."

"How are you going to get it to her?" Darthin asked.

"The guy in Yancy said the headmaster at the Kobold Retraining Center could help us. He's an Archivist, like Professor Zaida. He'll know how to find her. We just have to figure out how to get there."

"I'll see what I can find out about the place."

"He also told me a riddle. It's supposed to be a clue to where the entrance of the Great Library is located. Something about a Great Lady of Wisdom, and how there was a war, and she had to hide her children . . . No, she was angry and lay down to cover her children? But she's still crying, her tears haven't stopped, and a flame lights the way to her children."

It sounded so stupid when I said it out loud. A sleeping, crying, angry woman guard?

"Yipps said it's a statue in a fountain with a memorial flame," I added. "But there must be thousands."

"Is that all you have? A riddle about a sleeping woman who can't stop crying?"

"Tankotto's henchman said it's close to Westvolt Academy, but he doesn't know the clue to the entrance."

"Hmm," Darthin said, striking his thinking pose—eyes gazing skyward, hand on chin. "I'll do some research. That way you can finish working on your gift bag." He raised one eyebrow at me, knowing I'd put off that task.

I couldn't even think about the stupid gift bag. Did it matter, really? There were lives at stake, and one of them was mine. If one of those EOs destroyed the Great Library, I'd never find out where I came from.

The next morning, Boris, Frankie, and I sat in the dungeon conference room. I held a velvety gift bag that was taunting me with its emptiness. Boris and Frankie were folding programs that had just come back from the printer.

"What am I going to put in this thing?" I asked.

"I thought you were going to get a girl's help?" Frankie said.

"I asked, but they're all so busy." I sighed. "I can't focus on this stupid bag when Professor Zaida is out there somewhere, poisoned. In a few days, she'll be writhing in agony."

"We just have to get through this fashion show tonight," Frankie said. "Then we can find a way to get to the Kobold Retraining Center and warn the headmaster there. He'll take the antidote to Professor Zaida."

"And then she'll take me to the library," I said. "And I'll find out about the Broken Place and where the Oti come from. I'll finally know who I am."

"If Rufus doesn't kill you first," Frankie said. "Which is why I've appointed myself as your bodyguard."

"Thanks, Frankie."

"Boris too," Boris said. He put another program in his pile, which now held three folded programs. Frankie's pile was so high I couldn't count them.

"Thanks. But here's the thing: Janet wanted to go."

"I know. She never wanted to do the fashion show," Frankie said. He folded two more in the time it took him to say that. "I guess she thought anything would be better. Even facing a giant gorilla."

Dr. Critchlore burst into the conference room looking frazzled and carrying a large cardboard box.

"She wants a winner," he said. "Grand Sirenness Marissa wants this fashion show to be a competition. One guess as to who she thinks should win. Also, she wants to see all the dresses and have final say on who wears what. Mistress Moira is going to explode. You can't tell that woman anything." He sighed.

"I didn't know fashion shows were a competition," I said.

"They're not!" He dropped the box on the table. "This is not going to end well."

I opened the box. It was filled with cards that listed the girls' names and had a little check box after each one. Bianca's name was at the top of the list, in a bigger font than the rest.

"That Bianca," Frankie said. "Ever since her mom showed up, Bianca's been acting all stuck-up. Her head's as big as Frieda's now."

After we finished stuffing programs with ballots, we took the boxes up to the ballroom. Now completely decorated, the ballroom was ready to go. The runway looked strong, chairs filled the room and balcony, and the stage was cleared of Mistress Moira's dressmaking operation. The first set was in place—a mountain vista in the back, with trees on the stage. Everyone was getting ready for the last run-through before the show that evening.

Bianca's mother, surrounded by her entourage in the eaves, seemed to be evaluating a dress held by Mistress Moira. The silky fabric had swirls of white on a silver background.

"This will not do," Grand Sirenness Marissa said, shaking her head. "No. My daughter will not wear this." She signaled to one of her assistants. "I brought a dress for her. It's by Hermix Cleong, *the* top designer in Stull. She'll wear that."

She turned to her entourage. "Hermix and I go way back. I provide him with all his foreign supplies."

Mistress Moira sat there with her mouth open. "I don't think you understand," she began. "There's a theme—"

Marissa held up a hand. "I do not talk to the help," she said. And she strode away, her followers talking about how brilliant Hermix was.

Mistress Moira stood up with that look I'd seen on her face when she was angry and about to curse someone.

"Mistress Moira!" I said. "Don't do it."

She looked at me and I flinched.

"Runt," she said, softening. "It's just . . . I planned each of these dresses to highlight what makes each girl interesting, what makes them special. Bianca was going to have fun in this dress. That woman is going to ruin the show."

"It's really pretty," I said, pointing with my chin to the dress. My hands were still holding the box of programs. "Where should I put the programs?"

"Over on the table," she said, pointing to the side of the stage. She folded the dress and set it aside with a heavy sigh.

"Runt, would you tell Dr. Critchlore that I'd like to speak to him as soon as possible?" she said.

"You don't want to use your DPS? It'd be faster," I said.

"Derek never answers his e-mail, or texts, or calls," she said. "And I don't trust Vodum to pass on a message. Go."

"Okay."

A familiar scene greeted me when I reached Dr. Critchlore's office. He and Vodum were arguing, again.

"Go on and petition to block the takeover," Vodum whined from his desk just outside the office. "It won't do you any good. The vote of no confidence will pass, and the EOs will approve the merger. Dr. Pravus has promised the family that he'll turn this school around. You're the only one who doesn't admire the man. Many believe it would be a great coup to get him.

"But I believe in you," he went on. "And there's still time. All I'm asking in return for my help is a position as assistant headmaster, a seat on the board of directors, and a salary commensurate with those responsibilities."

"That's it?" Dr. Critchlore asked, standing up from his desk and packing some papers into an open briefcase. "You don't want a bedroom suite in the castle and full use of our dragons?"

"Well, I assumed those perks went with the job title."

"You are grabbing beyond your abilities, Vodum, and I will never submit to your blackmail."

"Then I will vote 'no confidence' with the rest of the family. And just so you know, Pravus made me an offer that I turned down, out of loyalty to you. But since that loyalty doesn't flow both ways, I have to consider it."

"What's that? Your own giant gorilla?"

"I'll be *his* assistant headmaster."

Dr. Critchlore laughed. "Well, good luck with that," he said, closing the briefcase. "I think I have some time left, so I may as well do my job. I'll be at the Evil Overlord Council meeting. When I'm done with that, I'll make sure to put in a little more effort to find you a job that suits your talents. The fish monster needs a new feeder, I believe."

Dr. Critchlore headed for the door, but I jumped in front of him.

"Dr. Critchlore?" I said. "Mistress Moira wants to see you as soon as possible."

"Tell her I'm off to the council meeting. I'll talk to her first thing when I get back."

"Grand Sirenness Marissa just called her the help and said her daughter will not wear the dress that Mistress Moira made for her."

Vodum laughed.

Dr. Critchlore sighed. "I'll speak with her when I get back."

CHAPTER 29

It is a truth universally acknowledged that an ambitious person in possession of a good fortune must be in want of a minion.
—FIRST LINE OF THE POPULAR NOVEL *PRIDE AND MINIONS*

Back in the ballroom, the girls were rehearsing the dance number. Bianca sat alone backstage, so I went to talk with her.

"It looks like fun," I said, nodding at the dancers. That was a lie, because I hated dancing, and to me it looked like the opposite of fun, but I knew Bianca loved dance class.

"Mother won't let me do it," she said. "She says I need to keep myself above the rest of the girls."

"Why?"

"Because I'm going to be a leader someday, not a common siren. I have the most enchanting voice of anyone my age, Mother says. I need to start acting like a queen."

"If you become Grand Sirenness, will you stop the feud with the mermaids? You know they aren't stupid."

"I wish I could, but Mother just gave me this huge lecture about how important it is to hate them. And they deserve our hate, she says. They are evil to their core."

"You know they aren't," I said.

"My mother is under so much pressure! She keeps saying that mermaids are untrustworthy, but everyone is talking about how we should work together, that the mermaids aren't so bad. She can't just change her mind all of a sudden, when she's been the biggest megaphone of hatred. She thinks she'll look weak if she agrees to cooperate with them now. She's in a really difficult spot."

"She just looks stubborn," I said. "Why don't you do something about it?"

"What can I do?"

I thought about it. After a minute, I said, "Well, here's an idea. What if you and Pismo did something at the fashion show to usher in a new era of friendship? Wouldn't that be amazing? You could show the grown-ups how to set aside their hatred and start fresh."

"Runt, you are so ridiculously naive." She shook her head and stood up to leave. "But you're right. I would be amazing."

After lunch, while the girls were getting ready for the show, I checked in with Darthin in Dr. Frankenhammer's lab.

"Any luck making more antidote?" I asked him.

He nodded at Dr. Frankenhammer, who was hunched over a table filled with bubbling and smoking liquids in glass beakers. "He's close," Darthin said. He put a hand on a huge stack of papers. "I've collected some information on the Kobold Retraining Center, and statues, and memorial flames," he said.

"Just a little information?" Leave it to Darthin to turn a simple request for directions into a six-hundred-page thesis.

"Don't worry. I'll summarize it. We should meet after the fashion show, and plan our—you know."

He meant our unauthorized leave. I nodded.

"Darthin," I said, "I know you're busy, but what would you put in a fashion show gift bag?"

"Isn't the fashion show starting in a few hours?"

"Yes."

"Then if I were you, I'd put in my resignation from the junior henchman training program." He laughed at his joke, and then said, "Just throw in some of Cook's saltwater taffy and some hair scrunchies."

"Misssss Merrybench'ssss perfume," Dr. Frankenhammer piped in. "She ordered it in bulk and kept it in her quarters. She doesn't need it anymore, obviously, and I would appreciate its removal. The smell of it fillsss the hallways upstairs."

I remembered that perfume. Just thinking about the smell made me feel like someone was angry with me. Ah, memories.

Soon it was time for the fashion show to start. I stood backstage looking at the huge crowd filing in. My stomach was twitchy with nerves, and I wasn't even in the show. Seating was arranged to face the runway, with the VIPs in the front row. These included the siren mothers and the wives and daughters of evil overlords. Behind them sat their bodyguards, as well as teachers and students and less important visitors.

I held one of my gift bags. I was going to get a third strike, for sure. Saltwater taffy, a vial of Miss Merrybench's perfume, and some thick rubber bands I was hoping to pass off as hair scrunchies. On a whim I snuck in the photophore gloves, because why not? What else could the sirens do to us?

Since my job was done, I stayed backstage to help as needed. It turned out that the needed part came up sooner than I'd expected.

Elise came out of the dressing room behind the set. "Where's Rufus? I was told he's the backstage manager, and I can't find my purse. It's my most important accessory."

The stage was crowded with people getting ready for the show. Rufus sat on a crate, trying to figure out how to work the headset that we'd been using in rehearsal. He hadn't gone to any of the rehearsals.

"How am I supposed to know where your purse is?" he said.

"Because it's your job," I said.

A surprised hush smothered the room. I didn't know who was more shocked that I'd criticized Rufus, him or me. Probably me. Darn that Pismo—he had me doing so many confrontation exercises in my head that one just slipped out before I could stop it.

Rufus stood up and got in my face. "Oh really? And maybe I could be doing my job if I wasn't so worried about Janet—thanks to you."

You know what? I was tired of taking his abuse. I wasn't going to stand there like an idiot and say nothing.

"Rufus, we're all worried about Janet. We still do our job. That's what we're trained to do."

"Right," he said. "Because we're getting such valuable training here, putting on a fashion show. At this ridiculous school that's run by a lunatic."

"If this school folds, it'll be because of kids like you. Kids who think they're too cool to try." I held out my hand. "Give me the headset."

"What?" Rufus looked around. People were watching.

"Give me the headset!" I said, louder. I wanted everyone to watch. He couldn't hurt me with other people watching, could he? "You don't know what you're doing, Rufus. I do. I've been at every rehearsal. Give it to me, or this show is going to be a disaster and everyone will know it's because of you. I'm saving your butt, you ungrateful jerk."

He growled at me, eyes flaring with anger. He threw the headset at my feet. "Have fun, loser."

"You're welcome!" I shouted at his back.

After that, I felt so full of energy and confidence I could've lit up a city. I'd just called Rufus a jerk, and I wasn't a shredded pile of human skin. This was amazing. I was ready to take charge of this little show, whether there were evil overlords watching or not.

I knew what to do. I gave Frankie the other headset, and we each took a side of the stage. We'd make sure the girls were ready to go from the eaves. I had ten girls on my side, and Frankie had nine on his. Syke still hadn't shown up.

I looked at Mistress Moira, who was wearing a very pretty white dress that seemed to float around her. It looked so brilliant next to her dark brown skin. She was calm, but she kept stealing glances at Bianca, standing at the end of my line.

Bianca really stood out. The rest of the girls wore Mistress Moira dresses, and even though they were different, there was something the same about them. They were different colors and lengths; some had capes, some didn't. I don't know what it was that brought them all together, but something did—a flamboyant subtlety, maybe, or an elegant casualness. *Yikes*. I could see why I hadn't been asked to write the descriptions for the program.

Bianca's dress was striking, but it was so different. Like seeing a fish monster frolicking with a pack of werewolves. She looked confident, though. Really confident. Smug.

"Bianca, you didn't come to the dress rehearsal," Verduccia said.

"Mother said I didn't need to. She thought it would be better to have my hair and makeup done by her people. It's just walking down the runway."

"What about the rehearsed stuff?" Verduccia said. "The dances—"

"I'm not doing those," she said. "Mother told me they're goofy and will make me look common. I'm just going last, so everyone will see how much better I am.

"I am so winning this thing," she continued. "As soon as Janet withdrew, I knew I'd win. It's not even this dress, although look at it. It's like I'm wearing gold and everyone else is in mud. It's ridiculous how good I'm going to be. Mother keeps saying that."

Verduccia rolled her eyes, but not so that Bianca could see.

Bianca was so much nicer when her mother wasn't around.

A tuxedo-wearing Dr. Critchlore walked out to the middle of the stage holding a microphone, and the crowd hushed.

"Welcome to the Inaugural Critchlore Fashion Show," he said. Listless applause greeted this announcement. It was the sort of applause that wasn't really interested in anything yet. "This is an entirely student-run event, except for the dresses, of course. I always strive to let the students practice the skills they've learned here in a completely new situation. Skills like logistics, timing, organization, and leadership."

He was covering himself should anything go wrong, I knew—everyone knew.

"I'm very proud of all the hard work these talented girls have put into this show," he went on. "And now I will share some words from Mistress Moira."

He cleared his throat and read from a card: "Every girl has that little something that makes her special and interesting. Perhaps it's a joyfulness that's a pleasure to be around, or an intellectual curiosity that makes us think, or maybe it's an infectious laugh that brightens our day. It can be any of a million things. We aim to find that little spark of character and kindle it, so that it glows for everyone to see. This is beauty. Not a physical beauty that lies as flat as a picture, but a personality that gives us something we want to return to. Let's ignite the inner confidence of these girls by celebrating the young ladies they are becoming."

The applause was even more tepid now.

"And to this I add: All our girls are beautiful!" Dr. Critchlore went on. "But don't take my word for it. Why don't I show you? Let's begin!"

I took a deep breath. I knew that the sirens were set on destroying my school once the show was over, but a part of me was hoping that they'd see their daughters onstage and change their mind.

On the other hand, I've been told many times that I'm too optimistic for my own good.

CHAPTER 30

Be evil.

—CORPORATE MOTTO OF THE SIREN SYNDICATE

D r. Critchlore returned to the eaves, microphone in hand. First up was Verduccia, and I nodded at her to take her position center stage.

"Frankie, make sure Trinka's ready to go as soon as Verduccia hits her last pose," I said in my headset.

"Got it," Frankie replied.

The lights went out and the auditorium was plunged into darkness. The music started, a thumping, dancey beat. The spotlights flashed onto the runway and Verduccia, who stood in the center of the stage wearing an emerald-green dress with long sleeves that reached her knuckles. A gold chain circled her waist and dangled down one side. Her auburn hair was styled into long curls.

"Verduccia!" The music faded in volume as Dr. Critchlore read from his note card. "Verduccia is a spirited and independent girl, calm under pressure when others are quick to panic. We are drawn to Verduccia's fearlessness and take-charge attitude."

The music rose again, and she began her walk. Cameras flashed from the audience. From my vantage point in the eaves, I could see the imps stationed at the aisles in the audience, dressed as minia-ture ninjas. This was the part I was nervous about. I'd seen the imps in rehearsal, and they didn't always get it right. I held my breath as I watched them sneak down the aisles. They crouched near the runway, watching Verduccia.

Verduccia walked with her head high, a slight smile on her lips. When she reached the halfway point on the runway, a large net dropped from the ceiling and covered her. She screamed. The imps jumped onto the stage to hold it down, smiling wickedly. Verduccia struggled, but the net held her in place.

Shocked audience members turned to one another, wondering what was going on. Some of the bodyguards rose to their feet, but Verduccia held up her hands to stop them.

She balled her hands into tight fists, and when she did, the sleeves of her dress erupted with short blades. With two swishes of her arms, she tore the net to shreds and stepped free.

Verduccia walked to the end of the runway, clapped her hands together, and the knives reset into the sleeves. She swirled back to the stage, smiling as the applause grew more enthusiastic.

Next up was Trinka, an imp. Dr. Critchlore read, "Whether on the playing field or in class, one thing shines through about Trinka—her ability to get out of tough situations. She's clever and crafty, thinking up solutions that others miss."

Trinka wore a pale purple dress with large green polka dots, each one the size of a saucer. She also wore a beret in matching purple.

"Frankie," I said into my headset. "The wall!"

Frankie nodded and pushed a ten-foot-tall wall prop out from his side to the middle of the stage.

Most people had to watch Trinka on the giant screens flanking the stage, because she was so little. The ninja imps were gathered at the end of the runway and, right after Trinka hit her pose, they popped up threateningly.

Trinka threw down her beret, and it exploded with a bang and a puff of smoke that made the imps jump back. She turned and race-walked back toward the stage. As she moved, she ran a hand down her dress, lifting off five polka dots in one pass. She threw them like Frisbees toward the wall, where they embedded into it, each one slightly higher than the last, like steps. When Trinka reached the stage, she climbed the steps to the top of the wall. She swung herself up, turned, and sat on the top. With a press on her sleeve, the steps disintegrated, so her pursuers couldn't follow. She waved at the cheering crowd as Frankie pushed the wall back to the eaves.

"Joelle," Dr. Critchlore said, "at first glance, seems like a shy and quiet girl. But still waters run deep, and everyone should get to know her quiet humor and intelligence. We are all just waiting for Joelle to soar."

Frankie and I had given nicknames to the dresses: The Slip-n-Slide, the Porcupine, the Magic Book, and the Side-Puncher, to name a few. We called Joelle's dress the Jetpack, and it was awesome.

"I would wear that dress," Frankie said in his headset as Joelle returned from her flight around the ballroom. "I love the Jetpack."

"Maybe Mistress Moira will make a boy version," I said.

The crowd was excited now. The cheers erupting from the audience made Joelle blush.

"I didn't know their dresses did stuff," Bianca said behind me. She chewed on a fingernail. "Do they all do something special?"

"Yes," I said. "Weren't you watching the dress rehearsal?"

She shook her head. "My dress doesn't do anything. What if everyone is expecting something, and my dress just hangs there? I'll be a huge disappointment." She started crying, which smudged her makeup. "I'm not doing it," she cried.

"You have to," I said. If she didn't compete, she wouldn't win. Her mother would be even more furious, and Dr. Critchlore would never be able to get back in her good graces. It would be a disaster.

I wanted to comfort Bianca, but I also really wanted to see Meika's dress, "the Flash Cape."

"Meika," Dr. Critchlore said, "has a bright smile for everyone, and her laughter brightens our day. She's the first to cheer up a friend who is down. You'll never hear Meika complain about anything."

I saw women in the audience, siren mothers and evil overlord wives, frantically scribbling in their programs. They pointed and nodded and laughed. They looked so happy. Everyone except Bianca's mother, who sat fuming. She stood up and walked toward the stage.

Bianca sobbed as Dr. Critchlore announced the next model. "We notice Elise's kind nature every day, whether she's helping classmates with their homework, or picking up that stray candy wrapper . . ."

"Frankie," I said. "Take over for me for a sec."

Someone had to do something about this impending disaster.

CHAPTER 31

It was the best of times, it was the worst of times, depending on whether you were an evil overlord or one of his subjects.

—FIRST LINE OF *A TALE OF TWO REALMS*

Mistress Moira watched from the eaves. I told her what was happening with Bianca.

"It serves her right, and her mother," she said. "They were completely rude to me. She called me the help. Me! I was a goddess back in the day!"

"It's not Bianca's fault that her mother is conceited. Yes, she's been obnoxious, but I think she's learned her lesson. Isn't there something you can do?"

"Tell her to meet me in the dressing room backstage. And hurry. Maybe we can work something out during the first dance number."

I turned back to Bianca just as her mother reached her.

"Where is the seamstress woman?" the Grand Sirenness asked, looking livid.

"Follow me," I said, and I led them backstage. Mistress Moira sat at a makeup table, waiting.

"You there, seamstress," Marissa said, snapping her fingers as if she were calling a puppy. "Where is the dress that you made for Bianca?"

"It's unfinished," Mistress Moira said. "When you told me you didn't want my 'common' dress, I stopped working on it."

"This is a disaster," Marissa said, pacing now. "You should have told me what these dresses do!"

"I believe your exact words were, 'I do not talk to the help.'"

"Bianca cannot go out like this. Everyone will expect her dress to do something, and it won't. Hers is completely different."

"Yes. I believe I said that," Mistress Moira replied.

Marissa stopped pacing and stood in front of Mistress Moira, squinting down at her. "Throwing my words back at me—do you think you've won your little battle here? Do you think you have bested the great Grand Sirenness Marissa? I can destroy this school."

Oh no. Confrontation. I hated confrontation, but I couldn't look away.

"Do you really think so?" Mistress Moira stood up. "Perhaps before the show you could have. But now? Now there is a ballroom full of evil overlords' wives who want these dresses for their daughters. Haven't you been watching them? If you cut off Dr. Critchlore's supply routes, I won't be able to make any dresses, and those wives and daughters will be very disappointed. Because of you."

The Grand Sirenness's face started twitching, she was so angry.

"Your position is an elected one, is it not?" Mistress Moira went on. "And right now you have the backing of those EOs. That will change if you so much as delay one shipment to this school."

The Grand Sirenness's twitching hardened into an expression

213

that looked dangerous. Mistress Moira was right. The Grand Sirenness had lost, and she wasn't used to losing.

The muffled bass from the show thumped in time with my heartbeat as I stood watching the women stare at each other. It was tense. It made me nervous. Sometimes when I'm nervous, thoughts jump to my tongue and escape my mouth before I can stop them.

"Bianca could wear the mermaid dress," I blurted out.

I looked from one woman to the other, waiting for a reaction.

The Grand Sirenness threw a water bottle at me.

"Runt, please," Mistress Moira said.

We stood in an awkward silence, which, for me, is just as bad as confrontation.

"Everyone says things are changing," I said to the Grand Sirenness. "Bianca told me you're in a tough spot."

"I did not," Bianca said, scowling at me.

"It reminds me of something that happened when my foster brother, Pierre, was a student here. One weekend, his friends wanted to go to the Caves of Doom to catch claw-worms—those snakelike creatures with front arms and claws. Before he left, I asked him why he was going, because he hates the Caves of Doom. He told me, 'If I don't go, then the next time they do something, they won't invite me. *I* need to be the one who decides what we do.'

"By the time they returned, Pierre was leading the way, carrying the sack of claw-worms, his arms covered with scratches. He was the hero of the trip, and they were all laughing and talking like it had been his idea all along."

And then he'd put one in my bed, but I didn't mention that part.

"You're saying my people will make peace with the mermaids, whether I want it or not," the Grand Sirenness said. "And I shouldn't fight it, or I'll be left out."

"Runt's right," Mistress Moira said. "Bianca *could* wear the mermaid dress. It's beautiful, and surprising."

"And I could pretend that was my idea all along," Marissa added, looking thoughtful.

"You could get out of two difficult situations with one move," Moira said.

The Grand Sirenness seemed to be fighting within herself, but eventually she turned to Mistress Moira and nodded.

"Do it," she said.

Pismo was watching from the balcony in disguise. When I told him the plan, and that I needed his help, he laughed in my face. I dragged him back to the wings with me, explaining how important this was for everyone—mermaids, sirens, Dr. Critchlore, the school. Everyone.

He agreed to go along with the idea, so I left him with Mistress Moira and hustled back to my position backstage, only to find Professor Murphy holding my headset and shaking his head.

The first dance number had ended and he'd just sent Devany out on her walk. He frowned as I approached.

"Leaving your post is a very serious offense, Mr. Higgins. That's another strike for you."

"But that would be my third strike," I said.

"You will be rejoining the regular minion program. In the meantime, finish what you started." He handed me the headset and left.

This was so unfair. What about Rufus? Doesn't he get a strike for not doing anything? Why should I be punished?

Devany returned, her dress sparkling as bright as her smile. Next up was Syke, which made me nervous. We hadn't seen Syke in dress rehearsal, but Mistress Moira told me she'd persuaded her to show up, so we waited.

"Do you see Syke?" I asked Frankie through the headset.

"No," he said. "And her cue is about to come up."

"I'm right here, idiot," she said.

"Syke!" I said, shocked to see her standing behind me, dressed in a long-sleeved tunic over black leggings. The shirt reminded me of a tree changing color in the fall. It seemed to be made of tiny metallic leaves, gently draping over one another.

"Wow, cool shirt. You ready?"

She shook her head. I've always loved the way Syke's hair looked like a hummingbird's chest. In the right light, it practically glowed with waves of color. Green, then blue, then black. She usually wore it tied in a ponytail, though. Now it was brushed out and flowing.

She held something in her hand. When she saw me notice it, she hid it behind her back.

"Syke, hand it over," I said.

She scowled at me.

"Syke, I thought you were brave," I said. "But look at you. Afraid to walk down a runway and back. So afraid that you'll cause a catastrophe just to avoid doing it."

She dropped her head and handed me the Tornado in a Can™ that she'd stolen from Dr. Frankenhammer's lab. "I wasn't really going to do it."

"And now, Syke!" Dr. Critchlore said, not reading from the script this time. "A loyal, brave, intelligent girl. A lover of nature, caring to all living things. Anyone would be proud to call her his daughter, and I'm lucky enough to call her my ward."

Syke looked stunned at that. She smiled and walked out quickly, like she was eager to get this over with. I wanted her to slow down, because watching the light hit her hair and the shirt was mesmerizing. At the halfway point, the imps jumped up at the end of the stage. Syke stopped walking and then shook one of her sleeves.

The tiny leaves detached and hovered in the air, like a swarm of insects. Syke swooshed her arm in the direction of the imps. The insect-leaves followed the air current to their target, speeding away from her so fast you'd have thought she'd shot a gun.

The imps turned and ran, except for one, who fell to the runway and covered his head. The metal leaves seemed to dart around his arms, trying to get at his face.

Syke walked to the end of the runway, kicked the imp off, which was not in the script, and hit her pose. The crowd laughed and cheered. When she turned around, I could see that she was smiling.

"That was awesome!" I said, high-fiving her as she passed me in the wings.

Frieda was next, and she was nervous again. She walked out to the edge of the stage and froze. The lights were in her face, blinding her.

"C'mon, Frieda, you can do it!" I said in a stage whisper.

She glared at me but seemed to gather some inner strength. Her expression turned dangerous. She flexed her arms in front of her. "Grr," she roared, and then she did it. The Frieda flounce.

The crowd loved that too, and they cheered her on with hoots and yells. Frieda, her confidence restored, strode down the runway.

We could hear the shouts of the ogre-men, who were watching the show with the other minions of impressive size on the boulder-ball field's giant screen.

Frieda hit the end of the runway, put her hand on her hip and struck a pose, then spun around and came back. Frankie rolled a giant brick wall out from the side. We put on our safety goggles.

When Frieda hit the halfway mark she held up her hand. She had a ring on each finger, and they were huge (both the fingers and the rings). She put her hand to her mouth and chomped down on what looked like a large gemstone. She swallowed, rubbed her belly, and then walked closer to the wall.

And burped.

It was a mighty burp. I don't think the world has seen a more powerful burp ever in history. The brick wall was reduced to dust. The crowd stood on their feet and clapped. Then they stopped clapping to wave the smell away. It was awful. I yelled in my headset to activate the fans and open the doors. Frieda turned around and bowed.

Frankie and I quickly swept up the debris, and then it was Bianca's turn. Heaven help us.

CHAPTER 32

*Two heads are better than one? Ha! I wouldn't show up
anywhere without at least ten heads.*

—ASTRID THE HYDRA

The lights went down, and the music softened to a melancholy tune. A spotlight hit Bianca, whose silver-swirled dress was as shiny as a polished coin. Her ruined makeup had been cleaned off, and her face looked fresh and sweet. Gone too was her elaborate hairstyle; her long blond hair flowed loose.

As she walked down the runway, the lights got dimmer and dimmer. By this point, the audience was accustomed to the unexpected, and everyone remained quiet.

At the midway point, the room was nearly black. Bianca pulled on the neckline of the dress, and when she did, Pismo's black tunic seemed to cascade down over the silver dress like water. In the darkness of the room, the photophores quickly activated and lit her up with pale blue dots. The crowd gasped.

The daughter of the Grand Sirenness was wearing mermaid clothes. Nothing that came before shocked the audience more than this. Stunned faces turned from Bianca to her mother, unable to believe the Grand Sirenness would sit still for this outrage.

At the end of the runway, Pismo stood between two imps. Dressed in a matching tunic of lights, he handed Bianca a pair of gloves. She pulled him up onto the runway and hugged him. Together, they walked back to the stage in their shining mermaid clothes, holding hands. Once there, they turned, flashing the finger lights of their gloves onto the Grand Sirenness.

Mistress Moira patted me on the back and then strode out onto the stage, microphone in hand.

"It was a very brave thing for Grand Sirenness Marissa to allow her daughter to wear a dress made by mermaids," Mistress Moira said. "I don't think I've seen a braver thing in a long time. Grand Sirenness?"

Marissa strode up to the stage and took the offered microphone. Mistress Moira joined Dr. Critchlore, who was watching from the eaves near my post.

"This feud between sirens and mermaids is old, and it should be put to rest. We are the same, inside." She tapped her heart. "We want the same things—to be loved, to have a safe place to raise our children, and to make ships crash on rocks. Why can't we do these things together?

"It is time to put away our hatred and start fresh. King Aquova and I will be meeting soon to discuss a new era of cooperation between the mermaids and the sirens. And I think we can all agree—it's the hydras who are the real problem in our coastal zones. How I hate those tentacly beasts! Am I right? As if one big head wasn't enough."

The stunned silence turned into wild applause, and then a standing ovation.

221

"Inside the gift bags, you'll each find your own pair of gloves," Marissa said, just like I'd told her to.

Everyone put them on, the lights dimmed again, and they all pointed their fingers at the Grand Sirenness so that she was lit up brighter than anything in the room.

Mistress Moira turned to Dr. Critchlore. "They did it," she said. "They wore the mermaid gloves."

The Grand Sirenness smiled and then held up her hand for silence.

"And now let us finish this wonderful event with the real stars, the girls."

She returned to her seat as everyone kept clapping.

"I really hope this doesn't get out," Dr. Critchlore said, shaking his head. "The last thing I need is a reputation as a peacemaker."

The crowd stayed on their feet as all the girls made one last appearance onstage. Dr. Critchlore strode out from the side, smiling.

"Thank you, thank you!" he said, hushing the crowd. "I'm so pleased you enjoyed the dresses that I designed for this show. Another hand for our assistant seamstress, Mistress Moira."

Did he really just say that? I looked at Frankie, whose eyes were wide with shock.

"We have a reception waiting in the courtyard. I hope you will all enjoy a little after-show treat. Evil overlord wives, please refrain from any physical attacks upon your sworn enemies. As Grand Sirenness Marissa has shown us, this is a time to put aside our differences and enjoy a day of fashion."

‡‡‡

Everyone seemed happy at the reception, but Mistress Moira was nowhere to be seen. The Grand Sirenness flitted through the crowd, telling everyone that she'd had this announcement planned for months and was waiting for a big event like this to make it. After a while, Dr. Critchlore came out to announce the winner, as the ballots had been counted. He stood on the steps and called for attention.

"I really hate to declare a winner, because clearly all the girls were amazing. At any rate, we've tabulated the results and our winner is . . . Frieda!"

"Frieda!" the girls squealed, covering the lower half of her body with hugs. Frieda looked genuinely pleased and shocked.

"What happened?" I whispered to Frankie.

"The sirens were told they couldn't vote for their own child. They voted for Frieda, thinking that she couldn't possibly win. They all thought that."

"That's great!"

"Syke should have won," Frankie said.

"You should tell her that."

Frankie, Syke, and I snuck out of the reception and headed for Uncle Ludwig's secret library. We needed a quiet place to plan our trip to the Kobold Retraining Center. We had no time to waste. We had to find the headmaster there and give him the antidote so he could pass it on to Professor Zaida. If we couldn't find him, then we had to figure out the Lady of Wisdom riddle and get to the Great Library ourselves.

Darthin was already there, sitting at a table covered with papers.

He was illuminated by a small pool of light shining from a desk lamp. The rest of the library was dark and quiet.

"The Kobold Retraining Center is north of here," he said when we sat down. He picked out a map of Stull and pointed to a remote region of the Neutral Territory. "Way north. At the border of Burkeve. It can be reached by road, but there was an explosion outside Stull City yesterday, and the main road heading north was destroyed.

"Here's what I know about the KRC. Kobolds are small creatures, usually helpful, but they go bad if they aren't thanked for their work. And by bad I mean completely malicious. The KRC captures bad kobolds and takes them to the retraining center, where they are turned back to good. Here's a map so you can find the headmaster's office." He spread out more pictures on the table. "Here's an aerial photo, and a photo of the main building. Here's a photo from their brochure."

"Looks pretty," Frankie said. "All those trees and the mountain range."

"That's Mount Izta," Darthin said. "It's an active volcano."

I picked up the picture of the mountain. There was something about it . . .

"I also researched statues of women with memorial flames." He plopped down another set of papers. "And I've come up with seventeen possibilities, but none are in Stull."

"That can't be right," I said. "Tankotto's henchman said it's close." I pointed at the picture of Mount Izta. "Is that a waterfall?"

"Yes," Darthin said.

"We need an excuse to go there," Syke interrupted. "We can't just decide to leave the school for some random outing. Someone will report us as absent without leave."

"Even if we could," Frankie said, "how would we get there? The road is out."

"I could get you there." A voice from the shadows startled us.

"Pismo!" I said. "What are you doing here?"

"I saw you guys slink down here and decided to follow." He sat down at the table with us. "This room is fantastic! Much better than the library upstairs."

"It's a secret," I said. "If word of this room got out, it could destroy the school. You have to keep it quiet."

"Believe me, I can keep a secret." He leaned forward. "Now, why do you want to go north?"

"We have to find the headmaster of the Kobold Retraining Center," I said. "Professor Zaida has been poisoned, and he can take the antidote to her. How can you get us there?"

"The Wallippi River comes down the mountains near there, eventually winding its way to our very lake. Swimming upriver is tough, but I need a good swim. My fin is atrophying something terrible. The lake just isn't much of a challenge, because the water just sits there. It doesn't fight you, like tides."

"You could take me, but what about everyone else?"

"I'll get some of the other mermaids to help."

"Other mermaids?" I asked.

"Yeah, you didn't think I was the only one, did you? There are a few more here. They're just hiding, on account of the sirens and the mean jokes and stuff.

225

"Boynton will love this," Pismo said, clapping his hands together. "He's anadromous."

"Does that mean he can use both hands?" Frankie asked.

"Not ambidextrous, you dolt. Anadromous means his family migrates from freshwater to the ocean. He's also got great magnetoception."

"Which is?" I asked.

"He can always find his way back. Did you ever wonder how homing pigeons find their way home? They sense the earth's magnetic field and use those cues to orient themselves. Same with anadromous people."

"I can't believe Boynton's a mermaid," I said. "What about the sirens? Won't they stop us from using the river without authorization?"

"Grand Sirenness Marissa gave me an official river pass at the reception," Pismo said. "She told me to use it to go home and arrange a meeting between her and my father. But I can use it to go upstream."

I thumbed through more pictures of the school and surroundings, focusing on that mountain again. The shape was almost the perfect silhouette of a woman lying on her back.

"Darthin, did I tell you that Uncle Ludwig believes the Great Library is in a mountain fortress?"

"No, you didn't."

"I probably forgot about it, because Yipps was so sure it's underground. But look at this." I showed him the picture again, pointing at the mountain.

"What was the riddle again?" he asked, frowning at the picture.

226

"The Great Lady of Wisdom was angry—" I began.

"Like a volcano erupting," Darthin said, pointing to the mountain.

"She threw her body on top of her children to protect them—"

"Her children, the books."

"Then she lay down and cried herself to sleep—"

"The waterfall comes out right from the mountain's head."

"A fire burns beneath her tears, lighting the way to her children."

"The Great Lady of Wisdom isn't a statue," Darthin said. "She's a mountain. This mountain. Runt, the area is rich in natural gas. One leak could be lit and stay lit forever, even beneath a waterfall. An eternal flame."

I looked up at everyone. "If we can find that flame beneath the falls, we'll find the entrance to the Great Library. We can find Professor Zaida ourselves. We don't have to waste time looking for the headmaster.

"Guys, we have to go tomorrow, right after breakfast," I said, looking up from the picture. "Pismo, can you be ready?"

"Sure," Pismo said. "Let's go find that library."

"And save Professor Zaida," Syke added.

CHAPTER 33

The next morning in the cafeteria, I piled my tray with a huge breakfast and sat with Darthin, Pismo, Frankie, and Syke.

"I was thinking," Darthin said, stating the obvious. He was always thinking. "These are some pretty huge stakes. Professor Zaida's life depends on us getting her the antidote. The safety of all the world's knowledge depends on us making sure Tankotto doesn't find it first."

"What's your point?" Pismo asked.

"I think we should tell Dr. Critchlore," Darthin said. "We're just kids. It's kind of silly to think we can go up against an evil overlord and his army."

"But I promised Professor Zaida I wouldn't tell," I said.

"Everyone here already knows about it. Tankotto knows, his henchman knows," Darthin said. "I think it's safe to say the secret is out."

"What do you guys think?" I asked, looking at Syke, Frankie, and Pismo in turn.

"I think Darthin's right," Syke said. "There's too much at stake."

Frankie nodded.

"As much as I hate to tell grown-ups secret stuff," Pismo said, "you gotta do it here."

"Okay, I'll go see him after morning announcements. The rest of you get ready to go."

The cafeteria grew noisy as kids came to breakfast. Boris and Eloni joined us. It wasn't long before Dr. Critchlore's face filled the screen and everyone quieted down.

"Students! Once again thank you for all your hard work this past week. It was a wonderful success, and I think you all deserve credit for that." He clapped his hands at the camera.

"Right before the show, I went to the Evil Overlord Council to present my case against Dr. Pravus, who was petitioning to take over another minion school. I have video from the council meeting, which I will share now. You may find it interesting."

Dr. Critchlore's face was replaced on the video screen by a shot of the council chamber. The seven Evil Overlord representatives sat in their judges' chairs on the right. On the left were two podiums for the petitioners. Dr. Pravus had no notes; he stood confidently behind his podium. Dr. Critchlore sat in a chair behind his podium, reading a book. It looked like a contest to see who was the least interested in the proceedings. Dr. Pravus spoke first.

"This hearing is just a formality, surely," Dr. Pravus said, smiling his winning smile. "Obviously, the Evil Overlords know that something must be done about the failing school and the lack of quality minions graduating from it. Equally obvious is the fact that the Pravus Academy is up to the task. I see that Dr. Critchlore has come to present his case, which is a surprise, but if you really think he's up to the job, let me take a minute to contrast our different styles."

He cleared his throat and paced in front of the judges.

"Comparing the Pravus Academy to Dr. Critchlore's School for Minions is like comparing a thoroughbred horse to a pony. An old pony, past his prime and perpetually confused. A pony that may have had a few lucky breaks, that manipulated others into believing he was a champion, that people are now seeing as the also-ran that he is."

He looked apologetically at Dr. Critchlore, who turned a page of his book to show he wasn't paying attention. Dr. Pravus sneered and went on. "Critchlore's has been teetering on bankruptcy for a while now. Has Dr. Critchlore lost his touch? How can you lose something you never had?

"Pravus minions are superior in every way. They are stronger, faster, more intelligent, and better trained. Period. That is all that matters. You need look no further than our sports teams. Boulderball, stealthball, Mixed Monster Arts, tackle three-ball. We crush Critchlore's teams in every competition. We play to win; we are trained to win. Who would want to recruit a loser? Who would want a loser training his minions?

"If you allow me my takeover, as you should, I will be able to meet demand for my exceptional minions. EOs won't have to settle for the poor quality that Dr. Critchlore regularly provides."

Dr. Pravus gave Dr. Critchlore one last glare, then sat down at the table behind his podium and began inspecting his fingernails.

"Dr. Critchlore?" the secretary said.

Dr. Critchlore looked up. "My turn? Wonderful." He stood and took his place behind the podium. He looked at each council representative, as if he was memorizing the faces. Then he began.

"Steel sharpens steel," he said. "You don't become stronger without being tested by the strongest opponent. I have to thank Dr. Pravus for providing my minion trainees with the practice that has made them stronger. Dr. Pravus's teams play to win, and for that, I thank him."

He looked over at Dr. Pravus, who was still examining his nails, though with a confused expression now. Clearly, he was listening to Dr. Critchlore.

Dr. Critchlore sighed. "I'm sorry we were unable to return the favor. Not because my minions are less capable, or my coaches poor strategists. My sports teams lose because that's what I instruct them to do."

I looked at Eloni. He shook his head. He didn't remember receiving these "instructions" either.

"You'd think that Dr. Pravus would have noticed this strategy, but as with all strategic thinking, Dr. Pravus is the last to catch on."

He walked out from behind his podium. "Why would I help my business rival train his minions by trying to win? Why would I train his minions for him?

"If my sports teams played to win, then we would be teaching his minions the lessons that come from losing—and those are the most important lessons to learn." He stopped walking and looked at the judges. "I repeat—losing teaches the most important lessons.

"Winning is easy. Everyone is happy and complacent when you win. Winners are overconfident, like Dr. Pravus here, who came to this hearing unprepared. He was so certain he had won before the competition even started. Is that what you want in a minion?

"Losing shows us where our weaknesses lie, where we need to improve. Losing teaches a minion to persevere, to be humble, to take chances, and to work harder. A minion should always strive to improve, and I teach my minions to be relentless learners. Even if you are the best, you can be better. You can work harder.

"My minions have been honed to the strongest, sharpest point because they are losers. They have suffered defeat, learned from it, and come out stronger, better minions. Dr. Pravus's have not. Like he said, his teams win every competition. To this, I say, what a loser you are."

Pravus stood up and shouted, "You aren't buying this insane rationalization, are you?"

"'Insane rationalization'?" Dr. Critchlore said. "Hmm, let's put my theory to the test. Dr. Pravus, your best-trained minions are what? Your dragon militia? Your river trolls?"

"My giant gorillas, you fool."

"Right. You've trained them to win, to destroy, to terrify a populace until they are cowed into submission. Let's take a look, shall we, at the recently conquered town of Rampersly in Delpha. This video was taken yesterday."

Dr. Critchlore pointed to a screen on the wall of the chamber. On it, a video feed showed a giant gorilla helping the townsfolk stack debris into a large pile by the side of a road. I thought I saw

Janet standing by the road, directing the gorilla, but the camera quickly panned away from her.

"Is that a cowed populace? It looks like that man just asked the gorilla to pick up a broken flagpole, and, look, the gorilla is obeying him. Is that part of his special Pravus training?"

The representatives gasped. One pulled out a phone and started pushing buttons.

Pravus leaned forward, his face purpling. "This is some kind of trick."

Dr. Critchlore ignored him. "And now the gorilla is playing with the village children. I wonder what could have defeated this Pravus-trained minion and turned him into such a peace-loving, happy creature? Oh, wait. I don't need to wonder; I know. It was one of my very own minions.

"So, council members, if you want more minions trained in arrogance, who collapse as soon as they start to lose, go with Dr. Pravus. Allow him this takeover and he will flood the employment market with his subpar minions, while mine will enjoy the rich premiums they deserve."

"Ha!" Pravus said. "I will destroy you! My minions will destroy your minions in any battle they engage in."

"And my minions will continue to lose in insignificant sports competitions. They will develop a teachable personality that will have them always striving to do better. We shall see who comes out on top in the end."

The Evil Overlord representatives were all smiles. They loved a good head-to-head competition.

234

The video went out after that, and Dr. Critchlore's face refilled the screen.

"Ha! That was fun. In the end, they ruled in my favor, and here's the funny part—Dr. Pravus wasn't petitioning to take over my school. He was after the Kobold Retraining Center! He thought I was there to bid against him. The council rejected his proposal, and they've allowed me to pursue that school, should I wish. The Kobold Retraining Center!" He shook his head. The screen went out, but we heard him mutter, "What would I do with a bunch of kobolds?"

I could feel the color draining from my face.

"Wait a second—Dr. Pravus wasn't after this school?" Frankie said. "He was after the KRC?"

"The KRC?" Pismo said. "Why? That place is so far away."

"He doesn't want the KRC," I said, as it all clicked into place. "Pravus has been after the Great Library this whole time. 'Knowledge is power,' that's what he said. He trained Tankotto's henchman, who knows where the Great Library is. He bragged to Yipps about it. Pravus must know it's in Mount Izta, but the mountain is huge and he wants to find the entrance. Come on. We have to get there first. You guys pack up. I'm going to tell Dr. Critchlore what's happening."

CHAPTER 34

We retrain kobolds.

—THE KOBOLD RETRAINING CENTER'S RATHER

UNINSPIRED MOTTO

D r. Critchlore looked unnaturally stiff sitting behind his desk.

"Where's Professor Vodum?" I asked, because his desk was not only vacant, but also spotlessly clean. I knew that Vodum hadn't cleaned it, because he's kind of a slob.

"I sent him back to his wife, my cousin, in Yancy," he said. "He was scheming to undermine the school for his own gain."

"What? How?"

"When he heard that Pravus wanted to take over another school, Vodum, like most of us, assumed he was after this school. He then contacted Dr. Pravus, my worst enemy, and offered to help him. He claims that I drove him to take such drastic measures because I refused to give him a job with enough prestige. Ha! Well, Pravus laughed at him and told him that he wasn't after my school.

"But rather than inform me of this, Vodum decided to make it look like Pravus *was* interested in taking over, to trick me into giving him a better job. Vodum staged that visit by the man who wanted to change my hedge maze into a Gauntlet of Pain. He wanted to scare the students and the teachers and ultimately me so that I'd give him anything he wanted in exchange for his support with the family. The fool!"

While he talked, Dr. Critchlore hadn't moved a single muscle, except his mouth.

"Are you okay?" I asked.

"I'm fairly certain Mistress Moira just hexed me," he said. "I can't move, and it's getting worse."

"You can't move?"

"I can talk, apparently," he said. "But I cannot move my head."

"Good," I said. "I need you to listen. I know why Dr. Pravus wanted to take over the Kobold Retraining Center. The Great Library is hidden in the mountains near there, and that's what he's after. And if he gets it, he'll be able to translate *The Top Secret Book of Minions*. He'll be able to create an undefeatable minion."

I told him everything. How Professor Zaida had been poisoned, and how we stole the antidote and got Dr. Frankenhammer to make more. I told him about the old lady in the capital, and Professor Yipps. I told him that the Great Library, THE Great Library, was located in the mountains there, and the entrance was beneath the waterfall. And I told him it would be a catastrophe if Pravus got there first. He didn't interrupt me once; he just sat there staring straight ahead.

"Dr. Critchlore?" I asked. "What do you think?"

"Hooper," he said. "Could you please find Mistress Moira? I would like to speak to her."

He stared at his bookshelf; a line of drool escaped from his mouth and slid down his chin. He didn't seem to notice. "Moira," he said again, and then he closed his eyes.

I ran out of his office, down the hall to the corner of the castle, and to the entrance to the tall tower. I looked up at all those stairs. *Ugh, not again.*

When I got to the top, I saw that Mistress Moira's entry room was filled with packing boxes.

"Mistress Moira!" I shouted. "You're not leaving?"

"Runt, I have had it with that man." She barely looked at me. She just kept packing fabric samples into a box on her coffee table.

"Please, come with me," I said. "He wants to talk to you."

"Of course he does. He's stuck. But as we know, he does everything around here, so I'm sure he'll free himself soon."

"You know he won't."

"I do," she said. "And I don't care. Runt." She looked at me. "I worked day and night on those dresses. Look at my hands." She held out her calloused red hands. "For him to take the credit . . ."

"I know," I said. "But there's a bigger problem now. I have to save Professor Zaida. She's been poisoned, and I need Dr. Critchlore's help. Please talk to him. You can rehex him after he helps me."

She stopped packing and sighed. "Oh, all right," she said. "Maybe I'll think of a better hex."

We started down the stairs.

"Don't you get tired of all these stairs?" I asked.

"No, I find them quite helpful."

"For fitness?"

"Yes, and my mental health too. I don't know if you've noticed, Runt, but I have a bit of a temper."

"Haven't noticed," I lied.

"When I get angry, I go to my quarters. After that long walk up, I find my anger is as exhausted as my body, which lets my rational brain reassert control over my actions. Anger and good decision-making are not compatible, let me tell you. Very rarely am I still angry after climbing. Dr. Critchlore is the only exception to that rule."

We made it back to Dr. Critchlore's office, where he sat, stiff as a dead person, one who hadn't been brought back to life.

"Mistress Moira?" I asked, prompting her to do something.

"Fine," she said. "Klamica Karvolt Fingleton Rip."

Dr. Critchlore turned his head.

"Moira," he said. He looked so sad. "I'm sorry."

"Derek, I told you the last time you took credit for my work that I wouldn't stand for it again—"

"I had to," he said.

"Why?" she asked. "Why take credit for everything? Is your ego so huge that you can't allow anyone else a sliver of recognition?"

"No, of course not," he said, rolling his shoulders as feeling returned to his body. "I don't care what people think of me."

"Then, why?"

"Moira," he said, looking right at her. "I panicked. I knew that if everyone there found out what you can do . . . if people knew how great you are . . . if any EO knew you were even one-twentieth of the woman that you are . . . they'd offer you more than I could ever offer you. If I gave you credit, they'd know. And I'd lose you." His voice cracked and his eyes began to water. "I'd lose you. And that I could not bear."

The silence that filled the room was thick and uncomfortable, like wearing a scratchy wool sweater in the summer.

"Oh, Derek," Mistress Moira said at last. "You great, big fool."

Dr. Critchlore got up slowly, the hex finally wearing itself out. He walked around the desk and took her hands. "Moira," he said. "Beautiful Moira. I won't do it again. Please. You can hex me once a week, to remind me. If that's the price I have to pay to keep you, so be it."

"I will, you know," she said.

He hugged her. There was an awkward moment when they pulled apart, but didn't quite let go, and they just stood there staring into each other's eyes. It almost looked like they were going to kiss, and I tried to back out of the room without being noticed, but they noticed me.

Mistress Moira stepped away from Dr. Critchlore. "I'm a bit of a hypocrite," she said.

Dr. Critchlore cleared his throat. "How so?"

"I got mad at you for taking credit for the dresses, when I did the same thing to Runt."

"What?" I asked.

"Runt, when you asked me for a crush-proof jacket, that gave me the idea to enhance the girls' dresses. I knew I couldn't create dresses that would be considered high fashion. I'm just an amateur seamstress. Did I think I could compete with professional designers who've had years of training at design schools, who've worked in the field for decades? Of course not. I'm not that egotistical. Instead, I decided to create a new category—defensive fashion. Thanks to you, Runt."

"Really?" I said. "Does that mean you're gonna make me a crush-proof jacket?"

She laughed. "I'll try. Well, I'll leave you two to save my friend Professor Zaida. Do *not* disappoint me." At the door she turned and looked at Dr. Critchlore. "I also wouldn't be disappointed with an elevator of my own, for when I'm feeling fatigued and not angry."

"Consider it done," Dr. Critchlore said with a nod.

I looked to the sky and mouthed, *Thank you*, relieved that I wouldn't have to walk up all those stairs to visit her. I didn't need the exercise, and I was hardly ever angry.

I took a deep breath, expecting to have to tell my story all over again, because I didn't think Dr. Critchlore had listened the first time. But before I could start, he put a hand on my shoulder.

"I'll have Professor Murphy take the antidote to the old woman in the capital. We'll send some to that Yipps fellow, in case he has other colleagues who have been poisoned. I'll try to contact the headmaster at the Kobold Retraining Center and warn him of Dr. Pravus's intentions. I'll tell him we're on our way with help, and to find Professor Zaida and tell her to sit tight.

"I'll take the antidote by air, either by dragon or maybe Master Ping can persuade the harpies to carry me in a flying coach. I really hate flying coach, but what can you do? Coach Foley will take some of the antidote by road until he hits a roadblock, then he can continue on one of our new unicorn stallions. I need one more backup plan, though. I hate to do anything without at least two backup plans."

I told him about Pismo's offer to take someone upriver.

"Yes, but who wants to swim in the frigid waters of the Wallippi River?"

"I'll do it," I said. "Please, Dr. Critchlore. My future depends on finding the Great Library."

"No. It's too dangerous for someone of your age and experience deficiencies."

"You just sent Janet to go up against a giant gorilla! Besides, you need someone small. Pismo can't carry an adult."

He frowned at me.

"I can do this," I said. "And even if I can't, you have two other plans. Land and river and air. One of us will get through."

He shook his head. "I admire your loyalty to your teacher, but you must trust us here. I will go by air, Coach Foley by road, and Professor Twilk can finally put his off-road vehicles to a practical test."

I could tell he wasn't going to change his mind. I wasn't going to change mine either. I was going up the river, whether I had permission or not.

Whoa. What did I just think? Pismo's turned me into a rule-breaking, confrontational delinquent.

We left his office.

"You like Mistress Moira, don't you?" I said as we walked through the secretary's office. "That wasn't just an act to get her to stay."

"Of course I like her," he said. "The scary thing is, she reminds me of my mother—beautiful, powerful, and vengeful. But if you breathe a word of that to anybody, I'll bring Professor Vodum back to be your personal tutor."

"Breathe a word about what?" I asked.

"Good lad."

CHAPTER 35

If it's flying, it's spying. Shoot it down.
—POPULAR QUOTE. ALSO WHY NOBODY TRAVELS BY AIR
ON THE PORVIAN CONTINENT.

I met the guys at the lake—Pismo had two mermaid friends, so we decided that Syke, Frankie, and I would go upstream while Darthin, Eloni, and Boris stayed behind.

Eloni and Boris had gathered supplies—wet suits, watertight backpacks, and food. Darthin handed us each a vial of the antidote, Dr. Critchlore's advice about having two backups still fresh in my mind.

The mermaids donned their battle slings, which we could wedge ourselves into to ride on their backs. The battle slings were long and stiff, and holding on was still hard work for us, but we glided upstream, fighting the current. I could feel Pismo get into a rhythm. Once away from school, the river ran wide and deep, the current just a whisper.

After an hour, we stopped to rest on a grassy bank surrounded by forest. The mermaids stayed in the water while Syke, Frankie, and I dried off in the sun.

"I'm exhausted," I said. "And I'm not even swimming." I rubbed my shoulders.

"Me too," Syke said. She leaned back, looking at the trees. "You know, this is what I want our new forest to look like. Dense, but not too dense, with mossy trunks and colorful leaves in the fall. A grassy meadow here and there."

"It'll be beautiful," I said.

"I still can't believe Dr. Critchlore agreed to the forest restoration project. He's always talking about how he wants to expand the facilities for the minions of impressive size. Give them more training space and stuff."

I shrugged. We lay in the grass, staring at the sky. I wanted to change the subject before she started wondering again why the hamadryads hated Dr. Critchlore.

"You know what?" I said. "I'm pretty sure Janet is a spy."

"Really?" Syke sat up, excited by this juicy bit of gossip. "Why?"

"Well, I don't think she's a siren. You once told me she can't sing. She didn't want to do the fashion show, and I think the reason is that she knew the siren mothers would ask who she was, and her cover would be blown. Plus I saw her talking to some shifty-looking guy in the capital."

"If that's true, I hate her even more," Syke said. "I mean, it was bad enough thinking she was a snobby, useless siren, but if she's a spy? That's so cool. I'd love to be a spy. How dare she be cooler than me? I. Hate. Her."

Frankie laughed. "I've gotta pee," he said, heading for the forest. Once he disappeared, I turned to Syke.

"Why do you like him?" I asked. Frankie was the best, but no other girls paid any attention to him. It made me curious.

"Because he's awesome and he doesn't act like he knows it.

One-on-one, Frankie could take anyone at school. Anyone. You see most of those guys—the ogre-men, the werewolves, the giants—they swagger around acting like they're the best at everything. They pick on guys who are weaker, just to show off how strong they are. They don't realize how insecure that makes them look. How mean and ridiculous. A strong man doesn't hold others down; he lifts them up. That's Frankie."

"Yeah, but those eyebrows," I said, and we laughed.

"I know, and he can be kind of dense," Syke added. "Hey, you know that new guy, Meztli? He's really cute."

"He's in my junior henchman class."

She grabbed my arm. "Introduce me to him when we get back, okay?"

We continued on our journey, taking breaks every hour or so. The mermaids were nearly spent, and Syke and I could barely hang on a moment longer. Frankie looked fine, of course.

"I had no idea I was so out of shape," Boynton said during another stop. "How much farther, Delray?"

"By my senses," he said, "we're about three-quarters of the way there. We're slowing, but we should get there before sundown."

We rounded a bend in the river and Pismo abruptly veered to his left and turned around. He surfaced near the riverbank, where some trees provided cover.

"Did you see that?" he asked. Delray and Boynton surfaced, and we all looked upstream. Standing on a bridge, looking down into the water, was a giant gorilla.

"We're too late," Frankie said. "Pravus is here, and he's set up defenses. He didn't win the bid to take over the school. How can he get away with that?"

"Who knows? Let's get out of here and check the map," I said. "We might be close."

"We won't get past that bridge without being seen," Pismo said. "The water's not deep enough."

We snuck out of the river and hid in the nearby trees. Pismo, Delray, and Boynton took off their battle slings and lay down. They were snoring in seconds, completely exhausted.

I pulled out the map. "That must be the Leshy Bridge," I said. "So we're practically at the Kobold Retraining Center. If we'd stayed in the water, we would have gotten out just a few hundred meters farther up, at the Leshy Pier."

We changed out of our wet suits and into T-shirts and cargo pants. After a quick snack, we climbed a tree to get a better look at the terrain.

Syke had no problem scaling the trunk of the tallest redwood. I couldn't reach the lowest branch, so Frankie tossed me up and then jumped up next to me.

As Frankie and I climbed, Syke visited other trees in the neighborhood. The sun was low on the horizon, lighting up the mountain so that the waterfall sparkled. *Could that be it?* Could the entrance to the most secret place in the world be within my sight?

Syke returned, sitting on the branch next to me. "This is a hamadryad forest," she said, smiling. "Some of these trees knew my mother. Isn't that crazy?"

I didn't have time to ask how that worked and get a lecture about how humans are so ignorant of the workings of the natural world that they live in, so I tried to steer Syke back to the task at hand. "Can we get to the school from here?"

"Yes, but they tell me that the forest is filled with giant gorillas and other things, worse things. The gorillas have uprooted a bunch of trees to make a base of operations, over there." She pointed in the distance, where a clearing opened up in the trees.

"We need to get to the waterfall," I said, pointing to the mountain. "The entrance to the Great Library is there."

"What about the school?" Frankie said. "Should we try to find the headmaster?"

"Critchlore is heading there," I said. "But Professor Zaida went to the library. We don't have time to waste. We have to get the antidote to her."

"Look." Syke pointed to a clump of buildings near the river. "See the trees waving? I sent a message through these redwoods. They're telling us to stay away from the school. Pravus must have defenses there."

"Pravus's base is pretty far to the left of the waterfall," I said. "It's possible he hasn't found the entrance yet. Maybe we can beat him to it. We just have to get through this forest."

A thunderous BOOM tore through the air, and the ground shook so violently that I was knocked off my perch. Fortunately, Frankie grabbed me as I fell past him and pulled me up to his branch, which I clung to with both my arms and legs.

"What was that?" I asked.

Syke climbed higher, and when she came back, she said, "Pravus is trying to blast his way inside the mountain, just past the clearing. I can see smoke."

"Oh no," I said. "He's desperate. He probably knows that Critchlore is coming, and he wants to get to the library first. He's not waiting for a CLOUD to break and tell him where the entrance is."

The ground shook again, a long, rumbling shake that felt more like an earthquake than an explosion. "Look," I said, pointing to the volcano, which was now billowing smoke and ash.

"Can an explosion trigger a volcanic eruption?" Frankie asked.

"I have no idea."

Roaring red fire blasted up out of the mountain. Another BOOM shook the tree.

"We have to get moving," I said. "If we can make it to the waterfall and find the eternal flame in the water, we can find the entrance. Let's go." I started down the tree. Frankie swooshed by, jumping from three stories above the ground. Syke also beat me to the forest floor.

"I can take Runt on my back," Frankie said. "Syke, you move faster through the trees than on land. Go ahead. I'll stay with you."

"Think you can keep up?" she said.

"I could keep up carrying five Runts and a Frieda."

"We'll see," she said, and climbed back up. As she reached the branches, she was propelled forward to the next tree, which caught her and threw her onward. Frankie turned his backpack around to his front so I could jump on his back. He made his own way through the forest floor. I bounced along, clinging for my life as he bounded over fallen trees and boulders, zigzagging around tree trunks.

We raced toward the mountain. Twice Frankie stumbled when the earth shook suddenly. We could feel the air getting hotter and smokier as the mountain rumbled and the sky filled with falling debris.

We were getting closer. I kept my eye on Syke, so I could tell Frankie if he veered off course. She reached for a giant sequoia tree, but it slapped her away. Syke screamed as she fell toward the ground. Frankie caught her before she hit.

"What happened?" I asked as Frankie placed her upright.

"That sequoia is the sentinel," she said. "It won't let me go any closer. She says the volcano is going to erupt."

"Can you go on foot?" I asked.

"Let's try," she said.

We edged around the sentinel tree, thankful that its branches were too high to swoop down and reach us. Once past, we ran on until a loud roar split the air, sending us ducking for cover behind a pine tree.

I hoped whatever made that noise wouldn't see us. Syke pulled something out of her backpack as the thumps and huffs drew closer. The trees seemed to tremble with each thump.

A giant hairy arm swung across the three pine trees in front of us, toppling each one and exposing us. We looked up into the enraged face of a giant gorilla.

CHAPTER 36

It's usually best to run away *from an erupting volcano.*

—GOOD ADVICE

Two regular-sized gorillas followed the enormous silverback. Regular-sized gorillas are big and scary too, with forearms larger than my torso and giant teeth and angry faces. The silverback pounded his chest and roared at us. His mouth was big enough to swallow us whole.

Just as he began his charge, a blinding light flashed in his face. He covered his eyes and roared again, louder this time. Syke grabbed me and Frankie, and we ran for a new hiding place. We jumped over a boulder and looked back at our attackers.

Syke had thrown Meika's cape, the one we'd nicknamed the Flash Cape, at the gorilla. The bright flash was meant to foil aggressive photographers by overexposing their pictures with light, but the cape also had a cool attack feature: When thrown, it flew like a flying disk and wrapped itself around its victim.

The cape now clung to the giant gorilla's face like flypaper. Trees were toppled, the smaller gorillas scrambled to safety, and the big one roared. With all that noise, we dashed toward a thicker part of the forest and safety.

"You stole Meika's dress?" I said once we were well enough away.

"It's not her dress. It's Mistress Moira's," Syke said. She pulled out Verduccia's green knife-sleeved dress and put it on for better camouflage. "And I think she'd want us to have it, don't you?"

We took off, sprinting through the trees. Frankie led, followed by Syke, and then me. Frankie jumped over a fallen tree trunk, but when Syke followed, a branch swooshed down and wrapped around her middle, lifting her into the air.

"Let me down!" she yelled.

"Syke! What's happening?"

"They're trying to protect me by not letting me go farther." She pulled at the branch. Frankie reached for her, but the branch lifted her higher. "Hang on," she said. "Let me talk to them."

She disappeared into the canopy of branches above us. I looked at Frankie, wondering what we should do. His shrug told me that he didn't know either. We listened for the gorillas, but the thumps seemed to be traveling away from us.

Frankie and I crouched near a clump of pines, watching the sky as it rained ash and rocks and fire. A flaming log rolled by us, crashing into a dead tree and setting it ablaze. The heat was suffocating, and I felt panic rise inside me. What if we got trapped in this forest fire?

And where was Syke? Just as I was about to tell Frankie to climb up and investigate, Syke jumped down from the tree and landed next to me. She looked back up at the trees. Then she shook her head.

"What is it?"

"There are hamadryads in those pines," she said. "One of them said that this was the last straw, and that if Dr. Critchlore was going to risk my life like this . . . they want me to leave the school . . . I said no way . . . and then she told me about my mother."

The air was getting smokier, and I lifted my shirt to cover my mouth. A giant boom shook the air, sending us to the ground. It sounded more like an explosion than an eruption. We had to move.

"That's great, Syke, and I'm sure you guys will have time to catch up later, but we have to go save Professor Zaida."

"I know."

I jumped on Frankie's back, and we turned toward the mountain. I didn't hear Syke follow.

"Syke, come on," I said. "Jump on my back."

"It's just . . . she said I shouldn't have stayed at Dr. Critchlore's," she said.

"Really? Why?"

Syke looked confused, sad. "He killed my mother."

Oh no. No, no, no, no, no.

"He's always said that he saved me from a forest fire. But Silveria, the queen of this forest, just told me that he burned the forest down on purpose. Dr. Critchlore killed my mother's tree."

"That doesn't sound like him," I said.

"Are you kidding? Of course it does. He does whatever he wants, and he doesn't care who he hurts."

"Maybe he didn't know your mom was in the tree? Let's go."

She scowled at me. I looked away because I couldn't meet her gaze. She was so angry.

"Oh my goddess, Runt." She grabbed my arm, and Frankie dropped me to the ground. "Did you know?"

"What?"

"You knew, didn't you? You knew he killed my mother, and you didn't tell me."

A huge boulder rumbled down the mountainside, crunching trees in its path. We really had to get moving, but Syke was firmly planted, waiting for answers.

"Syke, I . . . It's like you not telling me I'm not a werewolf. I didn't want to hurt you."

She held up a hand to stop me, shaking her head. "Don't even go there. Me not telling you that you're not a werewolf is not the same as you allowing me to live with my mother's murderer! How can you even think that?"

"Syke, I only just found out. I didn't know how to tell you."

"Let's stop the lying right now," she said. "You've never been anything but Dr. Critchlore's obedient puppy dog. Should I just call you Pizza from now on?"

"Syke. I'm sorry. I know this is . . . a shock . . . and you're hurt . . . but Professor Zaida is probably dying right now. We have to save her, and then we can talk about this."

She shook her head, as if to clear it. "You're right. We have to save Professor Zaida. But I'm not going to forget this, Runt. When we get back—"

She didn't finish. A tree branch bent down and lifted her up and away. "Hey! I told you I'm fine! You don't need to protect me!" The tree lifted her higher.

"Syke!" I screamed. "Frankie, we have to get her down!"

"No!" Syke yelled. "Don't waste time! Go!" With a heave, she threw her backpack at us. "You'll need it more than—"

And she was gone.

"Syke!" I yelled as she disappeared into the trees.

I looked at Frankie.

"You knew?" he said.

"I only just found out. I didn't know what to do."

Thumping giant gorilla steps shook the ground, heading our way. Frankie picked up Syke's backpack and handed it to me, and I jumped onto his back. He ran so fast I thought I was going to throw up from all the jarring changes of direction and stops and starts. Twice I was hit by flaming pebbles that burned holes in my shirt as fire rained from the volcano.

The forest thinned out and I noticed black shapes in the smoky air above us. They swooped between the trees silently. For a second, I thought it might be Syke, but there were three of them. They were big and dark, and they were following us. Frankie sped through the trees almost as fast as my heart was racing. I was terrified. Who knew what other horrific monsters Pravus had stationed around here?

We had to make it to the waterfall. I knew we were getting close because I could hear the sound of rushing water ahead. We broke through the trees and faced a giant pool at the base of the cascade. Frankie screeched to a halt, and I jumped off his back. He didn't seem winded at all, but I was wheezing and unsteady on my feet.

The waterfall was not a straight drop of water, but more like a river on a tilt, the water sliding over a rocky path down the mountain. The pool was wide and calm, edged by boulders and shrubs and pine trees. A gravel path wound around the pool to the base of the waterfall.

I patted Frankie on the back. "Great job," I said. "We made it. Now we just have to find that flame under the waterfall." But as we started off on the path, three winged creatures, each as big as a full-grown man, dropped down in front of us, leering with menace.

CHAPTER 37

Sometimes you need to shake things up.

—DR. CRITCHLORE'S EARTHQUAKE IN A CAN™ PRODUCT MOTTO

They spread out, blocking the trail. Though they were big, they looked like teenagers, and they stared at us with the sneering gaze of a bully who'd just come across an unprotected underclassman.

"Those are ahools," Frankie said.

"Shh, Frankie," I whispered. "Don't be rude."

"Remember Rimbo? He graduated two years ago? He was an ahool. Looked like a giant bat. Got detention all the time for raiding Tootles's fruit orchard."

"Oh yeah," I said, remembering. Rimbo was kind of creepy. Like these guys, he had a stubby nose; huge, pointy ears; and big fangs. His wings were so large he had trouble navigating the hallways, and he was always angry. These guys looked angry too.

"That's a Pravus crest on their chest armor," I added.

I reached into Syke's backpack, hoping to find the perfect dress for this occasion. I pulled one on over my head as Frankie held the bats off by swinging a very large stick.

One of the beasts swooped right at Frankie, which was a mistake, because Frankie has crazy-fast reflexes. He easily dodged the attack, swung around to grab the flying man-bat by the legs, and flung him into the water, hard. The ahool sank down, only to come up with his wings smacking at the water uselessly.

"It looks like he can't swim," Frankie said to the others. "Better help him." The other two backed up a step.

I clapped my hands, hoping that some sort of defense would pop out of my dress, but all that happened was a blast of perfume filled the air. It smelled fruity, which just incited the bats more. I'd turned myself into a delicious-smelling snack.

"I would have gone with the Jetpack dress for this situation," Frankie said. "Maybe accessorized with some of Frieda's rings."

I yanked the dress over my head and threw it at the ahools, who swarmed over to it, drool leaking from their mouths. I reached in for another dress.

"I'll keep them off you," Frankie said. "Go up that trail and find the flame."

"Okay." I stuffed the dresses into my pack and took off. I kept checking behind me, the hairs on my neck prickling. One of the ahools tried to fly over Frankie to get me, but he underestimated Frankie's jumping ability by a lot. Who wouldn't? Frankie looked like a kid who'd get winded tying his shoes. But he sprang into the air like a flea and knocked the ahool into the water, where it joined its struggling partner. Their wings were just too big and unwieldy in the water. Frankie turned to the third, now hiding behind a tree.

I was on my own. No Frankie. No Syke. No Critchlore and no Coach Foley. Just me and a clock ticking down on Professor Zaida's life.

I hurried up the hill. My hand felt for the little vial of antidote in my pocket. I had to reach her in time. I had to.

The path disappeared into the rocks that lined the waterfall. I didn't see a flame anywhere, so I kept climbing. The rocks were slippery and steep. I stopped every few steps to scan the wide waterfall for any sign of a flame. But how could a flame keep burning under a waterfall? The more I thought about it, the more ridiculous it seemed. I kept climbing, my legs complaining with every step. The sun had also abandoned me, slipping away like a coward. Now the mountain face was draped in smoky darkness.

The ground kept shaking, and the sound of explosions reverberated around me. I heard a crackling sound that made me think of fire. Smoke rose off to the left, joining the ash that already filled the sky. Soon, there'd be fire everywhere, and my task would become impossible.

I reached a wall of sheer granite too high to climb. I pulled Trinka's dress out of my pack and flung the polka-dot disks at the wall, where they made a line of little stairs I could climb with my toes.

I pulled myself over the ridge and scanned the next section of the falls. There, a dark, curving space stretched beneath a flat granite ledge. Water rushed over the ledge in separate streams, joining up in a little pool before continuing downhill.

I stepped over wet rocks until I was parallel with that ledge. I crouched down, looking into the darkness beneath, but I didn't see anything. Carefully, I stepped closer to the middle of the falls, jumping over one of the streams until I was right in front of the cave, one hand balancing on the wet rock. I reached deep into my backpack and pulled out a pair of Pismo's gloves. The finger lights lit up the dark, empty space.

The little cave was only a meter high. I ducked down and snuck inside, hoping to see the sign, but I found myself in a cave with no flame.

This isn't it.

But it did smell bad, like rotten eggs. I pulled out my Dr. Critchlore's PocketTool™ and unfolded some attachments until I found the right one: not the screwdriver, or the tweezers, or the tooth floss, but the mini-flamethrower. It was only good for one short blast, so I aimed it at the back of the cave and gave it a shot. The cave filled with light for a moment and I had to shield my eyes. When I opened them, a small flame was burning on the floor of the cave.

Someone had put it out, and I had just relit it.

Zaida? Or Dr. Pravus?

I crawled forward. The cave was small and wet, and continued into the mountain. I was able to hunch through, bending low, and the gloves lit up the space around me. The walls were close; I could touch both sides as I made my way down the gently sloping tunnel.

The space widened, and soon I was walking upright. I flashed my fingers forward and saw a T-junction ahead, so I raced for it. My narrow tunnel came to a dead end at a much bigger tunnel road, big enough to drive a car down, and it was dark in both directions.

Which way? I tried to picture the mountain outside. If the waterfall was the Great Lady's head, her body stretched to the right, so I went that way. I didn't hear any sounds except my own panicked breathing.

The tunnel curved, and I felt like I was running farther into the mountain. It wasn't long before I reached another dead end. I faced a huge blast door that had to be a foot thick, and it was opened at a slight angle, letting the light from inside escape.

I slowly peeked in. Opening up before me was a room so massive it made me think the entire mountain had been hollowed out.

I tiptoed inside, awed by the enormous space in front of me. I forgot my panic as I realized I was standing in the Great Library. I was standing in history. In forbidden history. I was standing in the most important and secret place in the world, and it was spectacular.

I stood in a central walkway of a room that was longer than the boulderball field at school. The arched ceiling was seven stories above me, painted to look like the night sky. Thousands of stars seemed to glow like photophores up there, providing enough light for me to see the shine on the floor, and the spines of the books. Each story held row after row of stacks stretching into the darkness at the sides, and they were all filled with books.

The weight of the room—of all that knowledge—was over-whelming. I felt so small, so insignificant. I could live a thousand lives and not learn everything that was contained in that room. Pravus had said that wisdom is knowing what you don't know. He was wrong. I was staring at a mountain of books, an ocean of things I would never know, and I didn't feel wise. I felt like I'd never be more than a ripple in that ocean. We had learned so much in our time on this planet that I could never comprehend it all.

Maybe that was how it was supposed to be. Maybe we were supposed to feel humble. No matter how much any single person knows, it's nothing but a snowflake in an avalanche of knowledge.

I tiptoed over to the nearest column on my right. It was marked

with a code for whatever books were held on its shelves, but I didn't understand it. It was something library-ish, I'm sure. *GPC 1500–1502*. Across the aisle, the stacks were marked with *Fiction OIR Repulgio–Rexultor*.

I could find out about the Oti here. I could find out where I was from. But that didn't matter now; I had to find Professor Zaida. I walked forward, staying near the stacks so I could duck into an aisle if I saw Pravus or one of his henchmen. Thumps still echoed from outside, but this long room was quiet.

After walking for a few miles (not really, but it was a long way), I approached a place where a wider aisle crossed the room. The right side was dark, but weak light seeped into the hallway from the left. I ducked behind the nearest bookshelf and peeked through. A long table stretched down the middle of the wide aisle, and on one of these tables was the source of the light: a desk lamp.

And standing beside the table was Dr. Pravus.

CHAPTER 38

Gulp.

—THAT IS ALL.

I was alone in a room with Dr. Pravus, again. If a giant were squeezing me in his fist while a dragon got ready to blast me with fire, I would not have felt more terrified than I did looking at that man. It was a fear so paralyzing, so crushing, that I wanted to curl into a ball and close my eyes and pray for the world to end before he discovered I was there.

But I didn't. I peeked through the books, getting as low as I could, and spied on him. His attention was completely focused on a book that lay open on the table. It was a book I'd seen before, locked up in Dr. Critchlore's office. *The Top Secret Book of Minions.* Or it was an exact copy.

I crouched down, wondering what to do. I had to find Professor Zaida. I had to get that book. And I had to make sure Pravus didn't see me. I was mostly focused on that last one.

I peeked through again, slowly. So slowly. I assumed that Dr. Pravus had a keen sense of movement, like most predators. He examined the book with a gleam of victory, reverently turning pages, his smile widening as he discovered the secrets inside.

Footsteps approached from the far end of the library. I stayed hidden, listening to the uneven steps, coupled with the sound of a struggle. Two people turned down the hallway in front of me, and I caught a glimpse of them—a man and a girl with shimmering hair. Oh no.

"Look what I found sneaking in your new entrance," the man said. It was the chameleon, I was sure of it, and he held Syke roughly by the arm. "Seemed to pop out of the trees like magic and dropped in right behind our guards."

"Who is she?"

"She won't say," the chameleon said.

Syke was wearing Verduccia's green knife-sleeved dress. I rummaged in the backpack, looking for something, anything. But none of the dresses seemed like they'd be helpful here: not the Jetpack, or the Slip-n-Slide, or the Side Puncher. I needed something to incapacitate two villains while I saved Syke, and I had nothing.

"Tie her to the banister," Pravus said. "You remember the plan?"

Please say no, please say no. I need to know the plan.

"Yes."

"Then take this book and go."

Go where? To do what? What's the plan? C'mon, guys, now's a good time for a chat!

"I remember you now," Pravus said to Syke. "You're from Critchlore's. You play tackle three-ball, and you're quite good. How many more Critchlore minions are here?"

"Thirty-seven," Syke said. "We're on a field trip. Dr. Critchlore is here too. He'll probably be wondering why you've attacked another minion school. That's against the Directives. You'll be banished to Skelterdam if you don't get out of here now."

Dr. Pravus laughed. "Critchlore is trapped in a field on the far side of the river. We saw his dragon go down, thanks to the defensive measures of the librarians. Your PE teacher won't be here either; my giant gorillas intercepted him, and the man with the off-road vehicle too. That leaves just the two of us."

He put on some gloves, watching Syke intently. I edged down my row, to be closer to them. Syke was out of my line of sight, but Pravus stood tall and threatening.

"Perhaps I can squeeze some truth out of you." He reached down and Syke screamed. Pravus struggled to hold a thrashing Syke, but his face showed nothing but amusement. "Now tell me . . . how did Dr. Critchlore find out about the library? How did he know to stop my takeover? TELL ME!"

"I don't know." Syke's voice sounded raspy and weak.

"Pity."

Looking at his face, I felt it again—that hand on my throat. I felt the horror that he would squeeze the life out of me without a care. And now he was doing that to Syke.

"Leave her alone," I said. All of a sudden, I found myself pushing books off the shelf in front of me and crawling through. I don't remember telling my body to do that.

Pravus turned, releasing his grip. When he did, Syke screamed "Runt, run!"

The full power and evil of Pravus's attention was on me, and I wanted to run. I shook with how badly I wanted to run. Every nerve ending in my body screamed at me to obey her. But I couldn't leave Syke sitting on the floor, her hands bound to the banister next to the staircase.

"Another child," Pravus said. He laughed as he approached me. "I was expecting Dr. Critchlore to send some of his more . . . adequate employees."

"Where's Professor Zaida?" I asked.

"The dwarf? Dead, probably," he said. He lunged toward me, just as he had in Dr. Critchlore's office, but I was ready for the move, and I rolled under the table, popping up on the other side.

"Runt, listen to me," Syke said. "I heard screams coming from a room at the end of the hall. Run!"

Pravus had never taken his eyes off me. "Ah, yes," he said. "I remember you as well. That's what you do, isn't it? Run. Like a coward. Don't listen to your friend. I will go much easier on you if you don't run. If you do . . . it will be unpleasant."

My heart pounded so hard I thought I was going to throw up. Pravus pulled out a slim metal tube and blew on one end. A faint, high-pitched whistle came out of it.

"You have a few seconds," he said. "One of you will tell me how Dr. Critchlore found out about the library. The other will experience pain and terror so magnificent I will almost feel sorry for you."

I pulled out my medallion and looked at Syke. She was trying to tell me something. She nodded at her hands and made a silent coughing face. She wanted me to make some noise.

Pravus had backtracked around the end of the table and was approaching me again. I reached behind me and knocked a row of books to the floor, trying to stop his advance. I backed up and threw more books in his path. I kept throwing books, and he calmly stepped over them.

"I'll tell you," I said, my hands up in surrender. The truth was, Dr. Critchlore didn't find out about the library, and it had been his dumb luck that he blocked Pravus's takeover, but I didn't want Pravus to know that. I thought about Uncle Ludwig, and how he asked questions and then answered them himself, just to prove how smart he was, so I decided to see if that would work here.

"I'll tell you," I repeated. "But I'm surprised you don't know. Dr. Critchlore always tells us how clever you are."

He scowled and then closed a fist in anger. "It was my henchman Waverley," he said, nodding. I felt my eyes widen, shocked that my tactic had worked. "Of course," he said, taking my reaction as confirmation of his guess. "Waverley was careless, which is why I staged that little scene at the Evil Overlord Council. People knew he was talking to me. I had to make it look like he was only loyal to Tankotto. But Critchlore figured it out, didn't he?"

Probably not.

"Thank you for the information. Your cowardice has saved your life. The girl will not be so fortunate."

"What girl?" I asked.

Pravus turned around and saw only severed ropes next to the railing. As soon as his attention was off me, I turned and ran . . .

. . . right into a wall of Girl Explorers.

"You'll pay for this," Pravus said. "The girl too. You have a few seconds before my minions rip the skin off your body and reduce you to bones."

I laughed. I don't know why—maybe I was hysterical with fear. It wasn't the reaction Pravus had been expecting. He bristled at my laugh. Clearly he was used to intimidating people.

"Go ahead. Keep laughing," he said. He pulled a blue handkerchief out of his pocket and draped it over the desk lamp. I knew what he was doing. The blue light would cut through the beasts' glamours and reveal their true selves. He wanted me to see their monster forms. He wanted to see me in complete terror. What he didn't know was that I could already see through them, just by touching my medallion.

"You told me that knowledge is power," I said. "But that wisdom is knowing what you don't know."

He walked toward me, eyes blazing with hatred.

I stood my ground. "I think you don't know something really important here." I wasn't going to back down now. It felt good, not backing away. Stupid good. Or maybe just stupid.

"Good-bye, you insignificant nothing. I will leave here listening to your screams echoing in this magnificent library, which now belongs to me."

He smirked as he pointed behind me, expecting me to melt into a quivering, terror-filled lump. I was surrounded by the whole frightening pack of them, with their strange, hairy bodies; powerful hind legs; and long arms dragging to the ground. Claws and teeth that looked sharper than any knife I'd ever seen. Even their horns were sharpened to a point.

"Not so smug now, are you?"

CHAPTER 39

Speak Troll in ten easy lessons!

—ESSENTIAL TROLL SEMINAR, TAUGHT BY FRAGLICK GRROKEE

I'd made sure to pick out Sara from the pack before their glamours were deactivated by Pravus's blue light. I might not have Frankie's photographic memory, but I would never forget her face from when she pinned me, or sat in that dungeon cell, or skinned the flesh from that fish with her teeth.

"Hi, Sara," I said, looking right at her. "I've come to free you."

The circle surrounding me got closer and closer, until the snouts were practically touching my legs. I tried to stand bravely as they sniffed at me, but my heart was pounding so fast that I was sure I was shaking.

"Fameely," I said, raising my medallion.

They backed away.

"Attack!" Pravus screamed. "Eat him!"

"No," I said. I stepped toward Pravus. "They won't hurt me." I turned to the beasts. "Grab Pravus."

The beasts lunged for Pravus, except for one who stayed by my side. "Thank you, Sara."

"Thank you, little one," she said. "For finding us."

Pravus's mouth hung open in shock at the monsters surrounding him. But he quickly recovered and yelled, "What are you doing? *I* am your master. You are bound to me by the spell. *I* defeated the last of your family!"

"Not the last," Sara said.

He looked at her, at me, his eyes squinting with fury. "Who *are* you?"

"I wish I knew," I muttered. I turned to Sara. "I have to find Professor Zaida."

"The small one ees in the office down the hall, with the other preesoners. I take you." She motioned for me to get on her back, so I did, grabbing onto her shoulders.

"Keep him there," I told the others.

Pravus was purple with rage. "I don't know who you are or how you turned my minions, but you have just sealed your doom. I will kill you myself, and your friend too."

I felt something more than fear when I looked at him. I felt anger. How could he be so arrogant? It triggered something inside me. I didn't want him to think he'd scared me. I didn't want him to think he could threaten Syke and me, and I'd just curl into a ball and take it, even if that was what I felt like doing.

I jumped off Sara's back and looked at him. "With one word from me, these beasts will strip you to your bones," I said. "It's . . . unpleasant, as you said. I think instead of threatening me, you should be begging for your life."

The beasts closed around him, their jaws snapping with antici-

pation. They really wanted to eat him. Pravus could feel it too, and his anger faded a little. His expression now looked a little fearful.

"I'm waiting," I said.

I could practically see his inner struggle as fear and pride battled for control. Pride seemed to be winning. He did not want to plead for his life.

"Are you guys hungry?" I asked the monsters. In answer, one bit Pravus in the leg.

"No!" Pravus screamed. "Please! Please don't kill me!"

"Keep him here, but don't eat him," I said. I jumped on Sara's back with one last look at Pravus. He looked like he was plotting my murder in his head, and making it as painful as possible.

Sara took me to a pair of double doors at the end of the long central hallway, and we entered a large room dominated by a long table, like a conference room. Around it sat a dozen worried grown-ups and one troll. The troll made a move toward me with his giant fist clenched, but Sara stepped in front of me and growled, and the troll backed away.

"It's okay. She's not going to harm any of you," I said. "Where's Professor Zaida?"

"*Blaggify wecknerk booooofree,*" the troll snarled at Sara. "*BOOOFREE!*"

The nervous people looked to the floor, and I ducked down and saw her. Next to the far wall, Professor Zaida's head lay unmoving in Syke's lap, an empty vile of antidote on the floor next to them. As I watched, Professor Zaida's eyelids fluttered and then opened. I crawled under the table to join them on the other side.

"Syke? Runt? How did you find us?" Professor Zaida asked.

"Um, long story," I said. "But you're all safe." I pointed to Sara. "They're with me now."

Professor Zaida gasped.

"It's okay," I said. "She won't hurt you. She saved me from Pravus."

"Pravus!" she said. "Where is he? He can't get away."

"The Girl Explorers are watching him," I said.

Professor Zaida wiggled her fingers. I watched her as she felt the antidote work through her body. She closed her eyes and breathed in deeply.

A dark-skinned woman in a gray suit helped Professor Zaida sit up. She knelt down so their heads were together.

"Do you trust them?" she asked Professor Zaida.

"Yes, look at his medallion," Professor Zaida said, reaching for my chest. "And like he said, the vaskor obey him."

"And the boy will obey you?" she asked.

"Yes," she said.

"Very well. We need to deal with the intruders first. Asim, you know what to do," she said to a short, bearded man. "Take this vaskor with you, to control the rest."

"My friend Frankie is near the waterfall, holding off a bunch of ahools," I said. "I was hoping Sara would go help him."

"I weel help your friend," Sara said. "The rest of us weel help your new friends here. We know they are friends of the fameely. We always knew, but the code binds us. The spell ees powerful."

"Thank you," the lady in charge said. "Go now, and keep Pravus from leaving. We need to continue what we were doing before the intruders arrived. The entrance must be closed and all signs to it obliterated. We will use the emergency exit that leads to the other side of the mountain. We must see how far the breach of information has reached." She handed out assignments to the people in the room. The troll stayed behind, not taking his eyes off this important lady.

"Valerie, does the boy know?" she said, nodding at me. Professor Zaida shook her head.

"You know what to do," the lady said. She put a hand on Professor Zaida's shoulder and left with the others.

Professor Zaida stood up, and when she did, Syke collapsed to the floor.

"Syke!" I looked for an injury somewhere but didn't see anything. Professor Zaida checked her head, her pulse.

"My head hurts," she whispered. "Those trees really shook me up. And my arms hurt, and my ribs from when that henchman threw me against the railing."

"There's a doctor at the school," Professor Zaida said. "I'll have our troll take you there immediately."

"I'll go too," I said.

"No," Professor Zaida said. "You need to come with me."

"I'm not leaving Syke," I said.

"She'll be fine."

"Go on, Runt," she said. "I don't need you."

Professor Zaida took me back to the library's central hallway, where we headed away from Pravus, to another hallway that was lined with arched alcoves, each one holding a statue.

"Runt, I have so much to tell you," she said. "When I got here, I

276

knew I was going to die soon, so I wrote you a letter. But we're here now, so I'll tell you. Look around."

I did. This end of the library looked like a shrine. Between the alcoves were stone inscriptions, filled with dates and histories. On the wall facing us hung an enormous portrait of a family in royal clothing.

"This is the shrine to the Natherly family, the onetime rulers of a country called Andirat, and the descendants of the royal family of Erudyten. In fables, the Erudyten king is called by a different name—King Wellread, because he loved reading. He collected books from all over the globe, and at the height of his rule, Erudyten was very advanced."

"Darthin told me that story," I said. "Other countries grew jealous and attacked it."

"That's right. Centuries ago. What are now the realms of Carkley, Delpha, Riggen, and Brix used to be Erudyten. Before it fell, an order of librarians worked tirelessly to save the books. They were smuggled out of the country and brought upriver to this place, which was an abandoned mountain fortress called NORAD, the National Overlord Restricted Area Defense.

"The librarians set up the Kobold Retraining Center as a ruse to be near their secret library. They continued to collect books as realms throughout the continent changed hands, and their histories were rewritten by new rulers. This is the only repository of true history, Runt. Protecting this sacred place has been the life's work of countless loyal people. We've hidden it well, and it has never been discovered by outsiders. Until today."

She sat down on a padded bench and sighed. "You know, this mountain used to be a volcano. The early librarians made it appear like it was still active. We've never had to use all our defenses before, but we did today. The volcanic eruptions, the falling debris, the flames. Nothing stopped Pravus's army of gorillas. They blasted through the mountain until they found us."

"That eruption was fake?" I asked.

"Yes, this mountain is dormant. We have staged eruptions from time to time as part of our cover. Many field CLOUDs are volcanologists, which provides them with an excuse to come here with books—they say that they are coming to study the volcano. Plus nobody would think a library would be hidden beneath a volcano. That would be ridiculous."

That was very interesting, but I wasn't sure why she was telling me all this. "Professor Zaida? Maybe we should get you back to school, to make sure you're okay."

"I have to finish telling you this story." She patted the bench seat, and I sat down next to her. "When Erudyten fell, the rulers fled across the sea and landed in the peaceful kingdom of Andirat, on the Currial continent. They were welcomed guests because they shared their knowledge with Andirat's rulers—knowledge of economics and trade, education, and public works, how to run a country so that it doesn't get split into two groups who disagree about everything—those kinds of things. There were marriages between the two royal families, and over many generations they became entwined together. Andirat's royal family took over the job of protecting the Great Library. They were our patrons, funding our operation here."

"Were?"

Professor Zaida nodded.

"Fearing a repeat of the attacks that led to pacifist Erudyten's downfall, the rulers of Andirat built a very strong army for defense. Unfortunately, the military grew too strong, and soon there was strife within the country.

"Eight years ago there was a military coup. The country's generals murdered the royal family and took over, splitting up Andirat among themselves and carving out their own realms. Soon, the generals were fighting one another. It was chaos, and the country is still in disorder."

"The Broken Place," I whispered. "Sara said she came from a broken place. And maybe me too."

Professor Zaida nodded. "There were rumors that the young prince had been saved by a loyal advisor, who brought him across the ocean to a place where he'd be safe from the generals. Look at the last portrait of the royal family—it's there above the shrine."

I got up and walked over to the end of the hall. The portrait was huge, the people in it life-size. A king and queen sat on thrones, and four children surrounded them: a tall teenage boy, a girl who looked like his twin, a younger girl, and, finally, a young boy. Flanking the royal family were two wolves. No, not wolves; they were too large, each one as big as a horse. I looked at my medal. The faces of the "wolves" matched the face on my medallion.

I looked at Professor Zaida. "Those aren't wolves, are they?"

"No, they are vaskor. Your friend Sara is a vaskor. They adopt the glamour chosen by their patron. The Natherly family chose a monstrously large wolf. The vaskor were tasked with protecting the family. Nothing was more important than the family. But that's not important. Look at the youngest boy."

The boy, like his brother, wore a light blue coat with gold trim over a ruffled shirt. He looked sullen, like he didn't want to pose for a painting. He also wore a medallion, just like mine.

It suddenly dawned on me what she was thinking. "That's not me," I said.

"Yes, it is, Runt. I believe that you are Prince Auberon Gabriel Titus Kenton Valdemar Natherly." She took an envelope out of her pocket and handed it to me. Inside was a picture of me with Cook and Pierre. It was an old picture; I looked about four years old. "Cook gave this to me before I left," she said. "Now look at the portrait."

I did, and while we looked very similar—same hair and eye color, same high forehead, same everything—I knew that the prince wasn't me. I don't know how to explain the feeling, but that guy wasn't me.

"Runt, it all fits," she said. "The timing of when you showed up at the school—right after the coup—your medallion, the resemblance to the royal family, the clothes you were wearing when Cook found you. Runt . . ."

She came over and stood next to me, putting a hand on my arm. I looked down at her.

"What does it mean?" I asked.

"You wanted to know who you were, where you came from," Professor Zaida said. "And now you know."

"If that's true, my family is gone."

"I'm sorry, Runt—er—Prince Auberon."

"No. Don't call me that."

"You're right. We should keep this between us until we figure out what to do. Runt, this library is your family's heritage. You belong here, and you can stay here. The librarians live in the village. The vaskor can stay and do what they were meant to do—protect the library. Protect the legacy of the Natherly family. They are forest creatures, and there are forests on every side of the mountain."

I suddenly felt so tired. It was too much to take in. I sat down on the floor and then toppled over, closing my eyes.

CHAPTER 40

Dr. Mancini's Curse-Testing Kit. Guaranteed accuracy in detecting and identifying curses!
—SHAM PRODUCT. CURSE IDENTIFICATION IS NOTORIOUSLY DIFFICULT.

Back at school, I stumbled through class, not really aware of what was going on around me. The events in the Great Library had left me shaken. I felt like I'd lost something huge, like my purpose in life. I'd always been driven by a need to find my family, but there was no family waiting for me to find them. They were gone. They hadn't abandoned me, though, like I'd always believed. They'd loved me and tried to keep me safe.

I'd lost my best friend too. Syke wouldn't talk to me. If my Shun Box was faulty, hers was a steel-plated, inescapable dungeon cell.

And then I found out that I had to report for a disciplinary hearing in Dr. Critchlore's office that would determine whether I'd be expelled for Repeated Acts of Disobedience.

I sat in Dr. Critchlore's office with Cook, there to testify on my behalf. As we waited for everyone else, I showed her my wrists. While I was in the Great Library, two thick, pale reddish bands had appeared on them, and they wouldn't wash off.

"Maybe it's some kind of rash," Cook said. "We'll go to the infirmary after dinner."

Dr. Critchlore entered, dropping a book on his desk after he passed us. I glanced at the cover, *Retraining Kobolds for Fun and Profit*.

"Cook, Higgins," he said, smiling. He laughed suddenly, and then noticed Cook glaring at him. "Forgive me, I know this is a serious situation, but I am in an exceptionally good mood right now."

"We're thrilled to hear it," Cook said, with a touch of sarcasm. "Maybe you've come to your senses about this ridiculous hear—"

"I just have to share this news with somebody!" Dr. Critchlore interrupted, leaning over his desk in our direction. "Dr. Pravus has to appear before the council. He's being brought up for Acts Inconsistent with Proper Minion School Stewardship!"

"Because he attacked the Kobold center?" I asked.

"No, they don't know about that. Fardaglio, Fandango, what's his name? The headmaster there didn't file a complaint." Dr. Critchlore sat down. "He's doesn't want the publicity.

"No, the council has gotten several complaints from other minion schools about sabotage, and they all blame Pravus."

"How did Pravus think he could get away with attacking another school?" I asked, because it still stunned me that we'd found Dr. Pravus at the Kobold center with an army.

"Simple. He assumed the evil overlords would grant his petition to take over the Kobold center. They've all been sucking up to him, hoping to get his giant gorillas, so of course they'd give him anything he wanted, right? And once he got his greedy paws on the school, he could move his army there and break into the

Great Library. Nobody would care, because it would look like minion training.

"But when the evil overlords gave permission to me instead, Pravus panicked. He decided to risk an all-out assault on the mountain. He was desperate to get to all that knowledge, and now it's lost to him. Ha!"

"Except for the book his henchman took with him when he left."

"Yes, that concerns me. The librarians told me he took *The Top Secret Book of Minions—Translated Edition*. Hopefully he'll be banished to Skelterdam before he can use it."

This was great news. I knew I shouldn't be afraid of Dr. Pravus, because he couldn't hurt me. The librarians had kept him prisoner until Dr. Frankenhammer arrived and erased his memory, so he wouldn't remember our confrontation. But he still scared me.

"If only I could have kept those beasts of his," Dr. Critchlore said, turning to gaze out his window. "Fearsome!"

Sara and the rest of the vaskor stayed at the Kobold center to protect the Great Library. It was a win-win—the librarians finally got some warriors to protect them, and the vaskor got to live in a forest. I'd been charged with assigning their new glamour, and after discussing it with them, we went back to the original wolflike creature on my medallion.

Rufus entered behind Professor Murphy, taking the seat next to me. He held my backpack in one hand.

"Hey," I said. "What are you doing with my backpack?"

"You left it in the classroom. Thought you could hide the evidence, did you?" He leaned over to whisper, "You're gone, loser. And nobody will miss you. Especially not Janet."

Mistress Moira was the last to arrive. When everyone was seated, Dr. Critchlore nodded at Professor Murphy to begin. He looked so serious that I began to doubt my chances.

"What we have with Mr. Higgins is an escalating pattern of misbehavior," Professor Murphy said. "In the first two weeks of school, he received three detentions, he started a food fight in the cafeteria, and he showed blatant disregard for authority, barging into your office whenever he wanted.

"We are now a month into the term, and he's been thrown out of the junior henchman program after receiving three strikes. He's in possession of a banned book, which could get this whole school shut down." Professor Murphy pointed to Rufus, who opened my backpack and pulled out the book I'd been hiding there. "And Rufus is willing to testify under oath that Runt Higgins snuck out during Friday movies to free Dr. Pravus's minion in the dungeon. A blatant act of insubordination.

"In addition, he was absent without an excuse for the last two days. This sort of flagrant violation of rules and standards of behavior should be more than enough to expel him from this school for good."

Yikes. I was a terrible, terrible person. I had no idea.

Dr. Critchlore sat behind his desk with his fingertips tapping against each other.

"Cook?" he said. "You wanted to say something?"

"Dr. Critchlore," Cook said, standing. I could tell she was trying to control her temper, but her anger was visible in the scowl she directed at Professor Murphy. "Runt Higgins is no more the delinquent painted by Professor Murphy than I am the master chef at Le Petit Chateau." Then she sat down.

"Thanks, Cook," I said.

"Mistress Moira?" Dr. Critchlore asked.

"As you know, Derek, I have a way of knowing what goes on in this school." She paused until Dr. Critchlore nodded his agreement. "The fashion show would not have been the success it was without the help of Mr. Higgins, who filled in for Mr. Spaniel here"—she pointed to Rufus—"when Mr. Spaniel deemed the task beneath him. In addition, his keen observations led to a major design breakthrough with the dresses, helped you find a solution to the giant gorilla problem, and led directly to the return of your precious book." She nodded to his new copy of *The Top Secret Book of Minions*, which the librarians had given me in thanks.

"A book that he allowed to be stolen," Professor Murphy said.

"As if any student here could stand up to Dr. Pravus," she said. "Not many adults can either." Professor Murphy looked startled, and then his gaze fell to the floor.

Dr. Critchlore stood up and turned his back to us. He gazed out his expansive window, and then came around from behind his desk to address us.

"Professor Murphy, what are the three traits every junior henchman must have? The traits you are teaching our third-year students this term?"

"They are going to learn how to problem solve for their EOs, how to get a disparate group of minions to work together, and how to take on their EO's enemies. I've only gotten as far as the first one, though, because of the fashion show. They'll—"

Dr. Critchlore held up his hand. "Runt Higgins solved Mistress Moira's problem with the dresses. He helped me figure out how to

286

defeat Pravus's gorillas, although I would have gotten there myself, eventually. So he has already accomplished the first trait—problem solving.

"Then he single-handedly got the sirens and mermaids to work together—and I can think of no two groups that are more disparate. That's trait number two.

"And finally, trait three—he stood up to my worst enemy at the Kobold center and saved the life of our most beloved teacher, two accomplishments I deem worthy of an unexcused absence, don't you?"

"Well . . . 'most beloved' is a bit subjective . . ."

"Professor Murphy," Dr. Critchlore admonished.

"All right, yes, those are worthy accomplishments."

"Runt Higgins is staying, and I'm reinstating him into the junior henchman program."

Rufus fumed. Thick hairs erupted from his arms as he clenched his fists in anger.

"But the illegal book!" Professor Murphy shouted. "How can you overlook a transgression that serious?"

"It's not Runt's book." We turned and saw Syke standing in the doorway. "I hid it in his backpack so I wouldn't get caught with it," she said. "It's my book. And you don't have to have a stupid hearing about it, because I'm expelling myself. Good-bye."

She turned and left, swinging a backpack over her shoulder.

"Syke, no!" I followed her down the curving stairs to the castle foyer.

She stopped but didn't turn around. "Runt, I'm leaving anyway."

"Syke . . . please. Stay."

"I can't. You should know how I feel. You've been looking for your family for years. What if you found out that Dr. Critchlore had killed them? What would you do?"

"I did find my parents. In the Great Library. I found out who they are, but they're dead."

"What?"

"Professor Zaida figured it out. Syke, I'm the lost Prince of Andirat."

She stared at me for a second and then burst out laughing. "Termites, Runt. You really think you're a missing prince?"

"My medallion, the Girl Explorers, the timing of when I arrived here, my resemblance to the missing prince. Look—"

I showed her the picture I had of the royal family.

She took it from me and looked at it closely. "That's not you," she said. "I've known you since you got here, and never in my life have I seen you make an expression like that. That kid looks evil."

"Professor Zaida thinks it's me."

"Runt, don't go pretending you're something you're not. It's dangerous." She handed the photo back to me. "Good-bye."

"Syke, just listen to his side first."

A dark fury seemed to overtake her, and she balled her hands into fists like she was going to punch me. "Are you kidding me? He killed my mother, and you're standing here defending him? Damn it, Runt! You still love him!"

"Syke . . . it's just—"

"No, don't say anything else." She held up a hand. "You'd still do anything for him, for this stupid school. I need you to hate him, like I do, and you can't. And that's so disloyal and weak. I hate that you need him to love you, when he doesn't love anyone but himself."

She stared at me, like she was waiting for me to say something. I wanted to beg her to stay, but she'd just called me weak. If I begged, I'd just prove her right.

She turned and stomped out of the castle.

I sat down on the steps and slumped by the wall. I felt squashed, like something on the bottom of a giant's shoe. It all poured down on me—all the stuff I'd miss if she left. We did everything together. How was I going to find out who cursed me without her help? How would I fend off Rufus? Who would make me laugh with her impersonations of professors when I complained about them?

I didn't notice Mistress Moira until she spoke.

"What are those marks on your wrist?" she asked, sitting down next to me.

I looked at them again. "I don't know. They just showed up while I was in the Great Library. They won't wash off."

She held my arms as she examined the marks, each about an inch and a half thick. "Interesting."

"Do you know what it is?" I asked.

"I think it's your curse."

"Really?" I brightened. "I'm cursed to have wristbands? That's much better than being cursed to die."

"No, Runt. This is not good," she said. "It's a tether, to prevent you from going outside the range of the curse's power. You traveled to the northern edge of Stull, and these marks showed up as a warning. If you hadn't returned, they would have turned black, and then tightened. This means that your curse is not only powerful, but also inescapable. And the person who cast it is quite talented."

"You're right. That's not good."

"On the other hand, there are very few people who can successfully cast a tethering curse on top of another curse. This just might make it easier for us to find out who did it. And Runt"—she took my face in her hands so I had to meet her eyes—"I will not rest until I find out who cursed you."

"I know," I said. "Thank you, Mistress Moira."

She got up to leave. "You did good, Runt Higgins. Real good."

"Thanks," I said to her back as she flitted off to her quarters.

Kids streamed into the foyer, heading to the cafeteria for lunch. Janet entered, surrounded by admirers. She'd returned from her mission a hero, because everyone at school knew she'd tamed the giant gorilla in the video. She saw me sitting on the stairs and winked at me. My heart fluttered like a million bats lifting off in happiness, and I felt like I could do anything.

I'd found the Great Library, after all. If I could do that, then I could find out why Dr. Critchlore had burned down Syke's forest. I could get her to come back. And together, we could find out who'd cursed me, and why.

ACKNOWLEDGMENTS

I'm so grateful to my family for the inspiration and support they give me every day. Thank you, Juan, Rachel, Ricky, Alex, and Daniel! Thanks also to my parents, Joan and Bob Jack, and my siblings, Lisa and Gordy Jack. And a huge thanks to the whole extended Grau, Jack, and Smith clans—you all make my life so rich.

A very special thank-you to my editor, Erica Finkel, and my agent, Molly Ker Hawn, who make everything they touch better. Thanks to the talented Joe Sutphin for his gorgeous covers and interior art. Thanks to my early readers, Ashley Shouse and Gordon Jack. And thanks to all the fantastic people at Abrams who brought this book to life and continue to get it into the hands of readers everywhere: Chad W. Beckerman, Jessie Gang, Jason Wells, Jim Armstrong, Christine Ma, Zachary Greenwald, Elizabeth Peskin, Jess Brigman, Elisa Gonzalez, Mary Wowk, Susan Van Metre, and Michael Jacobs.

E ver since she saw *The Wizard of Oz*, Sheila Grau has been curious about one of life's great mysteries: Where do evil overlords get their minions? Also: Who trains them? Unable to find the answers, she thought it would be fun to make them up.

Sheila currently lives in Northern California with her husband and four children and, sadly, still no minions.